THE HUNTER'S PREY

Debbie was marched to the front door, floorboards creaking under her feet. The man kicked open a door in front of her and suddenly she saw the dark outdoors. She had started to wonder if she would ever see outside again. It was night and there were no lights anywhere.

The gun stayed pressed to her back as Debbie was pushed through damp grass.

"Walk," came the now familiar voice from behind her, and she did as it said.

Debbie stubbed her toe on something and tripped. She fell forward, felt her balance go, and suddenly hands reached out of the blackness to grab her and hold her upright.

"Careful now..." came the voice.

After several metres, the pathway in the grass appeared to end at a wall of trees. Finally, the gun was pulled away and Debbie was in the middle of nowhere, facing the cold, dark forest.

It is time now, she thought. *Time to die....*

Other *Leisure* books by Tara Moss:

FETISH

SPLIT

TARA MOSS

LEISURE BOOKS   NEW YORK CITY

For my father, Bob.

A LEISURE BOOK®

July 2006

Published by

Dorchester Publishing Co., Inc.
200 Madison Avenue
New York, NY 10016

Extracts on pp. 66-67 from *Psychopathy—Theory and Research* (1970) by Dr. Robert D. Hare, Ph.D., reproduced with kind permission.

ISBN 0-8439-5643-7

The name "Leisure Books" and the stylized "L" with design are trademarks of Dorchester Publishing Co., Inc.

Printed in the United States of America.

Visit us on the web at www.dorchesterpub.com.

ACKNOWLEDGMENTS

First of all, I would like to thank my amazing literary agent, Selwa Anthony, for all her guidance and support, and the unique dedication that is her special calling card.

My research for this novel required a great deal of assistance and cooperation, and it is with much appreciation that I acknowledge Dr. Robert Hare, Ph.D., for his consulting on psychopathy and for making a cameo appearance in this novel, Dr. Tony Phillips, Ph.D., for his consulting on psychiatry, Steven Van Aperen of Australian Polygraph Services International for his consulting on polygraphy and the detection of deception, Dr. Kathryn Guy for the medical consulting, Penny Gulliver for the self-defence tactics, Tom Ryan "The BC guy" for all his facts, Thomas Claxton at UBC Security for his help, and the FBI Academy, the Royal Canadian Mounted Police, the American Association of Police Polygraphists and the Los Angeles Police Department for their assistance.

Thanks to Janusz for being positively amazing on every level (and for letting me be a nutcase), David and Glenys for Paradise Point, Urszula for the tango, Sheila Hammond for the voice, Marg McAlister for the encouragement, Marty Walsh and everyone at Chadwicks for their ongoing support, HarperCollins for their patience and faith, Gloria and Mark and little Jacquelyn for their friendship and Bo-sitting, and all my great friends for being there. That means you too, Bo.

Special thanks also to my sister Jackie, the tattooed, rock-climbing, computer-programming antithesis to Theresa Vanderwall, and my father, who, with no police background whatsoever, nonetheless takes the constant comparisons with Les Vanderwall in good humour. Love to Lou and the whole Moss, T'Hooft, Carlson and Bosch families.

Without all of you, this would not have been possible. Thank you.

split *vb* 1. to break or cause to break. 2. to separate or be separated from a whole. ~ *See also* split personality, split decision.

PROLOGUE

Rough hands startled her.

Instinctively, Susan Walker opened her eyes. She saw a dizzying flash of the room around her, a vision of her own flesh showing in patches through torn pantyhose, an unwanted hand on her leg—and quickly she locked her eyes shut again.

She could not bear to look.

The young woman felt the hands move over her body and she recoiled, but her binds were unforgiving. Even the slightest movement brought a sobering bite of pain to her bruised wrists and ankles. So she froze, absorbing the hurt once more, a moan of protest escaping her lips. She had long since accepted that she couldn't get away.

Susan could hear movement to her left—shuffling, scraping—but she did not open her eyes to see what it was. After what she had seen, she never wanted to open her eyes again.

Then the hands were on her once more and the odor of male—of deviance—filled her nostrils. She contracted, shrunk back, straining against the metal around her ankles and wrists, her flesh crying out in agony. She wanted desperately to disappear, to escape her body, to escape his touch. She didn't want to feel or hear or smell or taste or see—ever again. Somehow, by blocking out her senses, she prayed to be transported to another place.

God help me . . .

There was a twinge of relief. Her captor's hands moved over her torn pantyhose, and with a series of metallic clicks released the cuffs around her ankles.

The suggestion of freedom taunted her. *Will I be freed? Finally?* Her wrists were still tightly secured to the back of the chair, but mercifully, she could now bend her knees. She ached to stretch her legs—to stand, to kick, to massage away the pain—but reflexively she crossed her thighs.

What time is it?

What day?

How long had she been bound to that metal chair? Several days? Forty-eight hours? Or only a day and night? Her brain felt foggy and slow. No matter how she urged her mind to focus, she couldn't remember how she got there—or why.

Again . . . relief. Her arms were freed. But before she had a chance to move, she was shoved forward, her chest driven onto the tops of her knees. She hugged herself, closing into a tight ball. And still she kept her eyes shut. Her whole being ached from her confinement, and she felt her back stretch, her sore muscles welcoming the release.

But not for long.

Her arms were pulled behind her back—in her weakened state she only had the strength to resist momentarily—and her wrists were handcuffed together again, just as sharply as before.

She was ordered to stand.

Susan didn't move.

"I won't tell anyone, I promise. Please let me go," she begged, mumbling the words into her knees and holding herself protectively. She had lost count of how many times she had pleaded, and in how many ways. She didn't want to look up. She didn't want to stand. Susan didn't even know if she *could* stand.

"Up." Something cold and hard was jabbed between her shoulder blades. A gun. "Now."

Hesitantly, she unfolded herself and stood up. Her body cried out as she rose, her knees threatening to buckle. A warm liquid trickled down through her pinched thighs, adding to her humiliation. She felt a fresh wave of revulsion at the sensation.

Oh God, he's never going to let me go . . .

"Walk," came the voice.

She wanted nothing more than to crawl into the corner and collapse, but she obeyed the command.

"Please, let me go—" she said, stepping forward. No blindfold. No masks. She had seen too much and she knew it. "Please . . ."

She was marched several paces to a door. Floorboards creaked under her feet. She heard the door open and felt the slap of a freezing wind from outside. Only then did she open her eyes. They stung—they were dry and swollen, with salty sleep and the remnants of tears gluing her lashes together. For a moment her vision was blurry.

The sky was black as pitch. It was night. She had no sense of time. Her thoughts scrambled. What would her family think of her absence? They would be panicking by now. Her fiancé, Jason? How could she tell him what she had endured, what she had done? Would he forgive her? What would he do? How could she ever tell her mother?

Oh, Mom . . .

Her shirt, which had been ripped open, flapped against her chest in the wind, the collar whipping her neck. Goose bumps stood up on her legs beneath the torn nylon. Trembling, cold and scared, Susan stood in the doorway with death aimed at her back. She sobbed with dry eyes, muttering incoherencies.

Was someone out there searching for her right now under that huge night sky?

Thick woods surrounded her in every direction, stretching out into the blackness. Wind blew her hair across her face, leaving strands in her chapped mouth. She squinted and tried to make out where she was, but all she could see was the vague silhouette of trees in the night. There were no lights in the distance, no search helicopters—not one sign of life—only a forest forming an earthy labyrinth for which she had no map.

"I won't tell anyone," she said in a raspy voice she barely recognized. "I can keep quiet. I can keep secrets." She tried to sound strong, but instead sounded desperate.

The gun stayed pressed to her back as she was pushed down a path. She resisted the urge to look down. She didn't want to see herself that way—clothes torn, bruised and cut, utterly vulnerable with her wrists cuffed behind her back.

She could barely see a few feet ahead of her, but the gun barrel edged her forward. As the path narrowed, she stumbled on gnarled roots and rocks made slippery with recent rain. She slowed, but the gun just kept nudging her forward. "Walk," came the voice from behind her, and she did as she was told.

Eventually the path ended. The gun was pulled away from her back. She was in the middle of nowhere, faced with the cold, moist darkness of the forest. She prayed that the worst was over.

She felt a tug at her wrists, and again heard the click of the handcuffs. They were off. Her arms were free. She crossed them tightly over her chest and hugged herself, rubbing her sore wrists against her shoulders and neck.

"Run." The voice was emotionless. "Now."

Run? Her body felt heavy and weak. She had no shoes, and the forest floor was sharp and uneven, strewn with rocks and fallen branches. Run where? There was no path, no light to guide her way. She hesitated.

A gunshot rang out.

The blast startled her, the bullet driving into the ground only centimeters from her bare feet. She felt the air move from the blast and pieces of earth hit her legs. She jumped, her ears ringing.

"Run, *now!*" came the voice again.

She ran blind, stumbling and crying, the trees reaching out to grab at her with scraggy claws. Branches leaped out of the darkness, snapping and tearing, snagging at her legs, catching on her shirt, scratching and biting her skin. There was no path, but she scrambled as fast as she could, knocking into trees and tripping over slippery roots and sliding on moss.

Susan Walker ran like doomed prey through the woods, knowing that to slow was to die.

Behind her, the gun barrel followed.

She was fair game.

CHAPTER 1

RUN!

I can't run fast enough...faster...run! I must go faster but my legs won't listen, the uniform won't move quickly enough, the badge weighs me down. My gun is a hunk of useless metal, heavy and cumbersome in my slippery hands, I can barely lift it...QUICK! Before it's too late! The door is there and finally I reach it, knowing full well what horror awaits on the other side. I hit the door hard—*slam*—and burst straight through. It breaks apart into a million pieces, jagged shards flying all around like asteroids and I see her—my mother—tied to the bed and straining to escape the blade, and the devil looks up, looks straight through my soul with eyes that are flickering red flames. I raise the weapon—it is so heavy, and I struggle to aim between the flames. I squeeze the trigger but it will not give, it is frozen. The devil is smiling with great rotting fangs, he knows I am helpless, and flames leap from his eyes, shooting fire and a great rush of air to knock me down. He turns back to his prey, his captive—my mother—and he drives the knife down...

"No!"

A loud noise woke Makedde Vanderwall from her nightmare.

She sat bolt upright and inhaled sharply. *What?* When she realized the noise had come from her own lips, she broke into an embarrassed blush. She had dozed off again and cried out in her sleep. She surveyed her surroundings through puffy eyes, squinting with sleep-heavy lids. A couple of passengers were staring at her. A few feet away, a young man had looked up from his comic book and was smirking.

Damn.

Makedde looked away and ran clammy hands over her face. She was not steady yet. A deep breath. The strap of her purse was wrapped around her elbow and she untangled it and gathered it to her. She swayed for a moment when she got up from her seat, waiting out a dizzy head spin and adjusting to the roll of the ferry. She wiped the corner of her mouth and it felt wet. With long, slender fingers she pushed a lock of blond hair behind her ear, then straightened her head. Once she felt she had regained her composure, she made her way toward the doors that led to the outside upper deck of the *Spirit of Tsawassen*.

Cool sea air hit her with a sobering rush as she pushed the door open. Now fully awake, Makedde walked toward the edge, pitched forward in the wind, and leaned her forearms on the metal railing. She inhaled the salt air and looked out over the waves. The Gulf Islands stretched out around her as far as she could see— secluded outcrops covered in fir trees and surrounded by deep blue Pacific waters. The picturesque seascape was lit up with the scarlet and orange of a spectacular sunset, the sun a great ball of vermilion slowly dipping below the horizon. Sparks of gold reflected off the waves as they hit the sides of the ship and flew back in bursts of white foam below her.

Beautiful.

Makedde had taken this ferry trip between Vancouver Island and the west-coast Canadian mainland countless times throughout her life. At age five, holding her mother's hand, gripping her coloring book, her mouth and chin covered in chocolate ice cream. At ten, begging for more quarters to play Pac-Man and Space Invaders in the arcade room, dressed in acid-wash stretch jeans and a ZZ Top T-shirt. And at fourteen, checking her make-up in a compact, nervously preparing for her first big modeling casting in Vancouver with an agent from Milan.

She grew up fast.

Mak, as she liked to be called, had worked in Milan not long after that first casting, then Paris, London and New York. That was only the beginning. Thanks to the kind of statuesque genes that were currently in vogue, she had for the past decade modeled in cities around the globe. It was a job, and a pretty good one by most standards. Sometimes it paid well, and she got to travel, but the fabulous, fickle fashion industry never quite grew on her. Somehow she never felt like she fit into that lip-sticked world of smoke-and-mirrors glamor.

For the moment she was in neither Paris nor Milan. Mak was relatively close to home again, living and studying in Vancouver. Dreams of a Ph.D. and a life beyond modeling were now almost within her reach, but she still had bills to pay, just like any other student.

She pulled at the false eyelashes that clung stubbornly to her lids. She had washed most of her make-up off after the shoot, but the lashes she kind of liked. Now they were starting to itch. She tugged them free and sent them sailing through the salt air to the waves below, like tiny black insect wings.

Taking the hour and thirty-five minute ferry ride to the island home of her youth had become a bi-weekly ritual in recent months. She wasn't sure if she made the visits more for herself or for her father—maybe she was trying to make up for years of absence, or perhaps she was grasping to remember a time when things seemed safe and normal. Perhaps she simply enjoyed her father's company. She thought it was probably all of the above.

Her nightmare had dissolved into something distant and intangible, allowing Mak to turn her thoughts to the most prominent concerns in her waking life—her insomnia, her father and her thesis. She was aware that there were other subjects bubbling dangerously beneath the surface, but those were things she was not yet prepared to dwell on, no matter what their relevance.

Makedde sensed a presence and looked around to find a man walking behind her on the deck, a little too close, an older man with a dark mustache and a deeply lined face. He quickly turned his attention to the horizon after she saw him, and continued to walk by. She smelled the heavy, lingering scent of tobacco on him. Tense, Mak watched the stranger as he walked the length of the deck and disappeared down the stairs to the main level. His rubber-soled shoes made a dull clanging sound on the ferry's metal steps as he descended. Once she was sure he was gone, Makedde looked back out to sea.

Dusk was approaching. Swartz Bay terminal was visible across the water, a swarm of lights and bright structures on the shore. The ferry began to shudder and groan as it slowed its passage and prepared to dock. She watched the vessel move into the docking bay before leaving the rail with her hair wild and wind-tossed. Her cheeks were circles of rose, her skin refreshed by the brisk salt air—no longer hot with embarrassment. A line of mascara-stained moisture dipped just below the corners of her blue eyes, and she wiped it away with the palm of her hand.

By the time she made her way to the lower car deck, the *Spirit of Tsawassen* was almost ready to unload.

Deep in thought, Makedde failed to notice the posters tacked up on various community noticeboards around the ferry.

MISSING—HAVE YOU SEEN THIS PERSON?

The placards showed the smiling face of a young woman captured in a moment of pride and excitement. Her auburn hair was professionally styled and her dress formal. She wore a pretty heart-shaped locket around her neck. Bright eyes glowed with youthful optimism. The photo the Royal Canadian Mounted Police had used was a cropped section of a recent engagement portrait. A young man's hand was partially visible around her waist—her fiancé now cut out of the picture.

Susan Walker had been missing for three weeks.

CHAPTER 2

Fidelity.

Bravery.

Integrity.

The tall, fit, dark-haired man dressed in regulation cargo pants and a moss-green polo-necked FBI shirt looked long and hard at the seal of the Federal Bureau of Investigation as he passed it for the umpteenth time. The crest, consisting of the scales of justice surrounded by a ring of thirteen stars, also adorned an embroidered patch on the man's shirt.

Fidelity. Bravery. Integrity.

He knew the crest well, and the grounds on which he stood, but he was not a graduate of the Quantico Academy. The ID tags around his neck declared his standing. He was not an FBI agent, merely a guest—a member of an overseas law enforcement organization in special training. He wasn't one of them, a fact that was hard to forget in such a setting. But he had his allies and, fortunately, the strangers around him seemed to find his Australian accent disarming. It somehow endeared him to the otherwise insular group. Although he sometimes lamented the fact that his nation was stamped with an unfair stereotype, at least it was a friendly one.

Detective Senior Sergeant Andrew Flynn of the New South Wales Police was there to learn how to better track serial killers—something for which he had a natural talent. This was both a blessing and a curse, but a talent that was in dire need. He had little choice but to hone it. And Quantico was the place to do it.

Not so long ago, he had cracked the most violent and prolific serial murder case Australia had ever witnessed. Worse than the infamous Granny Killings, or the Backpacker Murders. Worse than the recent Snowtown Killings, where a routine missing persons' investigation had led to the discovery of several dismembered bodies in various states of decomposition. They had been neatly packed in oil drums in the sealed vault of a disused bank. A year ago Detective Flynn had caught the Stiletto Killer, a sadistic shoe fetishist who preyed on the attractive young women of Sydney, torturing and mutilating them.

The case had been complicated—and personal. Flynn's big career break had come at a heavy price. A price he would not have been willing to pay if only he had known. The burden of guilt hung like a yoke around his neck, impossible to ignore and impossible to forget. If only he had put the pieces together sooner, he told himself, lives could have been saved. Working that case had turned his own life upside down, and very nearly cost him his reputation as well. Plus there were other problems. The matter of a witness. A young woman. Beautiful. Clever. Irresistible.

Makedde.

He still thought about her—a lot. He had been lonely and stressed at the time, that much was true. But he had no excuse now.

Andy was so absorbed in his thoughts that he stopped looking where he was going, and that was dangerous on the deceptively quaint streets of Hogan's Alley. Day or night, it didn't pay to be preoccupied there. The moment Andy realized his lapse, he reminded himself to stay alert. Even at this hour, a tactical exercise could be underway.

He was right in the heart of Hogan, a short walk from the main FBI Academy building. It was dark and the buildings around him had lost the golden color of the sunset. The sky was clear above, the first stars now visible. He heard the rustle of trees, and watched a red leaf fall at his feet. The northern summer was over and winter wasn't far behind.

Andy peeked in the darkened windows of the Bank of Hogan, pressing his nose to the glass and cupping his hands around his eyes. He grinned for a moment, reflecting on its dubious title as the most robbed bank in America. But now the tellers were gone. The bank was quiet. There were no robberies underway; no agents arresting stunt actors and wielding guns loaded with pellets of paint. Similarly, the Dogwood Inn was still. He could see that the door to Room 101 hung broken on its hinges from an earlier exercise. How many times had it been kicked in? But the motel was empty now. It held no terrorists, drug lords or fugitives tonight. The little town of Hogan was finished up for the day, the deli closed and the faux criminals had gone home for dinner.

Or was it? Andy heard the thunder of running feet, and turned to see a group of FBI agents approaching from one of the many wooded trails. Their blue shirts, barely visible in the low light, indicated that they were new recruits. The young men and women looked like carbon copies of each other as they filed past, their FBI identification tags swinging in time. They were dedicated, focused and fit—not yet jaded, not yet riddled with the guilt of the cases they hadn't solved and the lives they hadn't been able to save. Each one of them would have fought like hell for the privilege of being in that group. Each one of them would have secretly felt a long-awaited thrill entering the academy for the first time, passing under the sign stating: "Through these doors pass the finest professionals dedicated to the service of law enforcement."

That's what they wanted to be. The finest.

And that's what Andy wanted to be too.

As he walked through the darkened Hogan streets, Andy Flynn was riddled with self-doubt. But then again, at that moment he had good reason to be. He was about to do something foolish.

By 10:00 P.M. he was settled into his modest room, reclining on the bed. He looked at his bare feet hanging over the edge and noted they were not his best asset. Once, in a state of extreme passion, Makedde Vanderwall had kissed his toes. He never quite understood how she managed that, but he'd liked it. That woman was capable of all kinds of surprises.

Focus . . .

The duvet was peeled back and he lay on top of the sheets dressed only in his boxer shorts. The room was cool, but he felt hot. A trace of perspiration beaded on his chest.

Mak.

Thankfully, he had managed to secure a separate dormitory room at Quantico this time around, and at this moment he was particularly grateful for it. It would have been embarrassing to have to ask another officer, or an agent, to leave the room while he made this call.

An overstuffed Filofax rested on his trim stomach. Mak

had kissed that too, but it was best not to think about that now. He opened the address portion and flipped to "V", then closed his eyes for a moment and once again considered the wisdom of what he was doing. *Just call.* He propped the pages up and scanned the row of addresses. There she was. Second entry on the right-hand side.

Andy only had the number for her father's place on Vancouver Island, but he knew she often spent her weekends there. Perhaps he'd be in luck. He rested the book in his lap and raised his index finger to the keypad on the phone, then hesitated.

Should I?

It had been almost a year since he'd last seen Makedde, and things had been messy. Although they'd spoken on the phone a couple of times at the beginning of the year, that was a far cry from seeing each other face-to-face. He wasn't sure how she would react to the prospect of seeing him.

He knew he couldn't put the call off any longer though. He would be attending a conference at the University of British Columbia in a couple of weeks. One of his mentors, Dr. Bob Harris, a Profiler with the FBI, was flying up to do a presentation on psychopathy and crime scene analysis. He had invited Andy to come along. That was how he had first heard about it. The conference would also feature a talk from highly respected psychopath expert Dr. Robert Hare, who was a Professor Emeritus at the university. The "Two Bobs" knew each other well.

The problem was that the University of British Columbia also happened to be where Makedde Vanderwall was studying. Of course, this wasn't really a problem as he saw it, but rather a good excuse to reestablish contact.

Until now, Andy had procrastinated over whether or

not to tell Makedde about his visit, but the UBC conference was fast approaching. Mak had done her Masters in Forensic Psychology, and there was more than a good chance that she would be attending the conference herself. He knew it would not be considered appropriate to just show up and surprise her, so he thought he'd call first.

Although he was looking forward to the conference, for the most part it was likely to be material he'd heard before. He had attended Dr. Hare's guest lectures at Quantico and he was quite familiar with the profiling techniques his friend Dr. Harris would present. The truth was, he wanted to see Makedde. Finally they were on the same continent. This was the closest to her that he had been for a long time, and as the distance between them shrank, his urge to see her had grown. If nothing else, seeing her again might get her out of his system. Perhaps seeing her would be a let-down, the spark gone.

Not likely.

His mind was suddenly filled with her, memories of Makedde grinning, playful and exciting. The weekend they spent together was impossible to forget—entwined in her bed, making love at all hours, lost in ecstasy as the candles slowly burned to the floor. And then . . .

Then it all went wrong.

Beep.

Beep.

Beep.

The phone emitted a rhythmic pulse.

Andy realized that his finger was still poised over the number pad. He shook his head, pulling back from that vivid memory and hung up the receiver.

He picked it up again.

Mak.

Hesitation.

Maybe I should cancel my spot at the conference and forget all about it?

Instead he dialed.

He was unsure of what exactly he should say to her if she answered. *Don't mention anything at first about flying over for the conference,* he told himself, *just chat a bit, feel things out.* He eyed the entry in his Filofax, staring transfixed at her name.

Makedde Vanderwall—*her name, her photo, her vulnerable body in the hands of that sadistic bastard. I find her, blood everywhere, she's bleeding on the bed, tied up and naked, and that bastard is grinning at me, he knows who I am, he taunts me and I aim and fire, tunnel vision, all I see is his perverted grin, everything else a blur, I aim for the heart, I pull the trigger, I shoot to kill, but . . .*

"Hello?" A male voice.

"Uh—" Andy hesitated, restraining a jealous reflex. He wondered if the voice belonged to one of Makedde's boyfriends. Did she have a boyfriend? Why hadn't he thought of that?

"This is Andy Flynn calling, is Makedde Va—"

"Ahhh, Detective Flynn."

"Mr. Vanderwall?" It was her father.

Of course it's her father, it's his house, you fool.

"Hello, Mr. Vanderwall. Please, just call me Andy, sir."

"Call me Les." There was a pause. "How are you?"

He'd almost forgotten that west-coast Canadian accent. It was quite different from the twang down in Virginia.

"I'm well, Les. Thank you."

"Good."

Another pause. That voice. Andy heard it for the first time in a hospital room in Sydney. He had met Les Vanderwall while Mak slept, bruised and full of stitches.

"It's been a while," Les said. Andy detected a tone of reserve.

"Yes, it has," he replied awkwardly. The line was rough with static. And there was a delay that made the moment seem more uncomfortable than it really was. With all the technology at the FBI's disposal, he would have thought the phone line would have been clearer.

"So, how have you been?" Andy said, trying not to ask for her right away.

"Very well, thanks. I suppose you want to talk to Mak?"

"Yes, if—"

"Well, she's not around." Andy's heart sank. "I expect her soon, though. She's coming across for the weekend."

Good. He didn't have the number for her flat in Vancouver, and he wasn't about to ask for it. He checked his watch. Just after ten o'clock in Virginia. That meant it would be seven in the evening on Vancouver Island. How late would she be arriving? What should he say now?

Makedde's father beat him to it. "How's the case coming along?"

"Well, it looks like it'll take some time. There's a lot of evidence to compile—"

"A lot of victims," Les said.

Andy felt a familiar pang of guilt.

Yes, too many. Too many victims.

Les Vanderwall was a retired detective inspector, and as with most in his line of work, this new phase was, for all intents and purposes, a mere technicality. Andy knew that Les had done some digging around on his daughter's behalf. He would have done the same thing if he were Makedde's father. But he hadn't wanted to talk about the Stiletto Murders with Les—not a good idea to discuss any case with a key witness's father.

He is a victim's father, Andy.

As soon as the thought came to him, Andy recalled Makedde's voice, cracking with emotion. "I'm a survivor, Andy. *Not a victim*. Don't *ever* call me a victim."

An uncomfortable pause.

The crackle of the line.

"It's in very capable hands," Andy assured him.

"You aren't handling it yourself?"

That was information Mr. Vanderwall would already know. Andy was sure of it.

"I'm doing some training at the FBI Academy at the moment," he said. "We're putting together a new Profiling Unit in New South Wales."

"Really?"

"I have a very good chance of heading one of the divisions in the unit."

"Congratulations."

"Thanks." Andy noted the lack of enthusiasm. "I will be involved in the trial, Mr. Vanderwall. Don't you worry about that. I'll make sure your daughter's treated with as much sensitivity as possible."

Les didn't respond. Courtrooms were not sensitive places. They both knew that.

"Well, I'll tell Makedde you called," Mr. Vanderwall finally said.

"Thank you, sir."

"Call me Les."

"Of course. Thank you, Les. Perhaps I'll try again sometime tomorrow."

"I'll let her know."

Andy hung up and exhaled. He flopped back against the headrest and folded his arms, the Filofax still in his lap.

In the cold room he was slick with sweat.

CHAPTER 3

The Pat Bay Highway was dark, the trees on the roadside silhouetted against the night sky. Makedde drove fast from Swartz Bay, white lines flashing by her on both sides, the remaining ferry traffic dotting the road behind her in a moving sea of headlights. Zhora, her turquoise 1969 Dodge Dart Swinger, needed a little prompting to get above eighty, but once she was there, she hummed along with the best of them.

Makedde felt that vehicles, especially older ones, deserved names. Before her Dart she'd had a Volkswagen Bug named Bette Davis. She had chosen the name of her current car as a reference to the ill-fated Nexus 6 Replicant in one of her favorite films. "She's trained for an off-world Kick Murder Squad," Bladerunner had said of her. "Talk about beauty and the beast . . . she's *both*." That was Zhora the Replicant. Zhora the car on the other hand was a temperamental, two-door, hardtop classic, with an original slant-six engine and leather bench seats—another kind of beauty and the beast. She was a rare find in original, though not perfect, condition. One day

21

Makedde planned to fix her up and maybe sell her to a Dart collector, but that day didn't look like it was coming soon. There was still too much to do.

In the past year she had learned all about the inner workings of cars. Unlike some of her other resolutions—learning to fence, speak Mandarin, juggle—she had reason to make it a top priority. Never again would she rely on someone else to fix her problems. Never again would she find herself caught out with the hood up and no idea of what she was looking at.

Mak negotiated Zhora through the residential suburb of Victoria and turned into Tiffany Street. At the end of the block, she pulled up at a two-story Tudor-style house, similar in design to many in the area.

Her father's house.

It used to be the family home. The home of Les and Jane Vanderwall and their two daughters, Theresa and Makedde. A family. Now its sole occupant was a widowed retiree, growing old alone.

The lights were on in the house when she pulled up. Almost every light, in fact. Despite the knowledge that her father had been very frugal with electricity when she was growing up, she was sure he was the only one in the house tonight. Makedde suspected this new habit was a way of coping with the loneliness of the place—lights on, the TV talking softly in another room. She remembered the time she discovered the radio left on in her mother's workroom downstairs, and she realized for the first time that the wooden easel was still sitting out—her mother's painting of the sandpipers on the beach, forever unfinished.

Makedde parked Zhora in the driveway—her father's white Lancer was tucked away out of sight in the garage—and made her way around to the trunk to fish out her overnight bag. A thin line of rust marred the turquoise paint near the rear fender. She looked at it and frowned.

Must fix that.

With her bag in tow and two heavy psychology textbooks under one arm, she walked through the front door her father had left unlocked for her. The warm smell of potatoes and hot butter greeted her as she entered. She heard the crackle of something frying on the stove.

"Hey, Dad!" she called in a loud voice. She put down her things and kicked her Blundstones off on the landing, leaving them in a heap beside some other, more neatly placed shoes. *Not enough shoes,* she thought. Three pairs in a neat row, all for the same two feet.

Her dad appeared at the top of the stairs wearing tan Eddie Bauer slacks and a Roots sweatshirt. The words "ROOTS CANADA" were written across it in big letters with the clothing label's crest of a beaver sitting beneath them. She once wore a Roots shirt in Australia, before it was pointed out to her that "root" has a very different meaning down-under. And as for the beaver . . .

"It's almost nine. You haven't had dinner yet?" she asked. He usually ate before seven.

"I thought I'd wait. Have you eaten?"

"Well, not really." She padded up the carpeted stairs in stockinged feet and met him at the top with a big hug. "The BC ferries don't really have that whole food thing down pat, I don't think. Spew with a view."

"Oh, Makedde, it's not that bad," he said, ever the diplomat.

"The buffet's okay, I suppose." Mak looked at her father. At six foot two, he was slightly taller than his leggy eldest daughter. He was still handsome in his mid-fifties, and had every single hair left on his head—and the silver-gray color it had turned over the years seemed to suit his striking, Paul Newman–like eyes. He seemed thinner every time she saw him though, and that worried her. He'd been losing weight since her mother died.

They ate dinner at the small round table in the kitchen, leaving the dining room to continue its task of collecting dust. He'd fixed a garlicky iceberg lettuce Caesar salad and a plate of potatoes and sausage. His cooking had slowly improved over the past year. The sausage actually tasted pretty good, which reminded Mak of how far she had strayed from her teenage vegetarian model days.

"How have you been? You look a little tired," he said.

She looked up from her food. "I've been fine. Studying a lot. Oh, by the way, I've got another shoot next week. Department store catalog crap, but they're using a good photographer. Should pay the bills."

"That's good. You better get some sleep before then. You look pretty worn out."

Oh, thanks.

"Please, stop with the compliments, you're embarrassing me," she said. "I'm fine, Dad. The shoot today was just a bit of a drag, that's all. It was for a billboard, but still . . . 'Last shot, last shot . . .' If I hear that once more I think I'll scream."

He looked at her fixedly.

"I'm *fine*," she repeated. She hoped he wouldn't start on the whole "insomnia thing" again.

"Hmmm," her father mumbled, sounding unconvinced. He brought a forkful of potato to his mouth and stared through the placemat as he chewed. Something was on his mind. Les Vanderwall rarely made such observations as light conversation. It wasn't his style. Perhaps it was because he had conducted too many interrogations, but the ex–detective inspector had a knack for pointed statements and loaded questions. As casual as he made it sound, the topic was not about to go away without being discussed further.

They ate for a few minutes in silence, but Mak sensed that there was a question her father wanted to ask. It made her tense. Finally she took the bull by the horns and asked, "What's up?"

"I was talking with a friend of mine recently about the way people react to stress, Post Traumatic Stress Disorder and so on . . . we saw a lot of it in the police force . . ."

Oh, here we go.

"Yes, I'm familiar with it. And?"

"And, Makedde, I'm worried. I was wondering if you had considered seeing someone about the incident in Sydney?"

The "incident in Sydney." That's how everyone referred to it.

"Considered seeing someone? I believe 'psychological therapy' is the term you're looking for."

"Just to talk it out with someone. Someone unbiased and experienced in these areas. You said yourself that you probably should." The furrow in his brow formed twin exclamation marks and his eyes were filled with real concern.

"That was an offhand comment I made a year ago, but I didn't end up needing therapy, and I still don't. Nothing has changed. I'm fine. There's no need to worry, Dad. I assure you, I'm totally fine." She looked at the food cooling on her plate. "I just can't see the point of rehashing all that stuff unnecessarily, especially now. I went over it with the police God knows how many times. Besides, there was that counselor in Sydney as you may recall. I talked about it with her. That was enough . . ."

Her appetite performed a Houdini and she was left

staring at a dinner of half-eaten dead flesh. From the recesses of her memory she got a flash of a mutilated corpse and immediately felt the hot sensation that precedes a fever. She blinked the vision away and concentrated on sipping from her glass of water. The glass felt refreshingly cold against her fingertips and the water she poured down her throat settled her down. Her right big toe began to tingle, exactly where the microsurgeon had sewn it back on. She ignored it.

"Mak, you talked with that counselor for a whole hour."

That was true.

She changed her focus, pushing any thoughts of Sydney back into a dark box and slamming the lid shut.

"Who is this friend of yours you were talking to about this stuff?"

Les Vanderwall caught his daughter's eye and held it. "Don't worry, I'm not using you as some kind of conversation piece. Remember how I told you I ran into that lady in the Starbucks on Robson several months back? Dr. Ann Morgan? Was married to Sergeant Morgan with the Vancouver PD?"

Mak recalled some mention of the chance meeting early in the spring. Her father was visiting Mak in Vancouver at the time and had been wandering around the shops on Robson Street killing time while she finished up a fashion shoot. He recognized Dr. Morgan in the coffee line. They had met before at a reception she attended with her husband. She'd heard about Jane Vanderwall's death and sent a card. They struck up a conversation.

Mak had met the husband, Sergeant Morgan, once, perhaps twice. Never much liked him, though. *Was married to* . . . hmmm. *Interesting choice of words.*

"Anyway, I was talking with her the other day," he went

on. "She's visiting some friends on the island at the moment. Ann has some idea of your situation. No specifics, of course . . ."

Makedde felt her throat tighten. Her temporal artery pulsed. "And what precisely would she know about my situation, specific or otherwise?" she asked. "What *is* my situation, exactly?" She knew she sounded defensive, but didn't care.

"Dr. Morgan is involved in this sort of area," he said in a cautious, soothing tone. "She's a psychiatrist. I may have mentioned it before."

He hadn't. In fact, this was the first time Makedde had ever heard her father talk about any psychiatrist in a particularly positive light. Many in the police force, particularly the older generation of officers, tended to view psychiatrists and psychologists with suspicion. The cynics regarded them as the thorns in their sides who would excuse criminals on the grounds of legal insanity or diminished responsibility.

Her father had protested when she announced her desire to pursue psychology as a career. Was he now suggesting that his own daughter ought to be seeing a shrink? If that were true, times had certainly changed. It threw her for a loop.

"Don't tell me you think I need to see a psychiatrist, of all things? Next you'll be saying I should be on antidepressants." She spat the words out. Mak felt that many psychiatric drugs were over-prescribed because of the influence of pushy drug companies. Her father knew very well about her reservations.

"Just relax. No one's talking about drugs. You've been under a lot of stress with your thesis and everything. You're not sleeping properly. Don't think I can't tell."

That stung. He could see right through her petty

protests. She couldn't keep anything from him. She fought the urge to push her plate away and leave the table. Instead, she pursed her lips, staring again at her half-eaten meal. Her father meant well. In fact, if anything, he was too well-meaning sometimes.

And besides, he was right.

"Just think about it. It might help to see someone."

Mak knew he was waiting for a response but she simply stared at her glass of water. A bead of moisture rolled off the lip, trickled down the length of the glass and stained the tablecloth with a small damp dot.

"Just think about it," he repeated.

She didn't say anything.

He changed the subject, knowing he'd hit his mark. He had her thinking about it.

"Theresa and Ben will be coming over for dinner tomorrow with little Breanna."

"Oh?" she managed. *Oh joy.*

"I hope you'll stick around this time. You and your sister haven't seen much of each other lately."

That was also true.

"And Ann might swing by at some point. It'd be nice if you were here to meet her."

If this is a set-up, I'll snap.

Makedde nodded and said nothing. If her dad had a new friend who wanted to visit, that was great. It was more than great, actually. But if he was meddling with her life again, and he had a shrink that wanted to corner her, that was a different matter altogether.

Mak reached for her glass and brought it to her lips. She sipped while he ate. She thought about how, after so many years of travel, being close to home seemed to both comfort her and give her an odd feeling of claustrophobia.

He's right, you know. You're starting to slip.

"By the way," her father said, "you got a call this evening."

"Mmm?" Mak mumbled. She was thankful he wasn't commenting on her lack of appetite.

"It was Detective Flynn."

Suddenly Makedde couldn't breathe. After a moment she somehow managed to say, "Oh," in a reasonably steady voice. She paled and then her fair complexion turned the color of fresh beets.

Her father pretended not to notice. He scooped up more potato covered in copious amounts of butter and salt, placed it in his mouth and proceeded to masticate with irritating leisure. Instead of offering further explanation, he used the salad tongs to lift some salad out of the bowl and onto his plate.

"Really? Andy?" she said. "Well . . . well, that's um . . . interesting."

He stabbed some lettuce with his fork and brought it to his mouth. He chewed. It sounded crispy.

"What did he say?"

Her father took a sip of Diet Coke. The ice cubes clinked in his glass. She hated it when he did this.

"For God's sake, what did he say? Was it about the trial?" Makedde blurted out.

"No. He didn't say much about anything. Just asked for you. He was calling from Quantico." He put the last forkful of salad into his mouth and chewed it slowly.

"Quantico? As in the FBI Academy, Quantico?"

"Yup."

Silence.

"He said he'd probably try again tomorrow," her father added.

Now she was the one to fork food into her mouth. The

remains of her meal were cold but she scarcely noticed. She silently chewed, failing to taste anything as her mind ticked over furiously.

She couldn't sleep that night. And by morning she had counted every point of stucco on the ceiling of her childhood bedroom.

CHAPTER 4

It was morning, and the Hunter watched dead leaves and pine needles float down the Nahatlatch River. He was listening for sounds beyond the steady flow of the water. The air was still damp, rocks were slippery, and the tall trees flanking the river on both sides disappeared into clouds of mist as they rose high up above the forest floor.

A heavy overnight rain had left everything wet, making the long drive from Squamish treacherous in parts, but the rough roads were familiar to him and he managed them well. Now he was near the Fraser River between Lytton and Boston Bar, an area for which he felt a special affinity. When he was a child, his father had taken him and his brother to this secluded and untouched wilderness. And now, on this damp morning, the fog seemed almost a part of him as he stood and listened, this quiet place sharing his dark secrets, a mute witness to his power.

He listened and waited. It was true that he was not always a patient man, but he could be when he wanted to, when it counted, and here in this damp place there was no rush.

Snap!

There was movement several yards away, coming from the trees. The Hunter sprang to life, crossed the slippery rocks carefully, moved away from the river and approached the edge of the woods, a safe distance from the source of the sound. He took shelter behind the large, upturned roots of a fallen pine tree, and waited.

His patience was rewarded. Before long a beautiful beast emerged, at first testing the open air timidly, then stepping straight into the clearing. It negotiated the uneven ground on thin, graceful legs, moving with footsteps delicate for its size. The Hunter admired the long cinnamon face and head, the thin, forward sweeping antlers. It was a fine white-tailed buck.

The deer moved away from the edge of the thicket, looking from side to side with large, dark eyes, like a child checking before crossing a road. Slowly it ventured toward the water's edge for a morning drink. Normally it would repeat the ritual in the late afternoon. But not today. The impressive rack would be a fine addition to the wall of the Hunter's den.

He waited for the deer to move fully into the clearing, considering how he could best ready his weapon so as not to alarm the sensitive animal. The deer moved forward a few paces, its long leaf-shaped tail raised to flash a white underside and rump. The Hunter watched its ginger movements with fading patience.

He wanted to kill.

Stealthily, he readied his shot.

He stood perfectly still, his feet shoulder-width apart with his left arm supporting the 270 Winchester. His right hand pressed the butt of the weapon firmly against his shoulder. His jaw flexed. Firing an accurate shot while standing requires a good deal of control, and the Hunter was a master at regulating his breathing and the delicate art of the trigger squeeze. He was confident. He was ready. He carefully lined up his shot; the deer's long, sloping neck in his sights. He caressed the trigger slowly, lovingly, feeling the power of death in his grasp. Slowly, he squeezed . . .

The animal turned its head. It snorted with alarm as if it knew what was coming, as if the grim reaper had tapped it on the shoulder.

You're mine . . .

Bang!

The startled deer fled back toward the edge of the forest with great undulating leaps, its broad white tail flagging. Gritting his teeth hard, the Hunter slid back the bolt and aimed slightly ahead of the quick beast for a second shot.

The animal screamed. The bullet pierced its neck and its huge, dark eyes rolled back to look in the direction of its executioner. The Hunter saw in those eyes a glimpse of wild, unbridled fear and the dumb shock of violence. It thrilled him. The once graceful creature stumbled to and fro on the wet rocks, its back legs seizing and its front legs reaching out, flailing uselessly. Its head hit the rocks when it fell.

The bag limit for Section 3 of the Southern Interior region was only one white-tailed buck. They were not as common near the Nahatlatch as they were near the Peace River.

This kill only added to the Hunter's reasons for believing that he was the finest and most accomplished hunter who had ever lived.

On the way back to his truck, he passed an area of nondescript undergrowth and slowed to consider the spot for a second. Looking at the unremarkable tangle of ferns and leaves he felt a rush of adrenalin a bit like the one he felt when he had killed the deer. An observer might have noted a subtle change in the tilt of his head, the slightly smug expression on his face. But it would have taken very keen eyes indeed to spot that the area of undergrowth he was looking at had been recently disturbed.

A young woman's body lay rotting beneath the earthy blanket. She'd said her name was Susan. She had not lied. The papers called her Susan Walker and her pleading mother had called her "my baby" on the news.

Satisfied, the Hunter moved past the shallow grave. He held himself tall and proud.

It was hunting season and the hunting was good.

CHAPTER 5

The phone rang several times on Saturday and each time Makedde jumped, nervously eavesdropping on her father's conversations until she was satisfied it wasn't Andy Flynn.

He didn't call. Then again, Mak didn't know what she would have done if he actually had. She wasn't ready to speak to him again, but her curiosity urged her otherwise.

What is he up to at Quantico? Why is he calling?

At three o'clock Makedde's father received a call from Theresa. She was coming over with her husband, Ben, and their little baby, Breanna, in less than an hour. Although she'd been forewarned about the visit, Mak wasn't really in the mood for her sister. When she overheard the call she promptly disappeared into her father's study and buried her head in *The Diagnostic and Statistical Manual of Mental Disorders* and kept her nose in the book until well after she heard the doorbell ring thirty minutes later.

* * *

"Makedde? Mak?" Her father punctuated his call with a round of soft knocking on the study door.

"Yeah, Dad."

The door creaked open.

"Your sister is here with Ben and Breanna. Come on out and say hello." He looked at her with bewilderment as she sat hunched over the thick textbook.

"Okay," she said and bookmarked her spot. "Sorry, I'll be just a sec." When she made motions to get up, he spun around and returned to his younger visiting daughter, whispering, "Bookworm . . ." or something similar under his breath.

It wasn't that Makedde didn't love her sister. She did. It was just that Theresa had the knack of irritating her at times—and Mak didn't have much tolerance for any kind of irritation these days. She wasn't sure if it was more from lack of sleep or overload of premenstrual hormones. It could be risky to have a visit from Theresa when she was like this. She didn't want to react badly.

Andy's mysterious call hadn't exactly helped Makedde's mood, or her sleeping either. That man was trouble, and she knew it. She wondered for a moment whether her problem was lack of sex. No, that was the kind of ridiculous statement that her friend Jaqui Reeves would make.

You're fine. You've just got PMS and a thesis to complete.

She shook any thoughts of Andy out of her head and walked down the carpeted hallway.

At five foot ten, Theresa was a couple of inches shorter than Mak, exactly the height their mother had been. Theresa was twenty-three, the younger daughter by three years. Her pretty face was a slightly paler, rounder version of Makedde's, and it rarely saw make-up. Her dark blond hair was naturally straight, and she had it cut in a neat bob just above her shoulders.

Theresa was always conservatively groomed and though no one in their family was particularly religious, she always looked ready for the pews. Mak rather thought she enjoyed being prissy. She wore a cotton shirt buttoned up one from the top, and a pair of Eddie Bauer slacks. She was the one who bought their father the pair he wore.

Her husband, Ben, was a nice-guy accountant who was born on the island and would die on the island. No threat of unpredictability. He was the same height as his wife, and his unlined face looked even younger than his twenty-six years. He wore a baby-blue plaid shirt, the kind that Makedde imagined yuppie lumberjacks would wear. It was also from Eddie Bauer. His hair was brown. She suspected he used Brylcreem to make it so smooth. Mak wanted to mess it up. Just a few strands would do.

Yikes. What's gotten into me?

Hugs all round. Mak felt stiff and formal. She was worried about being so negative. What exactly was her problem? Was it that her sister seemed so damn rational and perfect in their father's eyes? Married, with child. More often than not their father was worried about Mak, not happy for her, whereas Theresa was always the stable one. Predictable. Makedde was what one might politely refer to as "feisty." Always flying off somewhere. Always getting into trouble.

Theresa and her family made their way into the living room with Dad at their heels. Mak followed a fair distance behind, still trying to psych herself up for the visit.

Would she ever find herself wandering into that living room with her own baby and husband, and her father

37

smiling like a schoolboy at the sight of it all? Not any time soon, it seemed.

Back when Mak was twenty, the family had encouraged her to marry a local boy named George Purdy. When she found out he had cheated on her, Mak dumped him and flipped his engagement ring into a bagful of milk cartons and baked beans in the Safeway supermarket checkout.

They were forty-five minutes into baby pictures before Theresa started in. That was almost forty-five minutes longer than usual.

"Dad tells me you aren't doing too well," she said.

Mak blinked and looked up from a stack of photos of Breanna with a polka-dotted pink and yellow bow in her hair, just to check. Yes, the comment was directed at her. "Excuse me?" she said.

"Apparently you were up all last night, pacing."

"Insomnia," Les muttered under his breath from the safety of his easy chair on the other side of the room. He had the album of Breanna playing with an orange ball.

"Dad, I don't have insomnia," Mak said. "I just have a little trouble sleeping sometimes. It's no big deal." If he brought up the thing about the shrink, she'd strangle him.

Theresa had Breanna on her knee and was bouncing her gently. Her adorable little face turned to Mak and broke into a two-hundred-watt smile. It was contagious and Mak couldn't help but smile back. Breanna was very cute; there was no denying it. The toddler had soft white curls crowning her head, and ears that stuck out a little. Breanna's mouth was like a plump cherry, and her inquisitive eyes were the optimistic color of blue skies, and just as wide.

"Doesn't 'having trouble sleeping' *mean* that you have insomnia?" Theresa asked.

Makedde's smile dropped. She looked back to her sister, who, incredibly, was just getting started.

"I just can't understand why you would still want your damn Ph.D. after that whole nightmare in Sydney. Not to mention the incident with Stanley. I mean, Forensic Psychology? No wonder you're not sleeping. Always reading about psychos and rapists . . ."

Low bloody blow, sis.

The tiny hairs on the back of Makedde's neck bristled. The incident with Stanley was years before and he was in jail now. It had nothing to do with her Ph.D. It was totally irrelevant. And what the hell did "damn Ph.D." mean, anyway? She never bugged Theresa about her aspirations to be a house mom. If it wasn't about modeling not being "intellectual" enough, it was about Forensic Psychology not being "nice" enough. It seemed that Theresa just had to be negative about whatever her older sister was doing.

"It's not safe at university these days, you know. Especially a big campus like UBC." Theresa aimed her comment to the whole room as if it were an important public service announcement. "What did I hear the other day? One in three female students have been sexually assaulted or harassed there! I mean, one in *three!*"

"I think that particular report said one in six, which is shocking enough without your exaggeration," Mak said softly. "And those figures have since been disputed."

"One in six. Whatever." Theresa took a deep breath.

Oh no, she's not finished crapping on yet.

"And that missing girl . . . What is it? Walker? Susan Walker? She was a student at UBC, you know. Lived on campus. I saw her fiancé on the news the other day, pleading for information on her whereabouts. Her mother was crying. They figure she's been abducted. I don't know how you can feel safe there—"

Don't say it.

"*Especially* with what you've been through."

She said it.

Ben kept quiet. Theresa did not. "And the *druggings*. They've got girls waking up in strange men's beds and not even remembering how they got there. *Ropnol*, they use on them. It's an epidemic."

"Rohypnol," Mak corrected her gently. As a tranquilizer the drug was legal in sixty-four countries to treat sleeplessness, anxiety, convulsions and muscle tension, and although illegal in Canada and America, it had naturally found its way in the back door somehow. She was well aware of the reports.

"The kind of men who roam those campuses these days . . ."

Mak stared at the plain white wall beside her. If she looked really closely, she could make out her mother's brushstrokes. She managed to completely block out the familiar voice as her sister continued to make pronouncements on the perils of Vancouver, the UBC campus and Makedde's life in general. Mak wanted to tell her to stop encouraging their father to worry even more than he already did, but she held her tongue. Insomnia was sapping her strength, and she was too tired to argue.

Mak looked to Breanna for wisdom. The little girl was searching the room with wide eyes, her gaze moving from her mother's lips to her grandfather's, then back to her mother's, finally resting on the collar of her mom's shirt, which she then decided to yank. Theresa gently removed the tiny hand, still continuing to talk. Makedde watched her sister's lips move, hearing nothing.

Suffering from what felt like a loud steam train chugging around in her head, Mak excused herself to the study, citing deadlines on her thesis. She opened the textbook to her bookmarked section on Personality Disorders but couldn't keep her eyes open long enough to read anything. Before long, she lay her weary head on the textbook and slipped into a restless nap.

She emerged at dinnertime and walked down the hallway, rubbing her eyes and taking in the smells of cooking. She turned into the dining room, looked at the dinner table and . . .

Whoa.

There was a stranger at the table—a woman—and she was chatting with her father. The woman made eye contact and said, "Hi, Makedde," then pushed her chair out and stood, offering a handshake. "I'm Ann."

My God, the shrink.

Her face was warm and intelligent, framed by short, stylishly cropped wavy auburn hair. She was a compact-looking woman who Mak guessed was in her mid-forties. Not very tall. She was dressed in slacks and a loose blouse, smart casual, with little pearl stud earrings as her only jewelry. She was even-featured and pleasant-looking, with large brown eyes and a magnetic, Julia Roberts smile.

Mak shook her hand. "It's a pleasure to meet you."

"Likewise," she said. "I've heard lots about you."

I bet you have.

Ann read her expression and added, "All good things. I hear you're a brilliant student and quite an accomplished model."

Mak didn't know what to say. She couldn't say that she'd heard lots about Ann, because she hadn't. Last

41

night her father had obviously been hinting subtly that this woman was important to him, and Mak had been too paranoid and wrapped up in her own misery to make much of it. She had so quickly gone on the defensive.

How stupid of me.

Mak settled in at the table. Everything was already prepared. The food ready, the table set, the guests seated . . .

"I'm sorry I didn't help with anything. I passed out." Mak let out a nervous laugh when she realized she may have inadvertently opened herself up to that unwanted topic again. "I'm in charge of clean-up," she said.

She watched as her father served his new friend some rice and chicken and an assortment of vegetables. Ann flashed him a smile when she thanked him, and Mak thought she caught a slightly gooey look on her father's face.

Wow.

Is this . . . are they . . . interested in each other?

She stole a glance at Ann's ring finger. Nothing. *Wow, again.* "Was married to Sergeant Morgan," he'd said the night before. *Was.* Obviously she'd kept her married name. When did all this happen?

"So, you're visiting the island?" Mak asked casually.

"Yes. I have some friends here, but I live in Vancouver. You do as well, I hear?"

"Yup. Kitsilano."

"I'm not too far from there. Not quite as cool an area though, I'm afraid. Kits is nice."

"I like it."

"I still prefer Victoria," Theresa interjected over a fork loaded with rice.

"Yes, it's very pretty here," Ann said. "The 'Garden City.' We're not far from Butchart Gardens, are we? I haven't been for ages."

Les looked up. "Umm . . . Perhaps we could make a day of it when you come to the island next?" The words came out a little awkwardly.

Bold, Dad. Very bold, Mak thought. *Go for it.*

"That would be nice."

I can't believe I am witnessing my dad setting up a date.

"This chicken's great, Dad," Theresa said, oblivious to the conversation. "I just taught him the recipe," she added proudly.

He smiled good-naturedly.

"Well, my son Connor has just mastered toast," Ann said, and everyone laughed. "I can tell when he's sick of junk food because he shows up unannounced and cleans out my fridge—"

The pealing of the telephone broke the moment.

Oh no. Not now.

"I'm not answering the phone," Mak blurted out.

The call echoed through the house, its sound amplified in a chorus through several rooms. There were three phones in the Vanderwall home, and each person at the dining-room table looked up from their meal to stare at the nearest one, which was mounted on the wall in the kitchen. Everyone that is, except Les Vanderwall. He was looking right at Makedde.

"I'm not answering it," she said. "We're in the middle of dinner." Mak was sitting closest to the phone. Unfortunately her quick nap had not relieved her of her headache, which seemed to flare up further with each consecutive ring.

"Oh, for heaven's sake, I'll get it," Theresa said and pushed her chair back. She tossed her hair to one side as she stood, and her blond bob slid back into place perfectly when she straightened her head again.

"No, don't get it," Mak said, half standing now. "We're eating."

But Theresa was already a mere arm's length from the phone, saying something about how Breanna would wake up crying.

She snatched up the receiver and answered with, "Vanderwall residence, hello?"

Mak waited. Her heart was beating way too fast. If it was Andy, she didn't want to speak to him. Not now. Not with the whole family nearby . . . especially her sister, and her father's guest.

"No, this isn't Makedde. This is her sister, Theresa. Who is this?" Pause. "*Andrew Flynn?* Oh, *really?* I've heard a lot about you, Detective. Are you calling from Australia?"

Mak vaulted from her chair.

"The FBI Academy? *Reeeeeally?*" Theresa went on, her eyes bright with curiosity. She shifted her weight to one leg and put a hand on her hip, turning her back to the dining room.

Mak reached the kitchen and slid across the linoleum waving her hands to get her sister's attention and mouthing the words, "I'm not here . . . I'm not here!"

"Oh, really? How *fascinating* . . ." Theresa heard her approach and shifted her weight back to the other leg, looking over her shoulder and ignoring her sister's frantic sign language. "Uh-huh." When Mak was close, Theresa said, "Oh, here she is now—"

She was smiling as she extended the phone. Mak thought it looked like a "fuck you" smile.

Mak stood back and shook her head.

After the receiver was suspended in the air for a while, Theresa brought the phone back to her lips and repeated, "Yup, Makedde's right here, I'll put her on." She extended the phone again. The smile was really big now.

Smart ass.

"Uh, hi."

"Makedde?" That familiar voice.

"Hi, Andy. How are you?"

The line wasn't very clear.

"Good. How ya goin'?" The simple Aussie-ism pulled at her heartstrings.

"Fine, thanks." *Well, not really.*

Mak looked through the kitchen doorway into the dining room. Ann was the only one who was polite enough not to watch, everyone else was staring and Theresa was still standing in the kitchen, only a couple of feet away, watching intently.

"Just a second. I'll switch phones," she told Andy. "Can you hang this up for me when I get on the other phone?" she asked her sister, handing the receiver over. "I'll just be a sec."

Mak jogged down the hall to her father's study and closed the door behind her. She took the call standing up, the cord twisted and stretched taut. She didn't want to get too comfortable. By the time she picked it up, her sister was already having another conversation on the line.

". . . Really? So how long are you there—" Theresa was saying.

"Thanks," Mak said loudly. "I've got it now, thank you."

"Well, bye, Detective Flynn. Nice talking with you." Mak heard the phone click, then listened for a moment to make sure her sister was really off the line.

"Sorry about that."

"Oh, that's okay. Your sister seems nice."

"Yup." She leaned against the side of the desk and let her eyes wander around her father's study. A framed photo of his graduation from the academy was hung beside a plaque lauding outstanding service. Her mouth always curved into a lopsided grin at the sight of that photo. Her father looked so young and eager, his hair not yet gray, his face smooth and chiseled.

"My dad told me you called yesterday."

"Yeah, I did. You weren't in yet."

Yes, but how did you know I would be here? She knew the question would make her sound suspicious, so she didn't ask it aloud. Besides, it was probably just a lucky guess, right? He would know that she visited often, and he had her father's number. It was logical that he would call her father's place if he wanted to speak to her. *But to speak to me about what?*

Makedde turned her back to the wall of frames and plaques, and faced a shelf lined with dusty caps traded with police departments from all over the continent. She scanned the embroidered crests—Vancouver PD, Texas Polygraph Unit, Los Angeles Police Department SWAT Team, Federal Bureau of Investigation . . .

The phone line seemed to be quiet for an awfully long time.

"It's been a while, hasn't it?" she finally said. "So, you're calling from Quantico. Must be pretty late in Virginia?"

"Yeah. Past eleven. As I was just telling your sister, I'm here doing some training."

"With the Behavioral Sciences Unit?"

"That's the one. The Police Commissioner has okayed a new Profiling Unit in New South Wales. World-class technology. It'll be right up there with the best. Looks like I have a good chance of heading one of the divisions in the unit. Perhaps even heading the entire unit in the future."

For a split second she experienced an unexpected surge of anger, and knew that it was because she felt he was indirectly benefiting from the worst kind of tragedy and violence. But Mak knew it was unfair to feel that way and she pushed the thoughts aside.

"That's great," she responded.

The Australian accent. That voice. It triggered mixed emotions in her. She had fallen for him, but soon after mistrusted him, even feared him. He saved her life in Sydney and she hated being indebted. She couldn't shake that feeling every time she thought of him, and now, with his voice in her ear, her chest felt like it was filled with a swelling balloon, growing tighter with every breath. The fact that they had slept together made it even worse. Worse still was that she still thought about it.

"Look, I can't talk long. We're just having dinner," she blurted. She felt guilty about the way it sounded the instant she had said it, even though it was true.

"Oh, I'm sorry. I'll let you go."

"No, that's not necessary. I—"

"No, really, I'm sorry. Please get back to your family."

He had closed up like a clam. She knew from experience that he could do that.

Silence.

"Um . . . thanks for your call," she said.

"Take care."

"You, too. Bye."

Makedde hung up and stared at the phone. She was flushed. Her eyes stung. Did he just want to talk? Was there something he wanted to tell her? She fought a desperate urge to call him back. She sat in her father's chair and put her head in her hands. The last thing she needed was to start thinking about Andy Flynn again. She needed peace, and there was no peace to be found there.

Makedde thought her meal would be cold by the time she got back to the table, and it was.

Four sets of eyes stared expectantly at her as she sat down, but she said nothing. Theresa opened her mouth to speak, but something in Makedde's look stopped her before any sound came out. When she opened her mouth again it was to tell Ann all about Breanna.

That was good.

CHAPTER 6

"Call for you, Sarge," came Constable Perry's voice, intruding into a rare moment of peace by way of the telephone intercom on the desk. "Line four."

Sergeant Grant Wilson of the Royal Canadian Mounted Police sighed and pushed his paperwork aside. "Yup, I'll take it," he said, unsure if Perry would hear that acknowledgment. He picked up the receiver and pressed the flashing button that was fourth from the top on his far-too-sophisticated phone system. He preferred the old system. It was much simpler.

"Wilson," he said.

"Hi, Grant," came the familiar voice on the other end. "It's Mike."

He could tell that from the voice. "Hiya, Mike."

Corporal Michael Rose and he were mates from way back, despite the fact that Mike, at thirty-four, was ten years younger than Grant. They'd both done well with the RCMP. They lived in the same suburb and their wives were friends. The ladies kept themselves busy when they had to stay late, so it worked out well for everyone.

Grant's daughter Cherrie even thought Mike was kind of cute, but that was fifteen-year-olds for you. Mike and he still lifted weights together three times a week, and Grant was proud that he still managed to out bench press his younger friend (by two and a half kilos) even if his own daughter thought he didn't look quite as good.

"So whaz up, Mike?" Grant asked.

"Oh geez. We've got a bit of a problem out here."

Grant raised an eyebrow. "What is it?" He leaned back in his chair and began clicking and un-clicking his pen. Amanda hated that, so he tried to remember not to do it at home. "Your brother get himself in trouble again?"

Click. Un-click.

Mike's brother, Evan, was a real handful. He'd probably have to arrest him some day.

Click. Un-click.

"No, nothing like that. We got a call to check on a report out Nahatlatch way. A couple of hunters said their dog started digging around in something that looked like a body buried under some shrubs. We kinda figured it was probably an animal of some sort, but nope, it's a person alright. A dead woman."

Click. Grant's hand stopped.

"A dead woman?"

"Yup. Looks that way."

Grant thought about that for a moment. "Well, you been out there?"

"I'm out there right now. I'm here with Symmons and Kent. Not too far from the river itself."

"How's it look to you?"

"Looks bad, Grant. I can't figure why she'd be way the hell out here all by herself dressed like that."

"Dressed like what?"

"She's got on a sort of button-up shirt of some kind and a skirt from what we can tell."

"A skirt?"

"Exactly. And them black nylon thingies. She's no lost hunter or whitewater kayaker or nothin', that's for sure."

Grant nodded. "Street girl, you reckon?"

"Nah, I didn't mean it to sound like that. Hard to tell, but it don't really look like that to me. Kinda conservative even with the skirt and all. More like a church girl or something."

"How long she been there?"

"Not long, they don't think. A couple of days or so. Pretty fresh. In bad shape, but fresh."

Grant tried not to think about that. "Okay, Mike, I'll come out your way. Be there in about an hour . . ."

CHAPTER 7

Makedde Vanderwall always ran alone, and often after dark. Nothing could ever spook her enough to want to change that habit. She found beauty in darkness, in thunderstorms, and in those solo midnight runs.

But it drove her dad nuts.

Whenever she visited Vancouver Island, she always went for a jog around the nearby lakes. Her fastest time for the eleven-kilometer Elk and Beaver Lake track was forty-four minutes—not bad for someone who wasn't exactly petite, as the best medium to long distance runners always seemed to be.

During the day she often ran with her Discman playing, but when she ran at night she preferred the quiet, and the assurance of a small canister of bear spray as a defense. The woods were dark at this hour, but rather than being frightening, Mak felt protected, as if the night itself were a great comfortable blanket. The sky was clear, the moon and the stars lit her way, and Makedde knew the track like the back of her hand. There were few fellow joggers at night and she preferred it that way.

She hadn't come to the lake to socialize, or catch up with her island friends, she had come to run and to think.

Why did Andy call me?

Why is it that my sister and I aren't getting along? Is it my fault? Is it really that difficult?

Is Ann Morgan going to become Dad's girlfriend?

Ann seemed nice enough. And it had been almost two years since her mom died. Her dad was lonely. He would be so much happier with a girlfriend.

As Mak jogged she watched the still waters shimmering in the moonlight. Perhaps it was the time of year, but the sight of the bright orange moon hanging proudly in the sky above the lake brought to mind Halloween—that magical day she remembered so well.

Mom, leaning over me, waking me in the dark . . .

Her mother, Jane, had always fed Makedde and put her to bed early after school on October thirty-first. Mak would quickly fall into a deep sleep in the knowledge that when she woke up on what she believed was a new day, it would be Halloween—the day when there was no sun, and the ghouls and witches came out, smiling and ready to spook. It was a special day when all the chocolate malt balls and jellybeans she could ever want would be happily donated to her pillowcase carry sack. It was a special day when she could pretend she was a ghoul herself, and wander from door to door with her parents and with little Theresa in tow, and be greeted by even stranger beings—vampires and werewolves and aliens who would smile and give her candy and show her tricks.

It was a magic day, and a day of night.

Back on the mainland, under the same bright moon, Sergeant Grant Wilson of the RCMP found himself in a different set of woods, contemplating the senseless murder of Susan Walker—a girl not much older than his own daughter, a girl who was afraid of the dark, and who, in the end, never stood a chance.

CHAPTER 8

The Hunter sat quietly at a small table in the far corner of the student pub. He held a beer in one hand and a newspaper in the other, and his eyes watched every movement in the room.

It was a down-market sort of place, sparsely lit and furnished with plain wooden chairs and tables and an uninspiring green and brown carpet. A long wooden bar stretched out to his left. It was a quiet night and all the accompanying stools were empty. He only had the fox-faced bartender for company. The young man was leaning against the counter, a bored kid slowly polishing a mug, the fuzz on his unshaven young face visible in patches.

This pub was a prime hunting ground during the right season. And that season was now. It was September, the beginning of a new semester, and that meant a fresh crop of targets—girls from all over the country and some from overseas—smart girls, students, each one a challenge, all trying to find their way around, looking for new friends, looking for action.

Perfect.

He studied a group of average-looking men and women playing pool at the other end of the room. They were all wearing the same sort of clothes—jeans teamed with sneakers or hiking boots. The Hunter had got his look just right and he blended in well. But none of the women interested him.

Patience.

The pub was taking a while to fill up, but that was fine. No need to panic yet. He preferred to arrive early, secure a good position and get a feel for the growing activity in the room. He could become invisible. And if he sensed any unwanted attention he could leave.

He was in control.

The Hunter was smart. He knew the importance of planning. He had plans that were fluid enough to adapt to any unwanted elements, and he only ever made his move if things were perfect. He'd learned that lesson the hard way. Of course, after the catch it was different. Once you had won, you could do what you wanted.

He had just about given up when a young woman entered and immediately caught his eye. Almost as if he had picked up on some kind of radar signal, he raised his head and there she was, moving toward the bartender—a brunette, fairly short and plain, but not unattractive. Her black, square-heeled leather boots were polished nicely, and she wore stretchy dark denim jeans with a gray fleece jacket. She looked like she might have a decent figure under all the clothes. The girl appeared a bit unsure of herself and her surroundings. A bit flustered. That interested him the most. He immediately pegged her as a new student starting her very first semester of university.

A possible mark.

He lifted his newspaper slightly to cover the lower half of his face and stared at the girl through non-prescription glasses. He watched her pause a few feet from the bar and look eagerly around the room, and he lowered his gaze to the paper when her eyes came his way. She took no notice of the bespectacled man in the corner, and continued to look around the room. At a glance he thought her eyes appeared red-rimmed and a little puffy.

After a moment, the girl approached the bored bartender and asked where the phones were. The Hunter thought that was an interesting question, considering she had just walked past a bank of them on the way in. Obviously she hadn't been paying much attention. She was preoccupied with something. Distressed.

He felt the adrenaline surge. Conditions seemed good.

The bartender pointed back toward the entrance, barely raising his eyes from the mug he was polishing. She thanked him politely—with no obvious accent—and off she went.

The Hunter followed her, moving across the room quietly, one hand in his pocket and his head slightly slumped as if he were tired. He stuck close to the wall, inconspicuous.

The restrooms were in the direction of the phones, and he knew he would be able to hear the young woman's conversation if he listened through the men's room door. When he rounded the corner he raised his eyes ever so briefly and caught a glimpse of the bank of phones and the woman dialing. He entered the men's, which thankfully was empty. Good. He held his hands against the inside of the door, his ear flat against the hollow imitation wood panel.

"Brian? Brian, if you're there, pick up," he heard her say. "Pick up, please." Pause. *"Pleeease."* Pause. "Look, I'm at the pub. Where are you? Brian, I—" She stopped mid-sentence and let out a frustrated huff. The Hunter peeked around the door to see what she would do next. The girl hung up the receiver and fumbled in the pocket of her jeans for change. She had to pull up her jacket to get at her back pocket, and he caught a flash of pale skin. The girl found a quarter and redialled.

"Brian, it's Debbie again . . ." She stole a look at her watch and threw her hand in the air when she saw the time. "It's eight-forty already. I don't know how long I'll stick around, but . . ." She trailed off. "Just get here."

The Hunter waited until she hung up and quickly stepped out behind her.

"Hey, Debbie? I thought that was you . . ."

Many hours later, Debbie Melmeth woke to an unsettling quiet. It was so quiet she felt as though she had drowned and was tangled in weeds, wrapped up and trapped underwater in a freezing lake.

Nothing.

A breath.

It was her own breathing and it was ragged. She opened her mouth to see if water would come in. It didn't. She hadn't drowned. She wasn't dead.

She rolled her head to the side and tried to keep her eyes open. She was disoriented. Everything felt terribly wrong, and she didn't know why. The silence around her was disturbingly foreign. Even so, as she struggled back into consciousness, her ears began to pick up sounds. They were small, mysterious sounds, but they were something.

Debbie wasn't sure whether to laugh or cry. She felt dizzy and drunk. She remembered that Brian hadn't been at the bar. She had called him and he wasn't home.

But there was a charming man there. He spoke to her. She must have drunk a lot after that. Did he buy her drinks? Something was wrong. Her inebriated mind could not fully comprehend her circumstances, but she knew something was definitely wrong.

She tried to relax and concentrate on her breathing. She didn't know how long she stayed that way, listening to her own breathing, her mind spinning slowly in circles, taking in her body's confused signals, before she heard a new sound.

Clink.

Clink-clink.

It seemed to be coming from another room.

Her eyes did not want to focus, but she could make out that she was sitting in a chair in some kind of dimly lit room. It smelled odd, unfamiliar.

She heard the clinking again and fought a wave of nausea. She felt the urge to laugh, but a great blanket of blackness leaped up inside her and shut off the lights. Unconsciousness stopped her short.

Some time later, she tried to speak. She knew someone was there, someone who would know what was wrong with her, someone with answers, and she tried to ask, "What am I doing here?" It took all her effort to form the sentence, but still, the result was little more than a slurred string of incoherent vowels and consonants.

"Whhaaaayeee?"

Unintentionally, she laughed out loud. Her own ridiculous attempt at language seemed funny for a moment. But this wasn't funny. Nothing about it was funny. Why the laughter? Shut up and concentrate. She couldn't move her arms or legs—*Why in God's name can't I move my arms and legs?*—and it seemed to Debbie that her mind had failed her. It had turned to jelly. She had never been drunk like this before. How could she have let this happen? She couldn't even move her limbs! It was as if she were glued to the chair.

She tried to look down. Her vision was blurry—not working right at all—and now she could see why she was unable to move. Her ankles were secured to the chair with some sort of metal cuffs. It felt like her wrists—which she could not see because they were secured behind her back—were also handcuffed.

Someone had done this, and they were not far away. She had no concept of who or when or why, or even how close they were, but she sensed a presence and she tried talking to them again, this time more loudly.

"Whaaaaaaaa haa . . . ?" She stopped and tried again, confused at her inability to speak properly. *What is going on?* She tried again and it came out as, "Waaa waaa yaaaadee!"

She attempted to take in her surroundings, and that's when she first saw the animals. They were everywhere—bears, cougars, wolves, foxes, elk, deer. They were looking at her, staring at her, terrifyingly real. *This can't be real. It can't be.* But it was all she could see.

Debbie wanted to shield her face from their tearing claws and jagged teeth. She wanted to protect herself. The animals were coming at her from all directions and she panicked. She struggled in her binds and screamed. The room spun into a dizzy blur, the hard wooden floor leaping up to strike her in the face. She found herself on her side, her cheek pressed against the wood, her body heavy and awkward, folded onto itself.

She heard thunderous footsteps rushing toward her, making the floor rumble. Someone was approaching and she tried to speak but her mouth was squashed against the floor. Her lips moved uselessly, and with one eye straining upward, she saw that a man was leaning down. Then she was off the floor, pulled right into the air, chair and all, and shoved back into place. The animal faces were again snarling all around her, and now a human face joined them, a man standing over her. She was seeing double, now quadruple, now double again.

And then she recognized him. It was the man who had offered her a drink, only he wasn't wearing his glasses any more. He had done this to her. He had trapped her. She wanted to scream but what came out of her mouth was a distorted giggle, a hopeless, drug-induced giggle that was as far from joy as terror could be.

CHAPTER 9

Grant Wilson didn't like horses. He'd even had his leg re-set when he was little to prove to his father, also an RCMP officer, just how much he didn't like horses. The family nag, Daisy, had once thrown him about ten feet in the air and he'd landed in a tree.

But this didn't matter because, generally speaking, the Royal Canadian Mounted Police spent little time "mounted." There was the odd occasion—the famous "Musical Ride" when the Queen came to town, for example—but he didn't have anything to do with that. Nope, they had police cruisers now instead of those tall unpredictable bucking creatures, and in this part of Canada the jurisdiction of the RCMP went well beyond the reach of horses.

Grant was in the woods at the Nahatlatch River looking for clues. It was freezing, and he walked through the woods in his parka and layers of uniform, battling a deep, gnawing chill in his bones—and in his mind.

This was where the girl's body had been dumped. The spot was still lit up for the Forensic Team. She had been a real mess, just as Mike had said. The animals had got to her, they suggested. The area where she was found had already been gone over with a fine-tooth comb several times, and now the search was moving wider. And, like a fool, Grant had been roped into helping. He should really have been home with his wife. She needed him. *Damn.* He pulled his thoughts away from his ailing wife and focused on the job at hand.

They were finishing up the autopsy right now back in the city. She was a young girl, a teenager. That didn't sit easy with Grant. He thought of his own daughter, and he didn't like thinking about Cherrie while he was walking through the woods trying to find a murder weapon.

He didn't like that one bit. Once in a while they had to deal with an ill-fated hunter or two out here. They'd had a couple of bear attacks and a shooting accident as well. But nothing like this. Not that he could recall, anyway. That girl had no reason to be out here alone.

Grant didn't know if his body could take the chill much longer. It was getting late. They would have to pick it up in the morning. He spun around and headed in Mike's direction, sweeping the flashlight back and forth in front of himself as he walked. The forest floor was uneven and thick with exposed roots and ground-covering plants. He made his way into one of the clearings and looked around. Corporal Michael Rose was talking with one of the constables. He was using his hands a lot as he spoke. Mike looked up immediately when his friend approached. He ended his conversation and walked over.

"We should pack it in soon, eh?" he said.

"Yeah," Grant replied. "You took the words right out of my mouth. We'll make everyone sick if we keep 'em out here."

"Tomorrow when it's light we'll get a search team together and take them through the steps."

"Yeah."

Loud barking grabbed their attention, and they swiveled their heads around simultaneously, looking for the source. A voice broke through the darkness, and a flashlight flickered through the trees far ahead.

"Sarge!"

Grant started running and Mike was right beside him.

It was Symmons. He was with one of the dog handlers a ways back from the river. "We got bones here!" he cried. "We got bones!"

Bones? Mike and Grant exchanged looks as they ran. It could be something else . . . a deer perhaps? That was more likely. But the interminable barking continued at a terrible pitch. The dog was really worked up.

"Human?" Grant asked as they emerged through the trees.

"Hang on . . . I think so. Ella's going totally ape," Symmons said. He was breathless, even though Mike and Grant were the ones who had done all the running.

Ella kept barking and barking, circling the spot and barking some more.

"Good girl, good girl, Ella," the dog handler said, calming the animal down. "Such a gooood girl!" He turned to them. "Yup, she's definitely got something here."

A large bone stuck up through the forest floor a few paces away, stripped of flesh. It could have been anything. Grant felt a little disappointed after running all the way over. And a bit relieved, too.

A couple of members of the Forensic Team had followed them in. "Let's take a look," one of them said, and they brushed past.

"You know it could just be a—" Mike started to say, but he stopped short. Someone flashed a light across the area to the side of the bone Grant had initially seen, and that's when it became obvious that there was more, what looked like a whole ribcage was poking up through the dirt and the ferns, and it was definitely human. That is, unless the local deer had taken up wearing shirts.

"Let's get the lights in here!" one of the team called out. "Looks like we've got a second body."

CHAPTER 10

It was evening, and at last Makedde was feeling relaxed. She was curled up on the couch in her modest Vancouver apartment with an out-of-print copy of *Psychopathy—Theory and Research* by Dr. Robert D. Hare.

What more could a girl want?

She wanted to scrub up on the subject before the psychopathy conference the next day. The 1970 book was older than she was, but she thought that it would provide an interesting background to the cutting-edge research she would be hearing about during the conference in the days to follow. She was already quite familiar with Hervey Cleckley's *Mask of Sanity* and she had read Dr. Hare's classic, *Without Conscience: The Disturbing World of the Psychopaths Among Us*, a few times over, but in recent months her appetite for information on the subject had been insatiable.

. . . During periods of relaxation and painful stimulation, the pattern of adrenergic (sympathetic) and

*cholinergic (parasympathetic) activity is the same
for neurotic subjects as it is for normal ones . . .*

A half-eaten bowl of pasta sat on the coffee table beside her.

*However, following the termination of the stimula-
tion, the autonomic activity of the normal subjects . . .*

The phone rang, breaking her concentration. Makedde reached across and picked it up without taking her
eyes from the page. She was pretty sure she knew who it
would be.

"How's it going, Dad?" she said.

"Fine. And you?"

"Fine as well, thanks," she replied, and read another line.

*Experiments recently reviewed by Malmo (1966) are
consistent with Rubin's hypothesis . . .*

"How've you been feeling?" her father asked.

*The relevance of Rubin's theory to psychopathy is
that some of the characteristics of the psychopath
are more or less opposite to those of the neurotic . . .*

"Have you been sleeping?" he went on, his voice a little
louder this time, indicating that he knew she wasn't giving him her full attention. She took her eyes off the page.

"Hmmm, sleep?" Mak furrowed her brow and looked
to the ceiling, making a show of racking her brain even
though the only audience she had for her little perfor-
mance was her house plants. "Oh. Oh, that. Overrated."

"Makedde—"

She held the phone from her ear as he raised his voice, and with the other hand marked her page and lowered the book into her lap.

"Dad," she finally said. "Calm down. I'm fine. I'm sleeping fine." A lie.

"Who do you think you're kidding?" her father said. "Ann thinks she can help you. She knows all about that stuff. She said she would be very happy to talk to you about it, or perhaps recommend someone."

"Oh really?"

"I think you should take her up on it," he said.

"You do, eh? So, when did she get divorced anyway?" Mak asked.

Pause. "I guess they divorced a few years ago." *Bingo.* "What has that got to do with the price of tea in China?"

"Nothing." She wondered just how interested her father was in Ann. "I just saw how you were looking at her. I like her, Dad. She's nice."

"Good. Then maybe you'll consider taking her up on her offer. She wants me to give you her number, just in case you ever need it."

"Okay, go ahead." He gave her the details, and she took them down dutifully, with no intention whatsoever of calling.

"Now, you got another message from Detective Flynn."

"Andy?" *Oh, damn.*

"He left a number for you to call him at Quantico. I think he was afraid to ask for your home number. He said he would only be available on that number until tomorrow afternoon, though."

"Okay."

She took it down and stared at the digits after she hung up the phone. The piece of paper in her hand held two phone numbers of people she didn't really want to speak to. Talking to either of them would only open up a can of worms.

It was too late to call Andy in Virginia anyway. She'd leave it till tomorrow.

Maybe.

That night Makedde dreamed of psychiatrists, FBI agents and psychopaths. And the devil. Right before she woke up screaming, he shot flames from his eyes and Makedde—dressed in her father's police uniform—fell backward, her hands still frozen uselessly on the trigger of her gun. Once again the devil violently ripped her mother's life away before her eyes.

That was at 3:00 A.M.

She couldn't get back to sleep after that.

CHAPTER 11

Harold G. Gosper Ph.D., a Professor of Social Psychology, arrived at the University of British Columbia at eight-thirty and chose a seat at the back of the Graduate Center Ballroom. He wore his favorite forest-green cardigan and matching corduroy pants with a mauve button-down shirt. As he scratched at a spot of toothpaste on his pants, he vaguely recalled some protest from his wife when he had left the house, something about his wearing the same thing for four days in a row. But no matter. She'd hardly said a word to him the last few days and he didn't really care.

He wet the toothpaste mark with a bit of saliva, and once satisfied, pulled his hand away and ran a palm over his slick hair. He adjusted himself in the stiff plastic chair and licked his lips. Professor Gosper had picked a spot in the far corner of the room specifically so that he could leave quietly when things got boring. There were heavy exit doors to his right and his vantage point offered a full view of the room and its occupants. He liked watching people. More than attending psychology lectures; that was for sure. He was interested in social, not forensic psychology, and the truth was he didn't have a lot of time for "psychopathy" and Dr. Hare's theories on the psychopathic mind.

Sure, Dr. Hare had his awards and his honorary medals and his documentary specials, and his Hare Psychopathy Checklist (PCL) was widely accepted as the diagnostic tool for psychopaths. Gosper was all too aware of those facts. And of course there was his popular book, *Without Conscience: The Disturbing World of the Psychopaths Among Us*. He certainly couldn't forget that. But even so, Gosper found Hare's apparent guru status a bit hard to take.

In his own mind he was quite convinced that his secret animosity had nothing to do with the multiple rejection slips he had received for his own manuscript.

Perhaps one of Dr. Hare's publishers would be attending the conference?

With his arms folded, Gosper sat back and observed the slowly filling room. A clique of uniformed police officers filed in and eschewed the name tags offered at the entrance. They were from the local Vancouver PD, and they moved in a single pack toward the long tables of Danishes and choc-chip muffins. Upon noticing that the food was still covered with plastic wrap, they went for the coffee and ended up hovering around the coffee dispensers with empty styrofoam cups in their hands. Their caffeine fix wasn't ready yet. They would most likely have to wait until nine.

A number of students came in, dressed in jeans and running shoes, and struck up conversations with the graduates who were working as volunteers giving out the name tags and handouts. A couple of men, who Gosper guessed were plainclothes cops or Feds, leaned against the long row of coat racks at the back of the room and talked with animated gestures.

As the various attendees chose their seats, an obvious pattern emerged. Eager students and friends of the speakers sat up front in small groupings, and the police and RCMP sat along the back rows in segregated camps. Psych students, with their notebooks and knapsacks, filled up the middle rows.

A young man in casual pants and a dress shirt walked over and sat a couple of seats away from Professor Gosper. Gosper noted that he had brought his own coffee in a Starbucks cup.

The big room was now about half full and people were still arriving. There were students and cops, but still no one who looked like a publisher. The speakers hadn't arrived yet, either. Gosper kept watching.

At around eight-fifty, a female student walked in who caught his attention. She was quite striking and tall, and a number of other males in the room took the time to glance in her direction before resuming their conversations. She didn't seem to notice. She wore her blond hair straight and past the shoulders, and was dressed in black pants and boots and a turtleneck sweater the color of English toffee. No jewelry. Something about her dress sense, or the quality of her clothes, set her apart from the typical student.

Gosper knew her. Makedde Vanderwall. *And a strange name at that,* he thought. He had often wondered where someone got a first name like "Makedde" from. Was it Irish? Welsh? She looked Scandinavian but he didn't know of any Scandinavian names like hers. In fact, the closest name he had ever come across was the Japanese name "Makaira," which meant happy. Her last name—Vanderwall—was, of course, pure Dutch.

Professor Gosper also knew that she was bright and creative; that she sometimes worked as a fashion model; that her Masters was in Forensic Psychology and that she was currently working on her Ph.D. thesis on the subject of the variables affecting the reliability of eyewitness testimony. He knew that she had recently taken a great interest in the area of psychopathy, and he was sure she would be attending the conference today.

Makedde had enrolled in Professor Gosper's Psych 203 Introduction to Personality and Social Psychology course in her second year, but it was only recently that he had focused on her. Unlike some of the other people around the campus, he was not interested in her obvious physical qualities. His interest was purely professional. He had reason to believe that she would make a very enlightening subject, psychologically. Earlier in the year, one of the university staff had tipped him off about her involvement in a serial killer case in Australia during the previous summer break. Sensational stuff. Seems she'd been abducted by a multiple murderer and only survived because the cops managed to bust in the room and save her at the last minute. She was the only surviving victim of how many? Ten?

Makedde had worked hard to keep a tight lid on it once she returned to Canada. She had the geographical isolation of Australia in her favor, not to mention Canadian media laws that banned the printing of victims' names in criminal cases such as hers. But it was hard to keep such sensational news a secret for long. He had to admit she had contained it remarkably well.

Professor Gosper wanted very much to sit down with her at some point and discuss her experiences. He wanted to run some tests on her, the Minnesota Multiphasic Personality Inventory (MMPI), the Thematic Apperception Test (TAT), the Pain Apperception Test and the Holtzman Inkblot Technique for starters. Perhaps the Beck Depression Inventory (BDI) and Beck Anxiety Inventory (BAI) depending on what he saw.

What exactly happened? How much could she recall? How was she coping? How much had her experience changed her and altered her perceptions of the world around her? And in what ways? What was the accuracy of her own eyewitness testimony after what she had been through? Perhaps she should examine *that* for her thesis?

Professor Gosper hoped to publish an exclusive account of her torment and his findings in the professional journals, or perhaps even in a true crime novel. He had already left a couple of notes for her to contact him, but she'd ignored them. Women like that always thought everyone wanted to get in their pants.

Makedde walked in his direction and then veered off down another aisle of seats. He wasn't sure, but she may have spotted him. *Damn.* Now she was at least twelve rows away. He watched her struggle out of a shoulder bag and plonk a notebook and pen down on the seat. Her pants fit her nicely and the toffee color of her top complemented her fair hair. She was a very attractive young lady.

He noticed the young man in the next seat give Makedde a long appraisal.

"Look out for that one," Gosper said.

The man turned to him with a friendly smile. He was a good-looking lad, probably in his late twenties. "Why's that?" he asked.

"Ice Princess. Way too much baggage," Gosper said. "She's like Katharina from *The Taming of the Shrew*." It gave him great satisfaction to say it.

The man laughed. "Nice . . ." he said, exaggerating the "ice" in nice.

He looked Makedde's way again and Gosper followed his gaze. She was reaching into her bag to get something. When the man finished admiring her, he turned back and said, "I'm Roy Blake, nice to meet you." He extended his hand and the professor shook it.

"I'm Harold Gosper, Professor of Social Psychology."

Roy wasn't a student at the university as far as Gosper knew, and he didn't look like he was visiting from Simon Fraser or one of the other universities either. He was a little too clean-cut. Maybe a plainclothes cop, Gosper decided.

"I just started with campus security," he said, answering Gosper's query before he even had to ask it.

"Oh really?" That was interesting.

UBC had recently beefed up security but as far as Gosper was concerned, it was little more than a political move designed to appease the public.

"There's all that terrible business with the Walker girl, I suppose."

"Yeah," the man agreed. "Really put a scare into everyone. Then of course there was that poll—"

"That poll about the assaults on campus?" Gosper cut in. He was familiar with it. "They blew that story out of proportion on every bloody front page. It's crap." He shook his head with disapproval. "The numbers were totally exaggerated. They took the figures on sexual harassment, date rape and everything else and rolled it into one nasty-looking package. It made it look like we were hitting girls over the head with our clubs and dragging them by the hair. This campus is as safe as any. Safer than most." Gosper turned to find the security guard nodding absently. He was looking in Makedde's direction.

"I'm sure it is," the man said, "I'm sure it is."

CHAPTER 12

Sergeant Grant Wilson hated mobile phones. He'd rather wear a pager or an archaic walkie-talkie or even a satellite dish than one of those damned devices. He was convinced that the stupid things would give him a brain tumor, but his daughter, Cherrie, said he was just a Luddite and he should get over it. But he needed one now.

He was leaving McDonald's weighed down with a foam tray supporting an Egg McMuffin, hash browns and a tall Coke when the pesky thing rang. "Bloody hell . . ." he muttered, then hurried toward his car so he could rest his breakfast on the roof and dig around in his pockets for the phone. He didn't consider any call on his mobile to be a good sign, especially in the morning. He figured that either Amanda was having some sort of trouble, or else Mike had something dire to tell him. He caught it on the sixth ring.

"Wilson," he answered gruffly.

"Grant . . . we found another one," came the voice on the other end. It was Mike.

Grant closed his eyes and leaned heavily against the

side of his cruiser, nearly tipping the big Coke over as the vehicle shifted with his weight.

"Oh, Christ." He exhaled and the rush of air made a strange sound in the phone. "Hang on, Mike, I'm just getting in my car."

Grant pinched the phone between his shoulder and ear while he fished around in his pockets a second time, this time for his car keys. When he had unlocked the car and got in, he asked, "Same spot?" without really wanting to know the answer.

"Well, not exactly. Close by though. Within a coupla hundred meters. It's a woman as well."

"A woman," Sergeant Wilson repeated. His eyes rested for a moment on the little laminated wallet-sized photo of he and his wife, Amanda, taken a few years earlier, before she got sick. He kept it propped up on his dashboard.

"The dogs found her," Mike was saying. "She's only a few weeks old, they figure. So that places her before the Walker girl, but well after the other Jane Doe."

"No identification?"

"She wasn't wearing too much in the way of clothes considering the weather. Just jeans and a T-shirt. Couldn't find anything in the pockets. She was a real mess."

"I see," Grant said. Since Susan Walker, they had discovered another two bodies. How many more would there be? "We need an expert," he mumbled.

"What?" Mike said.

"I said, we need an expert. This is going to get uglier. I can feel it."

CHAPTER 13

Makedde popped the lid on a bottle of Visine artificial tears and tossed her head back. She raised the little clear bottle over one eye—*plop*—and then the other, and her aching dry eyes accepted the liquid gratefully.

Must sleep. Must sleep.

She wanted to be alert for the conference, and she cursed herself for not being able to get some good shut-eye the night before. There was no time for napping now—it'd have to be the trusty caffeine hit once again.

"Excuse me . . ."

Mak looked up. Liz Sharron, one of Dr. Hare's assistants, was standing at the lectern at the front of the room, talking into the microphone. She had been in charge of some of the organization of the conference. She was smiling, and her red corkscrew hair bounced as she spoke.

"Dr. Hare and a couple of the other speakers are running a few minutes late," she announced. "Traffic." Liz rolled her eyes, ever the entertainer. "We expect them in about twenty minutes. Sorry for the delay."

Yup, coffee break, Makedde decided. She went to

stand, but one of her black boots stuck unexpectedly to the carpet when she got up from her seat. The corners of her mouth turned down. Something tacky was wedged in the rubber treads.

What the . . . ?

Habib, one of the graduate students sitting near her, glanced down at Mak's feet and said, "Yuck," when she tentatively pulled her boot up again. She gave him a playful swat as she passed him on her way to the back of the room, moving with a limp as she walked on the heel of the offending boot. She found a quiet corner at the back and crouched down to inspect the problem. Oh great—a long, gluey string of pink chewing gum.

Wacky watermelon-flavored Hubba Bubba.

Nice choice.

The scent of artificial fruit wafted up from the pink goo as she peeled it away, and she was just attempting to flick it off her finger when someone spoke to her.

"Hi."

She stood up, goo in hand, and found a tall, good-looking man standing in front of her. She was pretty sure he was the one who had spoken . . . but to her? She had noticed him sitting near Professor Gosper. It was the tall frame and handsome profile that had drawn her eyes. She hoped he wasn't a friend of the professor. Did Harold Gosper even have friends? Mak thought that was pretty unlikely. If he did have any friends, she couldn't imagine they would look like this.

The man stared at the pink goo on her hand, and said, "Oh, let me get that for you . . ." Then, in a flash, he was gone. He jogged over to the name tag desk, said something to the girl there and came back with a piece of paper. Gratefully, Makedde scraped the gum onto it and he scrunched it up. Her fingertips still felt sticky.

The stranger was quite tall, perhaps six foot four, with curly, light brown hair and a handsome, even featured face. Before Mak realized what she was doing, she had recorded the essential details—clean-shaven Caucasian male, late twenties to early thirties, brown eyes, nice build, and no wedding ring.

Gulp.

"I guess they're running late," he said.

"Yeah." She studied his face for a moment while he looked at the ball of paper in his hand. She didn't allow herself to look for too long though, lest he notice. It had been nice of this stranger to help her. She considered what to do next.

"I'm Makedde," she said and offered her hand, then quickly pulled it back before he shook it, and offered him the less sticky one instead. "Thanks for the . . . umm, gum trick."

"Don't mention it. It's a pleasure to meet you, Makedde," he said, taking her clean hand in his for a firm handshake. *Strong hands*, she thought. "What a beautiful and unusual name you have."

"Oh, thank you. People get it wrong all the time."

"How is it spelled? I notice you decided not to wear one of those name tags."

"I notice you didn't either. It's spelled M-A-K-E-D-D-E. You can see the inherent problems," she added and rolled her eyes.

"But it is a beautiful name; no doubt worth the difficulty. I'm Roy. Roy Blake." He was smiling as he spoke. "I'm new with the campus security here. I thought it'd be a good idea to brush up on the whole criminal element thing on my day off," he said, and laughed. "I was told the conference should be pretty good. Are you a student here?"

"Yes. My Masters is in Forensic Psychology, so this is sort of up my alley," Mak explained.

There was some activity toward the entrance and she turned to see Dr. Hare and the missing speakers walk in.

"Oh, here they are. I'd better grab some coffee while I can," Makedde said. "And wash my hands while I'm at it."

They exchanged grins.

"Well, nice meeting you. Enjoy the conference."

She turned and headed across the room, for a moment regretting that they had to part. But what she noticed next, she regretted even more—Professor Gosper was coming her way.

All she heard Gosper say was, "Makedde, I wa—" as she rushed past him and ducked into the ladies' room.

Luckily, in her day-to-day work on her thesis she had no contact with him, but occasionally she bumped into him on campus, or rather, he spotted her and ran her over with all the subtlety of a steam train. Their contact usually consisted of him saying something along the lines of, "I want to speak with you," and her politely putting him off. It was only fairly recently that he had become that way with her. She wasn't sure what had changed, but she had a hunch that he had heard about the Stiletto Murder Case. She doubted his sudden interest was of a sexual nature, and it wasn't part of his official duties as a professor to hassle students he didn't even teach, so what else could it be? Given half a chance, she figured, he would make a lab monkey out of her—and feel proud of himself for it.

She stayed in the ladies' room long enough to be sure that Gosper had already returned to his seat, and when she finally came out of hiding, Dr. Hare was being introduced by a visiting professor she didn't recognize. Hurriedly, she poured her coffee, threw in a splash of milk, and forgot the sugar in her rush.

"As many of you would be aware," the man at the lectern was saying, "psychopathy has emerged as one of the single most important clinical constructs in the criminal justice and mental health systems of our time." The professor was short and rotund, with a head that was so completely bald it looked like it had been spit-polished especially for the conference.

"One reason for the surge in theoretical and applied interest in the personality disorder is the development and widespread adoption of reliable and valid methods for its measurement. Dr. Robert Hare, in his more than thirty-five years of groundbreaking research, has created the Hare Psychopathy Checklist, thereby finally providing researchers and clinicians with a common metric for the assessment of psychopathy. His Psychopathy Checklist has been proven to predict recidivism and violence with unprecedented accuracy, and will play a major role in the understanding and prediction of crime and violence in the future.

"Dr. Hare is the author of numerous books and academic texts on the subject of psychopathy, including his popular title, *Without Conscience: The Disturbing World of the Psychopaths Among Us . . .*"

At this there was a muttering in the crowd. Makedde heard a young woman beside her say to her companion, "Have you read that? It's amazing . . ."

"He consults with law enforcement organizations, including the FBI and RCMP, and is a member of the advisory panel established by the English Prison Service to develop new programs for the treatment of psychopathic offenders. His recent awards include the 1999 Silver Medal of the Queen Sofia Center in Valencia, Spain; the Canadian Psychological Association 2000 Award for Distinguished Applications of Psychology; the American

Academy of Forensic psychology 2001 Award for Distinguished Applications to the Field of Forensic Psychology; and the 2001 Isaac Ray Award presented by the American Psychiatric Association and the American Academy of Psychiatry and Law for Outstanding Contributions to Forensic Psychiatry and Psychiatric Jurisprudence. It is my pleasure to introduce the keynote speaker for this conference, Dr. Robert Hare."

Makedde ran over to her seat, quickly sat down and fumbled for her pen and notepaper.

Dr. Hare had stepped up to the lectern. He always wore his thick gray hair in a Caesar cut and beard, and his large glasses magnified the downward sloping pale-blue eyes of a world-weary intellect. He had given countless presentations in his career, but there was still a hint of shyness about him when he took to the podium. He had a humble demeanor, and always looked slightly ruffled.

"Thanks to all of you for taking the time to come along today to learn more about psychopathy, and thank you also to the many people who worked so hard to make this conference come together. No matter what your role is today—as a student, a member of the police, someone involved in criminal law or in any of the forensic fields, or simply as a member of the public—the subject of psychopathy is important to you. Statistically, psychopaths will affect each one of us in some way at some point in our lives. Newspapers are rife with headlines about the impact psychopaths make on our society, but even closer to home, many of us will have a relative who is unfortunate enough to have to deal with one, and many of us will have dealt with or will have to deal with psychopaths in the future ourselves. It is important for all of us to better understand the disorder and what it means in our lives.

"We estimate that one percent of the population are psychopaths. For those of you present today who are involved in the criminal justice system and its institutions, our research tells us that fifteen to twenty-five percent of the people who are incarcerated in this country are psychopaths. For our research we use the thirty-point cut-off on the PCL-R, so our criteria are quite strict. As some of you would be aware, some researchers argue that the cut-off point of twenty-five may be sufficient evidence of the disorder.

"This population of inmates does not respond in the same way to our existing treatment methods. We have not been able to effectively change their behavior. We need to find new solutions to this problem, and indeed a colleague of mine and I have developed a program specifically targeted at these individuals.

"Before I move on, I should begin with a basic definition of psychopathy. What is the first name that comes to mind when you think of the word 'psychopath'?"

He looked around the room. Eventually a hand went up. The hand belonged to a well-dressed, middle-aged woman. Perhaps a health care professional.

"Ted Bundy," she said.

"Yes. Who else?"

"Hannibal Lecter," someone else said, and laughed. Mak didn't catch where the voice came from.

Dr. Hare smiled. "Yes, these are the types of people most strongly associated with psychopathy, and yet 'psychopathy' is not synonymous with 'serial killer' or 'axe-wielding maniac.' The truth is, you are more likely to get fleeced by a psychopath than killed by one."

The crowd greeted this comment with a few chuckles, and Dr. Hare smiled again.

"Psychopathy is a personality disorder which is defined by a cluster of affective, behavioral and interpersonal characteristics including lack of guilt or conscience, shallow effect, shallow emotions, cold and manipulative behavior . . ."

By lunchtime, Makedde was hungry and her bottom was sore from the hard seat. She had made pages and pages of notes and her pen was starting to fade, along with the feeling in her hand. She tended to doodle on her notepad when lectures or phone conversations failed to grab her absolute attention—usually scribbling squares and chessboards—but there were no such doodles this morning. Dr. Hare's presentation was riveting, and each time she witnessed the Single Photon Emission Computerized Tomography (SPECT) scans comparing the brains of psychopaths and non-psychopaths, it sent a chill up her spine. She had heard some of Dr. Hare's initial material before, but it still gripped her every time she heard it, and the new research he revealed in the slide presentation was compelling. The functional Magnetic Resonance Imaging (fMRI) findings about psychopathic subjects not showing the appropriate activation of limbic regions during their processing of emotional words was an interesting bit of new information. Again, she wondered if the study of psychopathy was perhaps her calling. Certainly her lack of enthusiasm for her chosen thesis subject could be partially attributed to her obsession with this new area.

She couldn't help but wonder what might have happened if the Stiletto Killer had been identified as a psychopath in the years before he began his tirade of violence against the young women of Sydney—against her friend Catherine, and against herself. Would someone have stopped him before it was too late? She wondered how much Harold Gosper knew about all that.

Mak looked back to where Gosper was seated. She noticed that the handsome security guard was not with him but there was another young man in his spot, talking with the professor. He looked more like a body builder than a student. *I hope he's not trying to enlist him to persuade me,* she thought dryly. Gosper must have sensed that he was being watched, because he started to turn his head and Makedde quickly looked away before he caught her eye. The last thing she wanted was to encourage him.

After lunch, various international speakers were set to present their findings on the topic, and the conference schedule for the second day looked fascinating. According to the printed handout, an FBI Profiler, Dr. Bob Harris, was set to do a presentation on psychopathy and crime scene analysis. That was a topic Andy would surely be studying for his future with the New South Wales Profiling Unit.

Andy.

She hadn't called him back. She didn't know if she would, or should. She busied herself with some further notes, and tried to keep her mind on the subject at hand.

When she next looked up, the room was almost empty, the other attendees seeking midday sustenance outside. Of the people still milling about, Makedde recognized the student volunteers tidying things up and some of the speakers hanging around. Roy Blake, the handsome security guard she had met earlier, was talking with one of the professors in the far corner. Gosper and his beefed-up pal were nowhere to be found.

Mak got up from her chair and was pleased to find her passage unhindered by rogue bubblegum. But to her annoyance, when she reached the top of the stairs by the exit doors, she found Harold Gosper waiting for her. The instant she spotted him she did an about-face and headed straight back down the stairs toward the conference room.

Why won't that man take a hint and just leave me alone?

Oh!

She was mid-step when she ran straight into the security guard, Roy Blake, who was walking up the staircase alone.

Their collision knocked the heavy bag off Makedde's shoulder and it swung forward, narrowly missing Roy's privates. If not for his quick reflexes, she might have been responsible for crushing his family jewels.

Horrified, Mak put a hand to her mouth. "Oh! I'm so sorry!" Her heart was pounding fast, and all that effort seemed to result in pumping far too much blood to her face.

"Don't be silly," her gum-savior assured her. "I'm fine. Oh, you're blushing." He was standing a step down from her now, and was fractionally shorter than her, if only by a touch. *Wow, he really is tall.* She found that sort of height intoxicating. They were still standing fairly close to one another, and Mak realized that his cologne was having a dizzying effect on her hormones. What was it? Obsession? Envy? Not Azzaro . . . not Old Spice . . .

"Are you okay?" he asked.

She refrained from asking him about his scent.

"I'm fine. Well, sort of," Mak replied. She thought of Professor Gosper outside, and before she could edit herself she said, "Could you do me a favor and just walk with me out those doors?"

He looked a little surprised at her request. "Sure. Is there anything wrong? Is someone bothering you?"

"Oh no, nothing to be alarmed about. There's just someone I don't want to talk to."

"Well, I'm happy to help," he said. His expression was quite serious and sincere, and she realized that he probably put people at ease all the time, protecting them in the course of his duties at the university. This situation did not exactly require that kind of seriousness, however. It was only Professor Gosper, after all. Irritating, but harmless.

She thought she had better explain herself. "Actually, I saw you sitting with him earlier. Professor Gosper? Do you know him? He's not a friend of yours, is he?"

"Oh no. Just met him briefly this morning. He talks a lot of crap though, doesn't he?"

They both laughed. Oh, thank God . . . The tightness in her chest gave a little. She took a deep breath.

"Well, let's go," he said and pointed the way for Makedde with one hand, like a friendly and rather attractive tour guide.

They walked up the stairs and out the front doors. Gosper turned, opened his mouth to speak and then closed it again when he saw that Makedde was not alone. Perfect.

Roy and Makedde walked together for the five minutes it took to reach the cafeteria.

"Thanks," Makedde said. "I wouldn't normally enlist a stranger to walk me to lunch, but my God does he ever annoy me."

"I could see that."

He smiled again, and she felt a tiny part of the invisible icy fortress around her melt.

"Look, are you having lunch with someone? We only have forty-five minutes left before the next speaker. You better eat something. I don't know how familiar you are with the campus, but this is about the best you can do on short notice."

"I'd love to join you," he said.

"Great. It'd be silly to sit alone on opposite sides of the cafeteria and everything," she babbled.

Makedde ordered a tray of sushi and Roy ordered the same. They chose a bench and sat opposite one another.

"Is the sushi any good here?" he asked.

"I guess you're about to find out. It's not Tojo's by any stretch, but it's still my favorite option in this cafeteria." She smiled. "I haven't gotten sick from it, yet."

"And you've gotten sick from everything else?" he fired back, not missing a beat.

"No, not quite, but I have it from a good source that Professor Gosper caught Bovine Spongiform Encephalopathy from one of the burgers."

He blinked a couple of times and looked blank.

"Mad cow. Sorry, my twisted idea of humor. Not funny."

Who does he remind me of? A young Marlon Brando? No, not quite. Ah, I know who . . .

"Does anyone ever tell you that you look a bit like Vince Vaughn?" she asked.

"Who?"

"You know . . . the actor."

He clearly didn't know.

"He's been in lots of movies," she said. "*Swingers, Return to Paradise*. He played Norman Bates in the *Psycho* remake."

"I remind you of Norman Bates?" He seemed alarmed.

"No, no . . ." she assured him.

"Maybe it's just the conference that's making you think of him."

"Norman Bates wasn't a psychopath," Mak said.

Roy crinkled his face up. "He wasn't? Forgive my ignorance, but wasn't he running around killing people and dressing up like his mother?"

"Quite right, but he was more of a psychotic than a psychopath. That's a different thing altogether."

"Oh," he said and ripped into a packet of wasabi and generously coated his Inari with it.

"Why do you find psychopaths so interesting?" he asked.

His question sent a chill down her spine.

"Well, what can I say? It's an interesting area of research. Dr. Hare is widely recognized as the world expert, and he is a Professor Emeritus at the university, which makes for a unique opportunity to look into the subject. People come from all around the world to hear him speak."

"Have you learned much?"

"Yes, I think so." *I hope so.*

"So you think you could pick a psychopath, then? If one came up to you?" The blood must have drained from her face, because he was suddenly apologizing for his line of questioning. "Oh, I've made you uncomfortable. I'm sorry."

"There's nothing to be sorry about," she said. "It's a perfectly valid question."

"I just wonder how much these experts and academics really know . . . I mean when it comes to the practical stuff. Sure, it's fascinating to see those brain scans and everything, but when you are out in the field dealing with those types . . . Does it really help?"

Makedde's father sometimes asked her precisely the same thing. Dealing with psychopaths on the street was a very different experience to examining their brains in a laboratory. "I think it does help," she said. "Knowledge is the best defense."

He nodded.

"We need to learn more about human predators. I

have a great deal of respect for the researchers and what they can teach us." She was quick to change the subject. She had no intention of getting into her own experience with a psychopath. "So, what is it like in security? You kept pretty busy here?"

"Well, I haven't been at this campus too long. They've had a bit of a push to employ more security," he said. "There's been an increase in complaints lately . . . assaults and so on."

"And disappearances. I saw the poster for Susan Walker the other day. I think I remember actually meeting her once."

"It's awful, isn't it? I hope she turns up okay."

Mak nodded.

"I hope you take plenty of precautions yourself, Makedde."

She felt her big toe start to tingle. Soon it would itch like mad and she would want to take her shoe off and scratch it to pieces. "I do. I take self-defense classes and I carry pepper spray . . . for the bears, of course." *And I keep a little Saturday Night Special in my glove box, but that isn't quite legal . . .*

"Yeah, for the bears. Perfectly legal. You are a smart woman, Makedde. I try telling women to watch themselves, but some just won't listen."

Mak had a lot of reasons to listen.

"Why was that professor hanging around waiting for you to come out, anyway?" Roy asked. "I assume that's what he was doing?" He bit into his Inari. He choked for a moment and his face started to go red.

"Are you okay?"

He fanned his face and then reached for the water. "Wow, that's hot."

Did he think it was avocado instead of wasabi? It occurred to her that he may have copied her sushi order without having eaten it before. She thought everyone in Vancouver ate sushi these days.

"It's a long story. He seems to find me a little too interesting for some reason," she said.

"Now, I can understand that," he said and smiled, his cheeks flushed.

Lunch break flew past and their conversation became deeper and more relaxed as the minutes ticked by. Mak noticed that he kept the rest of the wasabi far from his food. Afterward, she excused herself to sit alone through the afternoon sessions. She wanted her space, and she didn't want to seem too eager. But she was certainly aware of his presence on the other side of the conference room. She had been pleasantly surprised to find that she was still interested in Roy Blake after he opened his mouth.

Karen Hughen, with her dreadlocks and her pale smiling face, came quietly over and sat in an empty chair beside Makedde midway through the first lecture. She was a former study partner, and the two were friends.

"He was cute," Karen said under her breath.

"Oh, you were watching all that, were you?"

Neither girl turned their head to look at each other. They both kept their eyes on the speaker, whispering like a couple of naughty conspirators.

"Did he get your number?"

Mak smiled to herself, still not turning her head.

"This is the new millenium, Karen," Mak said. "I gave him my e-mail address."

CHAPTER 14

It was 8:02 P.M. when the Air Canada Boeing 747 began its slow descent into Vancouver International Airport. The trip from Quantico had been rough, particularly leaving the rainy Los Angeles Airport a few hours earlier, and Detective Andy Flynn felt like he had traveled much more than the mere width of the North American continent that day. He felt like he had circumnavigated the globe.

The plane banked left and moved in a tight arc through the dark sky, the massive wing outside Andy's window tipping down to reveal the top of Grouse Mountain, lit up and floating magically above the city like Lando Calrissian's Cloud City in *Star Wars*.

Thrilled with the view, Andy looked to Dr. Harris across the aisle from him, only to find his mentor asleep, eyes closed and head hanging to one side. Bob's tie was loosened and crooked and his slack jaw gave the impression that he might be trying to eat the knot. Andy resisted the urge to gently nudge him back into the waking world. He knew that Bob was overworked and could use every minute of rest.

They sped above the city heading southwest to the airport, the engines roared on their descent, and within minutes they touched down, bumping along the runway, the flaps on the wing outside Andy's window jutting upward and straining in the air current. The aircraft shuddered and complained as it slowed to taxi toward the gate, and finally it was still.

Andy exercised a touch of defiance by standing up and stretching before the seatbelt sign was switched off. The rest of the passengers followed suit, and Dr. Harris came back to life as well, as if some mysterious force had flicked his ON switch. He stood up and grabbed his things out of the overhead compartment as if he were fresh out of a ten-hour sleep on a plush Sealy, not snoozing for half an hour crammed into a rigid airplane seat. This was not the first occasion when Andy had noticed the Profiler's uncanny ability to bounce back from all kinds of physical and mental unpleasantness. He felt sure that Bob could sleep on a hard wooden floor and not get a crick in his neck, despite his age.

The two didn't need to talk; they simply nodded at each other and followed the other passengers up the aisle and off the plane. Dr. Harris lugged his briefcase and laptop along with him, containing the all-important Powerpoint presentation for the next day. Andy carried only his simple overnight bag and a crinkled newspaper. He was glad he hadn't brought a lot of work to do on the plane. He probably wouldn't have touched it anyway. His mind was not particularly focused on work. He was tired, but more than that, he was distracted by his close proximity to Mak.

Andy watched his feet move over the carpet beneath him as they exited the ramp and emerged from the gate. It was only when he heard Dr. Harris's name being called that he looked up. To Andy's surprise, he found that two stocky men dressed in business suits were waiting for them.

"Dr. Harris?" the shorter of the two repeated in the same melodious Canadian accent.

The man stepped forward and his eyes flickered back and forth between them, searching for recognition. He appeared to be in his mid-forties and he looked to be quite strong. He had a thick knotted neck and a wide, faded scar visible across his nose that brought to mind a teenage bar brawl, or perhaps a school hockey game gone awry. This was Canada, after all. His partner was slightly taller and a fair few years younger, but shared his muscular build.

"I'm Dr. Harris," Bob said, raising a hand and stopping a few feet from the man. Andy noted his hesitation. He didn't seem to be expecting the welcome wagon either.

"I'm Sergeant Wilson. This is Corporal Rose." The man with the scar extended his hand and Bob shook it. "We're with the local RCMP. Can we speak?"

At that point they both turned and looked at Andy. It wasn't a friendly look.

"He's all right," Bob assured them.

"I'm Detective Andrew Flynn of the New South Wales Police Force," Andy cut in, moving forward to join them. "In Australia."

"You're sure a long way from home," Corporal Rose, the taller, younger one said. Andy didn't like his tone.

"Detective Flynn has been studying with me at the Behavioral Sciences Unit at Quantico," Bob said.

The men looked Andy up and down one more time, and then focused their attention on Dr. Harris.

"So, how can I help you, gentlemen?" Bob asked.

The four men walked slowly along the long concourse

toward the baggage claim, past the Coast Salish Spindle Whorl carved of red cedar, and down the steps suspended over a beautiful waterfall, where the soothing sounds of water cascading over smooth round stones calmed the busy minds of weary passengers.

The RCMP had come with a favor to ask of Dr. Harris, and as they walked past the cool flowing waters, the carved welcome figures and the slowly spinning baggage carousel, words were exchanged in an urgent hush. Sergeant Wilson painted a dark picture. The dead bodies of two missing UBC students, Susan Walker and Petra Wallace, had been discovered, and the unidentified skeletal remains of another victim had been found near their shallow graves.

When Wilson had spoken to Dr. Hare, a consultant with the RCMP, he had recommended that they approach the visiting Profiler.

Wilson believed that this was the work of a serial killer.

CHAPTER 15

Dead animal eyes stared down at Debbie Melmeth.

She sat vulnerable and exposed in the middle of a strange room, secured to a chair and surrounded by a plethora of unfriendly heads. Apart from the animals, Debbie was alone. She was hungry and afraid, and she prayed that someone would help her. She knew her captor would not. She'd begged and pleaded with him, but he gave nothing away, just stared at her with a half-smile.

Hunger and the dull ache of her body distracted her. She ran her tongue along her lips in an attempt to wet them, but her tongue had no moisture to offer. Time seemed to have stopped.

Since she had been confined to this horrible place—over a period of a couple of days was her best guess—the man had fed her some potato chips and occasionally made her drink beer. That was it. She hated beer, really hated it. Especially now. But it seemed that her captor lived on the stuff. He had taken to periodically walking around the room, pacing with an open bottle in his hand, staring at her. Very occasionally he would talk nonsense at her, but wouldn't respond to her attempts at conversation. He did not acknowledge her pleas. He would just pace and drink and pace some more, and sometimes even walk up to her unexpectedly, open her mouth with his brutish hands and pour the beer down her throat, ignoring her feeble protests. When he did this, he just stared at her blankly while she gagged and spluttered and tried to swallow. And then he would disappear again.

Debbie tried to figure out what was going on. She couldn't remember how she got there. She was calling Brian from the bar, and then what? She could not recall what happened after that. She only remembered the strange comings and goings of her captor.

Debbie was a smart girl. Surely there was some way she could get herself out of there? If she paid close enough attention and used her head there must be a way. If only she could figure out what he wanted and why. What made this man come and go? What were the times of the day? That part was almost impossible to know. There was no clock in the room, nor was any visible when the door opened into the rest of the house. There were no windows she could see to gauge the light outside.

A noise snapped her out of her ruminations. She heard movement, and footsteps on the hardwood floor. The man emerged through the darkened doorway, and although he had made countless such entrances in the past couple of days, her heart still froze at the sight of him.

He walked right up to her, stopping only a foot away. Debbie waited. She could smell him. He loomed over her and stared at her. The naked globe that hung from the ceiling threw light across him as he stood, leaving her in his shadow, her eye line positioned at hip level. She continued to wait for his cue. It was a game and she didn't know how to play. She didn't know the rules . . . or the aim.

Debbie couldn't move away, couldn't fight. She had been through it over and over in her head. Should she spit on him, just for the brief satisfaction of rebellion? Even if she wanted to her mouth was probably too dry. Was there something she could say? Something she could try? In Hollywood movies the main characters always came up with the most ingenious means of escape. But for some reason those means escaped her now.

As if in answer to her unspoken pleas his hands moved toward her. For a fleeting moment she thought she might be freed. But instead those hands moved from their position hanging at the man's sides to the front of his pants, less than a foot from her face.

He unzipped his fly.

A rush of panic swept through her. She screamed as loudly as she could. "No!" she yelled. "No! No! No!" she shouted again and again. She wanted to kick out, but her restraints would not allow it. The chair shuddered and jumped, guided by her frenzied movements. She tried to hop her way backward, away from the man and his open fly, but she could not.

Through all of this, the man seemed not to hear her.

He reached into his open fly, and exposed his penis.

She reacted to the display with a physical revulsion that began at her toes and crept up through her body to the top of her head and back down again. Knowing that she could not hop her way backward, she did all she could to turn her head. When she strained her eyes upward to look into his face, she saw that he was smiling— not a real smile, not the kind she was used to, but some cheap imitation of a smile.

After standing exposed for what seemed an eternity, her captor zipped his pants up again. Then he laughed. He laughed at her, making the most horrible, humorless sound she had ever heard any human being utter. Then he just walked away.

He hadn't forced himself on her. Yet. It would only be a matter of time, she feared. She needed to do something. She needed a plan, some semblance of control. Debbie even considered an attempt at seduction. She considered what she might achieve if she convinced him that she would cooperate, that she could love him. If he would just release her for a moment, to move her to a better position perhaps, then she might stand a chance.

What is this game? What does he want?

Debbie didn't know the answers, and she was afraid to find out.

CHAPTER 16

Les Vanderwall came home with a headache, having left some of his old mates downing beers at the Waddling Dog Pub. It was a bit early for him to pack it in, but for some reason he didn't feel well. Whenever that happened, he made a mental note of whether there was any link to his wife's death. He'd noticed that he became ill every month on the anniversary of the day she died. Sometimes it wasn't the right day of the month, but even just the time of day, or a reminder of some kind—a whiff of some special smell, a bit of her handwriting found unexpectedly in a cookbook, a memorable place, a phrase. The family doctor said this was not unusual, and that these reactions would ease in time.

Les was worried that he might become antisocial. His mates couldn't truly understand the impact of the loss of his wife. None of them had been through anything similar, except John and his divorce but that was hardly the same, as he'd instigated it. Now that Jane was gone, Les had no one to relate to emotionally, the way married couples did. He was alone in his grief. He didn't want to burden his daughters. They had their own lives.

Les Vanderwall felt like half a man. It was gradually forming a wedge between him and his friends. That could be a terrible problem. He had to make an effort to stay in touch socially. Les knew that if he became a hermit he wouldn't last much longer.

Wearily, he dragged himself up the steps and into the kitchen. The answering machine was flashing.

"Les, it's Christopher Patrick here . . ." His lawyer. *"It's about five-thirty, perhaps you can call me back tomorrow morning? There are a few issues with the estate."*

There were always a few issues with his late wife's estate. Eighteen months on, and there were still issues. How could there *still* be issues? The real issue was that she was gone. Nothing could reverse that.

The machine beeped and played the second message.

"Hello, Les, it's Ann calling from Vancouver. How are you? I, um . . . I was wondering when you are in town next. Perhaps we could grab a coffee? I was wondering if you had passed my details on to Makedde? It'd be a pleasure if I could help in some way. Anyway, talk to you soon. Bye."

His heart lifted at the sound of her voice.

I like that woman, he thought. *She's a good woman. Tony never deserved her.*

As soon as the thoughts came into his head, he felt a stab of guilt, but not for Tony Morgan. His life partner, Jane, was gone now, but he couldn't help but think of her watching over him. A partnership like that came along once in a lifetime, he believed, so was he doomed to be a lonely widower now that she was gone?

What would she want for him?

A second chance?

CHAPTER 17

Makedde woke with her heart pounding in her chest and the sound of an alarm drilling loudly in her brain.

Okay, okay, I'm awake already! I'm awake!

She sat up straight in bed, grabbed her tin alarm clock off the bedside table and fumbled for the OFF switch on the back. The small retro-style clock, which was round and stood on two legs, decided to protest by leaping out of her hands and falling onto the floor with a crash, increasing the dent on its right side while continuing to buzz with annoying insistence.

Oh, will you just shut up!

Irritably, she snatched the dented clock up off the floor and managed to flick the switch. Through bleary eyes, she read the silver hands. It was already 7:00 A.M. That depressing fact confirmed Makedde's suspicions that somehow not all sixty-minute time frames were of the same duration. The hours between midnight and 4:00 A.M. had crept past at an excruciatingly slow pace, whereas the last three hours could only have slipped by in a heartbeat or two—three heartbeats at the most. She felt like she had blinked rather than slept.

Makedde distantly remembered her life as "a morning person"—day after day of waking up fresh, all sweetness and light after another pleasant and effortless sleep. Where had those days gone? Where had that Makedde Vanderwall disappeared to? Luckily, there was no one around to see her in the morning these days, as she'd be quite a sight. But then again, perhaps she'd be in a better mood if she had company?

Too long. It's been too long without someone to hold me while I dream . . .

Such thoughts should really have been far from her mind. There was no one on the horizon, but still, her mind drifted back to the times in her life when she did not sleep alone. She thought of all the lovers in the world, and how she was not one of them.

Mak crushed the saccharine sentimentality as soon as it surfaced.

Foolishness.

Automatically, she reached beside her and pulled open the drawer of her bedside table. She took out a small arty-looking notebook she had bought at Sydney's Museum of Contemporary Art gift shop, and flipped it open to September 22. She slid the miniature pencil out of the side, and wrote:

Three hours sleep. 4:00 A.M. until 7:00 A.M. I had a nightmare about Andy chasing me through the woods. (Damn him for coming back into my dreams!) He was wielding a scalpel and I was wearing my father's police uniform again. I couldn't run fast enough. I woke up before he caught me. No devil this time.

She went to close the book and then opened it again and scribbled one last comment:

I feel like hell.

She flipped it closed and rubbed her eyes.
Damn. I really do feel like hell. How much longer can this go on?

In Makedde's research on sleep disorders she had discovered that one common recommendation was to keep a diary of sleeping patterns, and so each morning for the past week, Mak had dutifully scribbled down details of her sleep, or lack of it. Looking at it now, it made depressing reading. As she sat in bed contemplating her nightmares, she wondered skeptically whether a psychiatrist could really shed any new light on her problems. How? What would Ann make of her diary? Mak was well aware that her nightmares were the abstract manifestations of the trauma she had experienced in her recent past. But so what? It seemed unlikely that there would be any benefit in having a qualified expert point out the obvious.

Mak swung her legs out of bed and hopped up. She shook herself from head to toe in a halfhearted attempt to shake off the bad night, then slipped on a pair of fuzzy bed slippers and wrapped a thick white robe around her naked body. Her preference for sleeping in her birthday suit had little to do with Marilyn Monroe's famous comments, and everything to do with Makedde's own tendency to be an overactive sleeper, twisting PJ's, slips, boxer shorts, or whatever else she happened to be wearing around her while she slept. That is, when she did sleep. On more than one occasion she had woken up struggling for air with a T-shirt wrapped tightly around her neck and the bedsheets and duvet tossed on the floor on opposite sides of the room.

Robe-wrapped and vertical, Mak shuffled over to her computer.

"Welcome to AOL Canada," came the chirpy greeting as she logged on. "You have mail." Her saturnine mood lifted slightly, and the corners of her mouth curled into a sleepy grin. She had checked her mail a couple of times the night before but there was nothing there. Well, at least nothing interesting. She was kind of hoping to discover a little e-mail from a certain young man.

Hmmm . . . Word of the Day. Some mail from the Forensic Psychology list. *Aha . . . What's this?* An e-mail from one "BlakeR." Subject line: "A question."

Bingo!

> Hi Makedde,
>   It was nice meeting you today. I found the conference interesting, but of course you were a highlight. I won't be able to go tomorrow . . .

Damn.

> But I was wondering if we could perhaps catch up for dinner afterward?

Yes!

> I hope you don't think me too forward. Send me an email, or better yet, give me a call.

She re-read his e-mail. Twice. He must have sent it after she logged off at 1:00 A.M. Perhaps he was a night owl as well? She checked the time logged on the correspondence. Yup, 1:16 in the morning. That's pretty late.

Roy Blake.

Yes, she was intrigued. But a full-fledged date? It would have been better if he was just coming to the conference and they could chat a bit without any of the "date" formality. She hadn't been on a proper date in how long? A year? Well, not counting that disaster with Henry. But that didn't really qualify. She had left before the appetizer arrived.

She went to the kitchen and put on a pot of water, and then distractedly went about making a cup of coffee.

Mak found herself smiling as she considered her reply. She sat down at the desk, and sipped her drink. She was actually contemplating seeing Roy. Which was weird. But how to go about it?

Hi Roy,

Thanks for your message. It was nice meeting you, too. I must thank you for saving me from Professor Gosper and my bubblegum. :-) Thanks for your offer. Perhaps we could meet up for a quick coffee or a drink instead? Around eight would probably work for me, otherwise we could catch up sometime on the weekend. Give me a call.

She typed in her number, and was about to press "send" when a feeling of doubt overtook her. *This guy is a stranger, Mak. Do you really want to give him your number? Do you really want to meet him somewhere alone?*

Makedde recognized that her fear was a little irrational. She wouldn't be alone at all. She would be on familiar territory if she chose the bar or café, and she could excuse herself after a single beverage if need be. It was safe. Besides, he was a security guard . . . well, not that that really meant anything, but he did work on campus at least. Mak pressed "send" before she scared herself out of it, and then it was gone, dispatched into cyberspace.

At ten minutes to nine, Makedde arrived at the Graduate Center Ballroom at UBC and glanced around the gathering crowd. No Roy, just as he'd said in his e-mail.

Good. No distractions, she told herself.

Professor Gosper was nowhere in sight, so she could relax. Makedde noticed there were considerably fewer people attending the second day of the conference. Either that or they were all late. Dr. Hare had pulled a huge crowd of curious university students that first day, but only the more hard-core attendees had stayed on. There would probably be more people in the afternoon for the talk from the FBI agent on crime scene analysis and how that relates to the clinical construct of psychopathy. It sounded like an interesting lecture, and Mak was sure that any mention of the FBI would result in a standing room only situation. That was the *X-Files* for you.

The thought of the FBI steered Mak back to Quantico and to Andy Flynn, again. Since his call she'd had trouble getting him out of her head.

Should I try to call him back?

After what had happened in Sydney, whether she liked it or not, Andy Flynn was a part of her life. She didn't love him—or at least that was what she kept telling herself—but the experience they'd shared had forged a difficult bond between them, and like the branding of a red-hot poker, the events had marked them forever. But that wasn't love. That wasn't any reason to regret that he was so far away.

No, I won't try to track him down, Makedde decided. *Let it be. Move on, Makedde. Move on.*

A bitter lump formed in her throat, and she ignored it. She had a big day ahead of her.

CHAPTER 18

Andy Flynn arrived at the sprawling UBC campus just before 9:00 A.M. He parked his rental sedan, placed the ticket on the dash and began his walk to Crescent Road and the building that housed the Graduate Center Ballroom. He had left Dr. Bob Harris at the hotel to recover from the flight the night before. Although the Profiler needed to catch up on lost sleep, he would most likely have launched straight into work mode the moment he woke up, looking over the files the RCMP had given him the night before.

Even though Andy had heard a lot of his mentor's presentation material before, he was interested to see the way he handled the crowd, especially a crowd as diverse as this surely would be—students, professors, police officers, security guards, psychologists. Of course, there were other reasons why Andy was interested in who might be in that crowd. Reasons that didn't pertain to work, exactly.

It was Andy's first time at the UBC campus, and he couldn't help but think of Makedde as he walked across the green lawns and admired the panoramic views. It was a place she had spoken of several times in their brief time together, and to his surprise, it was even more beautiful than she had described it.

He had quickly decided that Vancouver bore a certain loose resemblance to Sydney. Both cities shared a spectacular harbor and bridge, and the five massive white sails of Canada Place graced the waterfront in a way that reminded him of the famous Opera House back home. But of course the mountain peaks that surrounded the city would always provide a dramatic point of difference to Sydney. Those who grew up near the Rockies, as Makedde did, thought of the Blue Mountains near Andy's home as the "Blue Hills." Now he saw why.

It took a while for Andy to get his bearings and it took him somewhat longer than he had anticipated to find his way to the ballroom. When he finally found the right building, a makeshift cardboard sign saying, "Psychopathy Conference" with a big arrow pointing at the front doors gave him a great sense of relief.

The room that held the conference was on two levels, with a sign-in area just inside the door and tables with coffee urns, and a spread of muffins, donuts and sweets to the left. To the right was a built-in series of numbered coat racks of the sort that Andy had not seen since his early school days.

"Hello," came a chirpy voice as he walked inside. He looked to the sign-in table to find that the voice belonged to an androgynous-looking female with very short-cropped hair, and a ring through her nose. He noticed that she wore a name tag that said "Billie Looker." Billie? He raised his eyes from the name tag up to the face again just to check. Yup, she was definitely a she.

"Hello. I'm Detective Andrew Flynn."

"Welcome to the conference," Billie said in a soft Canadian accent.

She flipped through her boxes of neatly organized cards and pulled one out with his name printed on it.

DET. ANDREW FLYNN

"Please keep this on throughout the conference," she said, and slipped the card into a plastic name tag holder with a safety pin through the back.

He took the name tag and thanked her, then made his way to the large sunken seating area where the first presentation was already well under way. He slipped the tag into his suit pocket, with no intention of ever wearing it.

Andy was definitely late. A crowd of a hundred and fifty or so people was watching the speaker intently. Luckily, there were still a number of empty seats left to choose from. He managed to slip quietly into a chair nearest the door, right at the back of the room, and his entrance caused very little disturbance.

Is Makedde here? he wondered.

He glanced furtively around the room and his gaze rested momentarily on a blond-haired student up the front, his breath stopping short. However it wasn't Makedde at all, but a somewhat bohemian-looking man. Men with long hair and women with brush-cuts and names like "Billie"—Andy was starting to feel very unhip and out of touch. Maybe he was getting old. Or maybe it was just a peculiar Canadian thing.

It wasn't until ten-thirty that Andy actually saw her.

A young red-haired woman thanked the speaker—a professor who had presented a lot of slides and graphs that Andy hadn't found very interesting—before announcing a coffee break. The entire room stood in unison, a mass of bodies moving hungrily toward the refreshment table. A very large man in one of the middle rows stood up with them, and Andy's eyes were drawn to him. He was at least six foot seven, and probably weighed a good three hundred and fifty, or four hundred pounds.

When he moved to one side, Andy did a double take.

Makedde was sitting alone and jotting down notes studiously in her notepad. She had been hidden by the man the whole time. Her hair was long and luxurious as he remembered it, and she was definitely female—not like the other long-haired blond he had been eyeballing earlier. He could see her profile as she wrote on her notepad, her head tilted down and her hair swept to the opposite shoulder.

She was even more beautiful than he remembered, and that realization was downright depressing.

She seemed absorbed in her notes, and she looked so wonderful sitting there with her hair hanging forward on one side, and that full mouth pouting in concentration that he almost didn't want to disturb her. Almost.

He took a deep breath, stood up and walked over.

To his surprise, he managed to make his way right up to her without her noticing him. She didn't look up from her notepad until the very last minute, and when she finally did, the most amazing expression came over her features. Her jaw dropped open and her blue eyes became perfectly round, showing the whites all around her pupils. The blood drained from her face as if she had seen a ghost, as if he, of all people, was a ghost, and then it took what seemed like an excruciatingly long time before she said anything.

It wasn't quite the reaction he had hoped for.

"Hi," he said sheepishly. Half of him wanted to crawl under a rock, and the other half wanted to take her into his arms.

"Andy?" Makedde said. His name still somehow managed to sound sweet on her tongue. "Andy," she repeated. "Well . . ." She closed her eyes for a moment and shook her head from side to side a couple of times. The corners of her mouth turned up. A light charcoal was swept across her closed eyelids, and her lashes were long and black with mascara. He noticed that her skin was still absolutely perfect. Andy thought she might have changed her hairstyle slightly, and she was perhaps a little thinner in the face as well. She opened her eyes again and focused them on him. "What on earth brings you to UBC?"

"I'm here for the conference. I arrived last night from Quantico. I'm here with a colleague, Dr. Harris."

"Umm," she said. "Dr. Harris, the Profiler. He's doing a talk this afternoon. What is it, 'Violent Crime Scene Analysis and the Psychopathic Personality'?"

He nodded. "That's right."

Mak pursed her lips together and looked down. "I'm sorry I didn't get back to you," she said.

"Oh, that's fine. It is hard to get calls through at the academy sometimes."

Andy knew perfectly well that she hadn't tried.

She nodded absently, and they both fell silent.

It was a novelty to stand next to such a tall woman. In her heeled boots she probably stood close to six foot three, almost as tall as Andy. He liked that.

"So, um . . . When did you get here?" she asked.

"Last night." He told her again. "I'll be here for a week at least."

He hoped that didn't sound suggestive. After the words came out he thought he probably should have said it differently, like, "I'm in Vancouver for a week," or "I'm just here for the conference," or something similar. He didn't need to add "at least," as if to suggest he might stick around if she could persuade him. Of course, saying, "I'm just here for the conference," wouldn't have been entirely true either.

"Oh," she said. The color still hadn't returned to her face. "That's great. So what do you think of Vancouver so far?"

He laughed, trying to sound casual, and said, "More like, 'What do I think of the airport and the inside of the Renaissance Hotel . . .'" He meant it as a joke but again, he immediately thought it could have sounded suggestive.

"I mean . . . I haven't really seen any of Vancouver yet," he went on. "I hope to see a few sights, you know, with my colleagues. Is there anything you'd recommend?"

"Oh, you should try to see Stanley Park, Gas Town, Grouse Mountain. The Capilano Suspension Bridge is kind of cool if you're out that way. And you really ought to get to Whistler if you can." She rattled the tourist info off and then stopped short, as if she suddenly remembered who she was talking to and found it all a bit too bizarre. Or maybe he was projecting his own feelings into her actions, he wasn't sure.

Makedde met his eyes, and pressed her lips into a tight smile. Her golden complexion had regained its warmth.

"So . . . Andy Flynn," she said and crossed her arms.

Andy was over-analyzing. He had his intense study of body language, Statement Analysis and Scientific Content Analysis at the academy to thank for that habit. Every word and gesture had some probable meaning. One of his instructors had said, "Don't try this on your friends, or you won't have any."

"So, how's it all going?" Makedde asked him, arms still folded across her body. "What have you been up to? You know, with the Profiling Unit and everything?"

"Well, the Police Commissioner finally got the thing a green light and it should be up and running sometime next year. We're looking to make it the center for Profiling and tackling major crime through all of Australasia."

She raised her eyebrows. "That sounds really exciting."

He didn't want to mention that the Stiletto Murder Case might have been an influencing factor in finally pushing the plans through. There was nothing like a public outcry to suddenly boost political support for a crime-fighting project.

"It looks like I may have the opportunity to have a high-ranking position. Perhaps even head the unit at some point."

"Like I said, that's great. Congratulations. Well, um . . ." She looked past him to the gathering of people at the refreshment table. "I guess . . ."

And then the redhead was back at the lectern, introducing the next speaker—coffee break over.

"Now, if everyone could please take their seats, I would like to introduce Professor Rickford from the University of Wales . . ."

No time for refreshments.

Makedde looked back to her seat, and then across to Andy.

"Are you here alone, or . . . ?"

"I came alone," Andy told her. "Dr. Harris will be arriving just before lunch."

"What time is his presentation?"

"At one. First up after lunch," he said.

"I'd love to meet him," she said, and motioned to take her seat.

He smiled, still standing. "You can join us for lunch if you'd like."

"I didn't mean to invite myself . . ."

And then Professor Rickford was at the lectern, starting his speech. It seemed inappropriate to cross the room to his seat, so Andy just sat down on the spot, right where he was, with one chair separating him from Makedde.

Mak smiled at him and shrugged, taking out her note-pad and pen, and gesturing toward the speaker. The room was quiet except for the professor, and they didn't speak again until the lunchbreak at noon.

Makedde picked up the conversation right where they had left off.

"I didn't mean to invite myself to lunch," she said as the room began to clear.

"I'm sure Bob won't mind," Andy said.

They both got up from their seats at the same time. The room had erupted into a busy chatter, and people brushed by them to head out for their lunchbreak. They stood awkwardly looking at each other, neither of them motioning to leave.

"No, honestly. You two will probably want to talk about work—"

"Not at all," he assured her. "Not at all." Perhaps she really didn't want to go. He didn't want to force her. "Hey look, the invitation is there for you," Andy said. Somehow that seemed to end the standoff, but apparently not in his favor. She had obviously made the decision not to go.

She gathered up her bag and notepad. "Will you be here tomorrow?"

"I may be."

"Perhaps we could catch up then?"

It was better than saying that she didn't want to catch up at all, but he still felt a little like he was being brushed off.

"Well, I'll talk to you after the lecture, anyway."

"Oh, of course."

Andy scanned the entrance and spotted Dr. Harris chatting with the red-haired organizer.

"He's right over there." Andy pointed to him. "Why don't you come over and I'll introduce you?" He didn't want to let her go.

"Okay, but then I am leaving you two to have your lunch. I don't want to get in your way."

Andy wanted to tell her that she could never possibly be in his way, but then she was gone, already striding toward the entrance, and he couldn't keep his eyes off her as she walked away.

She slowed her pace for a moment so he could catch up, and they walked up to Dr. Harris and his new friend together.

"Hey, Mak," the organizer said when they approached.

"Hi, Liz. How are you?" They exchanged friendly smiles, and Mak turned her attention to Dr. Harris.

"Bob Harris," he said, and extended his hand.

"Makedde Vanderwall. Nice to meet you." She gave him what looked to Andy like a pretty firm handshake. He noticed that the Profiler held her eyes for a moment while their hands were clasped. Bob sometimes did this when he first met someone, and Andy knew from experience that it felt like having an X-ray. Mak accepted this brief but intense scrutiny without flinching.

The other young woman turned to Andy and introduced herself. "Hi, I'm Liz Sharron." With her pale skin, and a head full of naturally red Shirley Temple curls, Andy imagined her classmates calling Liz "Carrot Top" or something similar at school. She had a good-natured smile, and a lot going on behind her eyes.

Makedde introduced him to Liz as "Detective Flynn."

Not very personal, he thought.

"Andy has been training down at Quantico with me for the past couple of weeks," Dr. Harris told her.

"Liz is an assistant to Dr. Hare in his Psychopathy Lab," Makedde explained.

"What exactly *is* a Psychopathy Lab?" Andy had to ask.

Liz laughed. "Well, we don't really have a conventional laboratory as you might imagine it, as with physics or chemistry labs. As a group we conduct research on psychopathy, some at the university here and some at various forensic laboratories and local correctional institutions. We use a lot of different techniques to measure for neuro-biological differences—SPECT scans, EEGs, MRIs . . ."

"Sounds like a lab to me," Andy said.

"No brains in jars or anything, though," Liz said. "Well, only a couple, anyway."

"Dr. Hare's past assistants? Or is that just a rumor?" Makedde said, grinning.

Liz smiled.

"It's actually quite an interesting area of study," Dr. Harris said.

"Yes, you should make sure to stick around for some of the lectures in the next couple of days," Liz added. "Some of our researchers are presenting really fascinating stuff."

Andy was about to remark that he'd stick around, when he noticed an odd look on Makedde's face. She was staring past them to the stairwell. A security guard had come down the stairs and was walking toward them.

"I should let you get to your lunch," she said a little too quickly.

"It was nice meeting you, Makedde," Dr. Harris said.

Bob was vaguely aware of Andy's former association with Makedde, and Andy guessed that he was watching the scene unfold with interest. Unless you knew Bob well, it was impossible to imagine the keen analytical mind that churned away behind his calm and casual exterior. He never missed a thing—not a gesture, inference, or expression went unnoticed. A man like him never shut that talent off. That's what made him so good.

Mak turned her attention back to their group. "It was a great pleasure meeting you, Dr. Harris."

"Call me Bob."

"Thank you." Mak faced Andy and then Liz, and said, "See ya later."

Her gaze flickered back to Andy before she walked away, and there was a strange, uneasy look in her eye that didn't sit well with him.

"See you later," Andy said as she wandered off. He tried to pull his eyes away, tried not to stare as Makedde greeted the tall security guard. He was a young, good-looking man, and Andy didn't like that one little bit. She didn't quite kiss him hello, but they certainly seemed friendly. Andy tried hard to contain the sharp surge of jealousy that flooded through his body. His jaw felt tight.

She's got a boyfriend. Of course she's got a boyfriend. Girls like that always have a boyfriend.

He corrected himself. He knew Makedde was different. She was a bit of a loner at times, not always attached, but that didn't mean she hadn't fallen for a tall, good-looking security guard at her own university—a guy who wasn't continents away, and wasn't wrapped up in some terrible time in her life that she would be eager to forget.

Cool it, Andy. She's none of your business anymore.

He regretted that fact.

CHAPTER 19

"Looks like they may have a nasty one here."

Andy glanced up from his cold coffee. "Sorry, what?"

The cafeteria was still busy, but Andy had never felt more alone. He noticed that Dr. Harris had almost finished his chocolate brownie and can of Diet Pepsi, and he was now looking across the table at him intently. Andy wondered how long he had been staring off into space. He hoped he hadn't missed anything important.

"Get your mind back on track, Andy."

"It's that obvious, is it?"

Bob looked at him incredulously. He didn't have to say anything.

"Sorry," Andy mumbled.

"I can see why you are interested in her. She's a very beautiful girl, and bright too, from what I can tell. But I think you might be barking up the wrong tree."

Andy said nothing.

"How was your meeting? How did she respond to you?" he asked, but Andy knew Bob well enough to know that the questions were not ones he was asking for his own benefit, but ones that he wanted Andy to ask of himself—a classic psychologist's strategy.

"I think she was surprised to see me, to say the least," Andy admitted.

"You didn't tell her you were coming?"

"I never quite got around to it."

His comment hung in the air for a while, without response. He wondered if it would be possible to feel any more stupid.

"Did it seem that she was interested in seeing you again?" Bob asked. When Andy didn't respond, he said, "I think you ought to move on, Andy. She has."

That stung. It was obviously true, but it stung.

Andy got up from his seat. "I'm gonna grab another coffee. Do you want anything?"

Bob shook his head.

Andy ordered a coffee he didn't really need, and when he came back and sat down he said, "So, what were you saying before about something being nasty? Are you talking about the case the RCMP wanted you to look at?"

Bob was far too busy to take on any new cases, but he had studied the files all morning instead of sleeping in, just as Andy suspected he would. Bob could not deny his charitable nature.

"It's a mess," Bob said. He looked off into the distance, his eyes unfocused. "I've got a bad feeling about this." He said the words softly, so he wouldn't be overheard. "We've got three victims so far, but what about that increase in campus disappearances? What if we've stumbled upon a series of campus murders?"

Andy leaned forward.

"I think the RCMP suspect it as well," Bob went on. "Both identified victims turn out to have been students here, and the third . . . if we can identify her I'd say she will have been a student as well. Let's look at what we've got. We have three bodies dumped in the same area, all in varying states of decomposition, and the two identified victims were killed only weeks apart. The unidentified skeleton is also of a young adult female and she could go back quite a bit longer, which is ominous when we consider how long this particular killer may have been doing this.

"The two recent victims, and possibly the other as well, all appear to have been shot in the back with a high-powered rifle. Not strangled or stabbed, like a rape that spiraled out of control, but shot. And in the back. Cowardly, isn't it? Sergeant Grant Wilson—likable guy if I may say, and pretty smart too—mentioned that it was like an execution of sorts. And he's partially right. If it was a single shot to the back of the head I would have said yes, execution-style definitely, but it brings hunting to mind, if you ask me. I think we're looking for a local. A hunting buff, or someone into weapons. Perhaps a student or former student, or a professor at UBC. I mean why were the two identified victims UBC students? They didn't appear to have known each other. There is no other correlation apart from their age and the fact that they were students at this university. Is this a coincidence? Is someone making this campus a hunting ground?"

At this thought, Andy felt a chill. Was the killer at UBC that very day?

Dr. Harris took another mouthful of brownie and went on. "I'm going to suggest that they note the plates on every vehicle found in the Nahatlatch area, and check ID's on the people living, visiting and spending time out there. They need to cross-reference those names with UBC students past and present, and yes, UBC staff as well, including the professors. Hunting licenses too. They

should cross-reference those names with people associated with the campus for any reason. Especially anyone
who has had a license revoked for some reason."

Detective Flynn had a hard time concentrating on Bob's
lecture after lunch. He couldn't stop looking in
Makedde's direction. Thankfully she hadn't noticed. But
after a while even that fact added to his misery. Why
wasn't she looking his way? He started to feel creepy
about staring at her so often, and more than that, he
started to feel creepy about traveling across the world to
this conference with an ulterior motive.

Dr. Harris was giving a great presentation. He was a
skilled communicator, both in interviews and in the public speaking arena and he also had a very professional-
looking Powerpoint presentation to back up his speech.
Andy noticed that most of the people in the room were
taking notes. Andy wasn't, but that was only because he
had taken many notes on the topic before.

"The crime scenes of psychopathic offenders are more
likely to show that the crime was well-organized and contained some high risk or thrill element," Bob was saying.
"For this kind of individual, it is not enough to simply
creep into the old woman's house and steal the money
from her purse while she is sleeping, he has to go to the
trouble to beat her senseless as well . . ."

Andy thought about the Nahatlatch case the RCMP
had asked for help on. Now that Bob had shared some of
his concerns with Andy over lunch, he felt somehow involved in the investigation. Bob realized this and had
urged Andy to keep the whole thing as quiet as possible.
If word got to the press there would be chaos.

But Andy was uncomfortable. He wanted to tell
Makedde about it. She deserved to know. For the first

time in his career, he hoped the papers would pick up the story, so the burden of his confidentiality would be lifted. Makedde didn't need to know exact details, but she should know that something was up, and that she had reason to exercise more caution than usual. It was a safety issue. He had to find a way to tip her off and still keep his promise to Dr. Harris.

"Psychopathic offenders show a complete disregard for their victims," Bob was telling the crowd. "There is always an element of control in the crimes they commit . . ."

Andy saw that nearly everyone in the room was on the edge of their seat. Bob was an FBI agent, and that title in itself was fashionable these days, thanks to popular entertainment like *Silence of the Lambs* and *Hannibal*, or the *X-Files*.

"They may employ staging if there is a close personal relationship between them and the victim . . ."

Andy knew all too well that the lives of FBI Profilers were not glamorous. In fact, neither were the lives of anyone who sought to deal with the aftermath of the world's most violent and disturbed people.

Andy grew up in the peaceful town of Parkes, in New South Wales, where the local cops were heroes. There was Sergeant Morris, for instance, who hung out at the milk bar and got all the attention of the pretty waitress there. He always had a couple of kind words for young Andy, and Andy hero-worshipped him.

But the reality of policing never quite lived up to his childhood expectations and he quickly discovered that not everyone loved cops. Many hated them, in fact. The public seemed to think of nothing but parking tickets and breath-alyzer tests. And now they thought of scandal, too. Corrupt cops were the only ones who made the press these days.

Even the woman he married had ended up hating him for being a cop. Andy was a cop, but he was hardly a hero.

He wondered if he could ever forgive himself for his shortcomings.

CHAPTER 20

"Come on, ya big wuss-bag. Five more."

Sergeant Grant Wilson looked up from his strained position below a two hundred and twenty-five pound loaded barbell and squinted in the direction of the voice.

Asshole.

They were deep into their regular weight session at their local gym, and Corporal Michael Rose was counting off Grant's progress "... eight ... nine ... good work ..."

"I could bench two fifty and practically double your reps," boasted Mike's brother.

"Jesus, Evan, would you just shut up?" Mike snapped. They didn't usually have company, and it wasn't working out so well.

When Grant finished his set, Mike helped him place the bar in its cradle. His brow was dripping, and his gray shirt was stained with dark patches of perspiration. He stood up and glared at Mike's brother.

Evan was a tall guy and he was pretty buff. He pumped a lot of weights and Grant suspected he did steroids too. He had a few too many tattoos and a lot too much ego for Grant's liking. He certainly hadn't invited him to this weight session. As a matter of fact, he doubted anyone had invited Evan along.

Damn, I wish I was taller. A glare is always better with height advantage.

"Go for it. The bench is all yours," Grant said with a sweep of his hand, and stepped aside.

"I already did my sets this morning."

Grant laughed. There was a time when he would have just flattened someone like that, but he had learned restraint. Besides, this was his best friend's brother, after all.

"I was just buggin' ya, Grant. Don't take it personal," Evan went on. "You lift pretty well."

For an old guy, Grant could almost hear him say.

"What are you doing coming to the gym in the morning? Aren't you doing the stocktake at K-Mart any more? They cut your hours?"

Evan frowned. He seemed to deflate a notch. "That used to finish before the store opened. But no, I'm working at the Fox now."

"Oh, the Blue Fox."

Mike didn't join in the conversation. You could tell that he wished the subject would change.

"What do you do there? You waiting tables, or taking to the stage?" Grant asked. The Blue Fox was a girlie strip bar.

"Bartending. You should drop by sometime, you'd like the atmosphere," Evan said.

Mike had moved on to the leg press and Grant joined him. He helped him place a few fifty-pound plates on the bar. Sure enough, before long Evan came over to join them. He wouldn't take the hint. "So, is it true that you handed your big case over to the FBI?"

What?

This time Mike cut in. "Like I told you, Evan, we are asking for some consultation with an FBI Profiler. It doesn't mean the FBI has jurisdiction or anything."

"It doesn't?"

"No."

Mike started his set, and Grant watched him, ignoring the uninvited third party.

"I saw him today," Evan said.

Both of them turned. "Saw who?"

"Your FBI agent."

Grant took pause, and Mike looked equally astounded.

"He did a lecture at UBC. There have been ads up around campus for ages. It's part of a big conference on psychopaths." He rolled his eyes and made bogeyman gestures at the word.

"Yeah," Grant said. "I wish we could have gone to that, but some of us had to work. A few of our colleagues went. Did you learn anything?"

"Yup."

"Anything you care to share?"

"Nope."

Grant was about to explode. "I gotta go home. Amanda is waiting for me."

"Oh, yeah. How is she, anyway? What a bummer . . ."

"Thanks. We'll be fine." He threw his towel on the weight machine and walked away. It was all he could do to keep his temper.

The last thing he wanted was to hear an ignorant prick like Evan Rose shovel some bullshit sympathy his way about Amanda. What would he know about taking care of someone you love? What would he know about Amyotrophic Lateral Sclerosis?

Grant had just finished dialing the combination for the padlock on his locker when Mike came in, apologizing.

"I'm really sorry about that, Grant. I don't know what's gotten into him."

"Forget about it. I need to get home."

"He's not usually that bad."

"What did you do inviting him, anyway? And telling him about the case?"

"I . . ."

"Just keep him out of my face."

"I'm sorry . . ."

Grant pulled his things out of his locker and shoved them in his gym bag. He didn't bother to shower or change. "Don't be sorry, Mike," he said. "I'm not the one who has to be nice to him just because he's family."

Mike looked hurt at the comment.

"Forget about it. I'm under too much stress." Grant waved over his shoulder when he left, not bothering to say good-bye to Evan as he walked out.

CHAPTER 21

He stayed on the library computer for hours.

To his delight, he found more than expected. It was exciting. The Internet was a treasure trove of information on his chosen subject. He clicked to the main page of the Australian news archive, and signed up using a false name. He gave his anonymous AOL account as a contact.

The search page came up. He typed in his subject.

Makedde Vanderwall.

He briefly considered adding more specific details, like "Makedde Vanderwall + murder + Australia," or something similar, but felt that her name was probably unique enough to provide him with what he wanted. He specified that all available publications were to be searched, over an unlimited time period.

He pressed "send," and his request was silently processed.

He could not have been happier with the results.

Result of your search: 184 documents matched your query "Makedde Vanderwall."

Results 1 to 20 are displayed on this page.

There were ten pages of articles. He could find out anything that had been printed about this girl, all those juicy details that any Australian press could dig up, but which she was so careful not to allow anyone back home to know about.

Herald Sun, Daily Telegraph, Courier Mail, Sun Herald, The Australian . . . the list went on and on. He began at the top, double clicking on the article titled, "Model Survivor Flies Home."

He stayed there reading until the library closed. His photocopy card, which he had restocked with extra dollars, was empty by the time he left, his backpack weighed down with the burden of Makedde's newsworthy secrets.

Now this is an interesting one . . .

CHAPTER 22

Roy Blake wasn't happy about getting a call just before his shift ended. There was a disturbance in the Monashee building at the Thunderbird Residence, one of UBC's on-campus student quarters. Roy was still on duty and he had to go and check it out. It was bad timing—he had a date with Makedde Vanderwall shortly after work. Despite that, he was quick in responding, ever the professional, and within minutes he was pulling up at Thunderbird Crescent. He parked the security vehicle at the entrance and went to have a look.

Okay, what have we got . . . ?

Roy didn't even have to step inside the foyer before he heard the racket. As reported, someone was banging unrelentingly on one of the apartment doors. He could hear shouting as well.

He frowned.

Roy rushed up to the second floor and in the hallway found a woman shouting, then sobbing, then shouting again. She looked to be in her late forties, was dressed in sweat pants and a leather jacket, and had brown, unkempt shoulder-length hair. Her eye makeup had run down her cheeks in long, dark streaks.

She looked set to begin another tirade of yelling and crying when she turned and saw Roy approaching. His appearance in uniform always made an impact. Her fists halted millimeters from the door itself, wavering in the air. Her mouth hung open.

"Hello there . . ." he offered, raising one hand as he approached. As he got closer, Roy saw that the woman's eyes had the red, glittery look of someone who had cried too much. Her lips looked puffy, her nose wet. She needed a tissue. Despite her disheveled appearance, she looked to be a middle-class citizen—not a junkie or a street person. Her hands were well manicured and she wore a gold wedding band.

"Excuse me, ma'am. Is there something I can help you with?" Roy asked, now only a couple of meters away. He was careful to use a caring but firm tone, just like he'd been taught.

For a long while the woman didn't respond. She went on staring at him, her fists poised at the door. He wondered for a moment if she had not heard or understood him. By now Roy was only a few feet away, and he was ready to take action if the woman caused any trouble. He still held one hand in front of him, palm open in a friendly gesture, while the other hand was at his hip, ready to use the pepper spray if he needed it. Even harmless-looking citizens could act in unpredictable and irrational ways.

Roy knew that it was when you got too confident that you could get yourself into trouble. Recently, an officer was trying to help an elderly lady on the street in the West End. She had simply fallen on the ground. But when the officer tried to raise her, he almost lost his eye as she swung a feeble fist at his face and scratched his eyeball

with the sharp stone of her antique ring. Now that un-
lucky sod had one eye that permanently looked like the
pupil was sitting in a sea of blood.

"Is there a problem, ma'am?" Roy asked, moving forward very slowly now, still holding his safety position.

Finally she spoke. "Officer . . . I . . ." she began. "My
daughter . . ."

"Yes?" he said, urging her on. "Your daughter, ma'am?
What about your daughter?"

"My daughter is in there and she won't open the door."

Perhaps there is a reason she won't open her door, lady,
Roy thought. Who knows how long she had been screaming and carrying on before someone called it in.

"Ma'am, you've been making a lot of noise and I believe that your daughter would have heard you if she was
in there. Are you absolutely sure that you have the right
residence? Do you have the right number?" He asked the
questions gently, trying not to provoke her.

"Do you think I'm some kind of a fool?" she screamed
back at him. "I know where my own daughter lives!"

Well, that didn't work.

Roy thought of Makedde waiting at the bar for him. He
wanted to be there on time. He needed to get home to
shower and change first. How long would this take?

"I don't think you're a fool at all, ma'am," he assured
her. "I'm sure you know where your daughter lives. May I
ask your name, please?"

"Marian. Marian Melmeth," she said.

"Okay, Mrs. Melmeth. Let's just go downstairs and
speak to the manager of this building and see if we can't
just give your daughter a call. Simple as that. What is your
daughter's na—"

"No! I've already called her. She is refusing to pick up
the phone, just to spite me!"

"Mrs. Melmeth, we aren't going to be able to settle this here in this hallway. Clearly, anyone in that apartment would have heard you. I think we need to just go downstairs—"

"Can't you make her come out?" Tears were flooding down the woman's cheeks.

Okay, maybe this will bring her to her senses. "What is your daughter's name?"

"Debbie."

Roy paused. This name struck a chord with him. *Oh, Melmeth. Right . . .*

He tried not to react.

"Her name's Debbie? Okay." He leaned into the door and knocked politely, knowing full well that there would be no Debbie Melmeth inside. "Debbie, this is Security Officer Roy Blake. Are you in there?"

No response.

"Is there anyone in there at all?"

Nothing.

"If anyone is in there, could they please make some sign?" He knew this was ridiculous now. "Okay, Marian, let's go downstairs and we can sort this all out."

Suddenly the woman threw herself at the door again, pounding with her fists and wailing. "Debbie! It's your mom! Come out, darling! Pleeease!"

He heard a door down the hall open. He turned to look, and saw that it had only opened a crack. His efforts were being watched.

"Ma'am, I'm going to have to take you downstairs now."

She continued bashing the door.

He seized Mrs. Melmeth's arms, pulled them behind her back and forced her away from the door, careful to contain his irritation and to temper the strength he used on her.

"I'm sorry to do this, ma'am. I'm going to take you outside."

Once he had her in his grip, she seemed to deflate, her strength leaking out of her as she fell sobbing against his broad chest. He didn't know how long she had been pent up like that, shouting and crying, but when he held her she finally let go.

Gently he led her from the building. A female officer, Larissa Greaves, had turned up and helped to calm the woman down.

Roy was only forty minutes late leaving his shift. He rushed home to shower and change and get to his beautiful date. Luckily he didn't live too far from the university. He still stood a chance of being on time to meet her. . . .

CHAPTER 23

The Chilli Bar in Vancouver's hip Kitsilano district is a carefully crafted study in modernity. Adorned with dried peppers hanging from the corners of rough mirrors and steel dividers, two large, deep-red wall lights continue the signature chilli pepper and their shapes creep up the walls on opposite sides of the room. The dim lights give off a faint red glow that splits the room into red and shadow, giving some of the patrons a slightly devilish look.

An American film crew was in town shooting an action flick, and Mak recognized a couple of actors in the far corner—Michael Ironside and that pock-faced actor from the old *Miami Vice* series whose name she could never remember.

The Chilli Bar was hopping on this weekday night, the watering hole overflowing with hip urban dwellers polishing off a few martinis with their friends at the end of a hard workday. Makedde was alone, sipping a decidedly non-alcoholic mineral water at the end of the central black lacquered bar, which curved and tapered like a giant stylized chilli pepper. If the mammoth chilli were an exclamation mark, she would have been the point.

This date with Roy was her first foray back into the scene since the fiasco with Henry, after which she had decided never to let her friends set her up again. They meant well, but it invariably was a recipe for disaster.

The Chilli Bar had been Makedde's suggestion. Roy knew where it was but had never been inside before, so Mak had a certain home advantage. It was also the only really cool bar that was in walking distance from her flat and also busy on a weeknight in autumn.

Mak pushed a lock of hair behind her ear and stared through the patent leather of her small Bally purse sitting on the counter top. *So what is this Roy Blake really like?* she wondered. He was cute, she couldn't have missed that, and he seemed like a nice enough guy, but she really didn't know much about him. Barely anything at all, in fact. He had been very attentive when they'd chatted at lunch, and she found that flattering. Some guys were too busy stroking their own egos to actually listen. They had sat together on a bench at UBC for about half an hour during her break, talking about the university, and his job, and the weather and the upcoming ski season, and by the time Mak grabbed herself some sushi, it was time for her to get back to the conference.

Makedde hadn't let herself enjoy any male attention for a while, thereby earning herself the title of "Ice Princess" from her friends. She had forgotten how nice it could be. With just this little bit of encouragement, she felt as if her femininity had been turned up a notch. Perhaps it was little more than the biological mating instinct, but there was still a thrill in meeting someone. In a sense she was a recovering romantic.

Makedde, who was naturally fashion-conscious in the best and worst of times, had found herself wasting too much time and thought on the way she dressed for this particular evening. But the "I'm not tying too hard" principle was an important one to stick with in times like these. Her strategy had meant that she simply switched her rubber-soled boots for a pair of sexy heeled shoes, and changed into an elegant black scoop-necked top. That, along with a slick of lip-gloss and a quick brush through her hair, and she was ready.

She should have been set for a pleasant little diversion from her worries with the help of a handsome young man whom she barely knew—except there were two problems. Number one, it was past their meeting time and she was still alone, which was irritating. And problem number two basically stemmed from problem number one, because the longer she waited restlessly for her date, the more she rehashed her surprise run-in with Andy.

What the hell is that man doing in Vancouver?

Mak shook her head and leaned forward on her elbows, gazing down at the counter to see her own reflection, distorted in the black lacquer finish. Her face appeared freakishly elongated, half of it red, half of it pale. To her eyes, she looked like a monster. Monsters reminded her of psychopaths—the modern Nosferatu who stalk the earth—and psychopaths reminded her of Australia and her experience there, and the man who saved her life, which brought her right back to where she started—Andy Flynn.

Andy bloody Flynn. Here. In Vancouver.

She had his sudden appearance to blame for her added stress. It had been bad enough since his call, but now she couldn't get him out of her mind. Only a couple of months ago she thought she'd got over that problem, and now he had ruined all that progress.

What am I going to do about him?

Do I have to do anything about him?

Mak sipped on her water, hoping the cool drink would calm her flushed cheeks. But the more she thought about Andy, the more agitated she became. She couldn't have been more shocked when he had walked up to her at the conference. It was like he had stepped right out of one of her dreams, or rather, one of her nightmares. The problem was, of course, that he was all too real. Okay, he wasn't chasing her through a field with a scalpel like he had in her nightmare, but she wasn't about to be saved by her alarm clock either.

Damn you, Andy, why did you have to walk back into my life? Why? Why now?

She had fallen for Detective Andy Flynn, unwillingly at first, but she really had fallen for him. She should never have let that happen. He was the detective in charge of her friend's murder case. He was going through a nasty divorce and an early midlife crisis or something as well, like so many of the men who suddenly decided that Makedde was the answer to their problems. In fact, Andy Flynn was many things that a wise woman would know to stay away from, but somehow that hadn't made any difference. She was drawn to him like a moth to a flame. It had become very complicated very fast, and she sure regretted it.

As Andy's effect on her had gradually worn off, Makedde had cursed herself for letting him get under her skin, and now that he was here, she cursed herself doubly. This was exactly the kind of distraction that would further interrupt her studies. And it certainly wasn't going to help her to get a good night's sleep.

She had missed him for a while when she first returned from Australia. But not now. Not now that she was trying to get her life together.

Makedde's blood was pumping fast—too fast. Her eyes were sore and she didn't like the way she felt. If she thought about the wrong thing—if she let her thoughts get away from her, she'd end up a pathetic idiot crying alone on a bar stool. What a sight that would be! She held the unexpected rush of emotion back, but was already caught in the grip of a nauseating vertigo. She closed her eyes and held her breath for a moment.

Relax.

Breathe. Breathe slowly.

Mak took another sip of her drink and wondered if what she really needed was something with a little more bite.

"Excuse me? Roddy?" she said to the bartender.

He turned. Roddy was in his early twenties, well muscled, eternally bronzed and a few inches shorter than Mak. During the day he worked as a personal trainer at one of the smaller exclusive health clubs nearby. Tonight he wore a tight lycra shirt that showed off his well-defined biceps. Despite his job and his outfit, she always thought Roddy seemed kind of shy.

"Um . . . Roddy, what's your favorite drink? A real good one." She hoped that a drink would help calm her nerves.

"You mean, alcoholic?"

"Yes, I sure do," she said.

He looked a little surprised. "Well, what do you like? We've got our Martini Special. What about Chi Chis? Daiquiris? Do you like shots, perhaps? Sex on the Beach? How about a Slippery Nipple?"

So much for the shy theory, she thought as he rattled off the provocative drink names.

Mak blinked once, reflecting on the name of the beverage, then said, "Sure. Um, give me one Slippery Nipple, please."

Maybe later she would have Sex on the Beach.

The shot would take the edge off. It had to. Makedde wasn't much of a drinker, but it was supposed to relax people, and that was the kind of thing you did at bars, right?

She thought Roddy may have given her a sideways glance before he turned his back to prepare her drink. Mak realized that she had never really ordered a serious drink from him. After busying himself behind the bar, he presented her with a milk-chocolate colored concoction in a shot glass.

Oh, boy. Is this a good idea?

"Here you go, Mak. This one's on me. Tell me if you like it."

"Thanks, Roddy. You don't have to do that."

"It's my pleasure. Enjoy." And with that, he left her to her drink.

Mak lifted the glass to her nose. It smelled creamy and sweet. Baileys. *Yum.* She wasn't sure about the mammary reference, but she imagined the little mixture would taste good. She stared at the lifted glass for a moment, overcame her hesitation, then downed it in a single gulp.

Whoa.

Very strong.

Mak might have choked on the heady drink were it not so delightfully smooth. It sent a charge through her nerves, followed by a deep, mellow sensation. *Very yum.*

She licked her lips and scanned the bar.

Where is that boy, dammit?

And then, inevitably, Makedde found that she was not on her own anymore.

"Hiya. Would you like another drink?" American accent. Definitely not the security guard.

Mak looked beside her to find a slick-looking man with graying hair, a deep and crispy foreign tan and the whitest teeth she had ever seen.

She obviously didn't respond fast enough to keep up with his routine, so the dental-poster boy continued without encouragement. "Hi. I'm Richard. What's your name?"

"Hi, Richard. I am waiting for someone, so thanks for the offer, but I'm just fine." She gave him a closed smile.

"I was just watchin' you sittin' over here all by yourself, and I wondered, 'What is that pretty lady doin' alone?' I'm up here from Hollywood shooting a film with—"

"Yeah, with Michael Ironside and . . . What is that other actor's name? From *Miami Vice*?"

"Which one?"

"Oh, never mind. Look, like I said, I'm waiting for someone so if you don't mind . . ."

"Well, I could just keep you company until she—"

"*He*," she corrected him, drawing the word out to make her point.

"Until *he* arrives," the man finished.

Makedde swiveled around to face him directly, raising her chin and giving him a steady glare down the end of her nose.

"Okay, okay," he finally said, throwing his hands up. "But if you change your mind . . ."

"Bye now," she said, turning back around to face the bar.

Out of the corner of her eye she saw him wander back to his table to receive some high fives from a few of his buddies. She overheard one of them say, "Ooooh, strike out for Richo!"

Irritating.

Makedde placed her coat on the stool beside her to avoid further mishaps and looked at her watch. It was well past eight o'clock and there was still no sign of her date. Now she was definitely feeling weird drinking alone, fending off strangers and waiting for . . . well, waiting for a stranger.

She looked around the room but he was still nowhere to be found. She pulled her mobile phone out of her bag and checked the messages. None.

Maybe I should just leave?

She decided she'd wait just a couple more minutes before leaving and never speaking to that Roy Blake character again. She looked at her watch, and counted down the minutes on the second hand. *If he isn't here in sixty seconds . . . fifty-nine . . . fifty-eight . . . .*

At twenty past eight, she felt a cool breeze on her neck and looked up from her watch. There he was.

Twenty minutes isn't so late, Mak.

Makedde took a good look at her date as he came toward her. Perhaps the drink gave her a little added confidence. He was impressively tall and masculine, and not overly slick. He was a bit of a cowboy, perhaps, and a handsome one at that. He had dark-brown eyes and a full, sensuous mouth. His hair was light-brown and curly, and he had it cropped short. She decided that he was good-looking in a raw kind of way. She liked that. Although he came across as charming and polite, Makedde suspected that there might be a bit of an edge to him beneath it. She imagined he could be intense and passionate.

Roy was dressed casually, and she realized that she probably liked him a little better in uniform. Or perhaps she liked him better when she knew Andy was around? Had she really wanted to make Andy jealous? No, she simply wanted him to know she had moved on, that was all. She wanted him to know that there was no possibility of a romance forming between them again. No chance at all.

Who are you trying to convince, Makedde?

She removed her coat from the stool beside her, and Roy took a seat. His lips were curved into a pleasant smile, and he smelled of Azzaro cologne. She could pick it now. It hadn't had the chance to settle into his skin, and it had a certain sharpness to it. Pleasant, but sharp.

"Hello." His voice was deep.

"Hi."

She found him very attractive, but she still felt the urge to bolt.

Oh, God, I'm not into this. Damn you, Andy! It's your fault!

"How was the conference this afternoon?" Roy asked. "I'm sorry I missed out."

"Oh, it was good," she said, managing to sound pretty much normal. She needed to slow down. She wasn't going to bolt. She was going to sit right there and enjoy herself.

"It was nice seeing you at lunch. I'm sorry my break doesn't give me much time."

"That's okay. I wasn't expecting any company." And suddenly there was company all over the place. "How are you? How was work?" she asked, trying to deflect attention from herself. She wished the drink would just take effect and calm her down.

"I'm so sorry I'm late," Roy said. Mak had been wondering if he would apologize. "It was work," he went on. "I was supposed to finish more than an hour ago but something came up right at the very last minute. Quite sad, really." He lowered his head and looked forlornly at the bar top.

Sad? "What happened?"

"Oh, I'm being so rude. Would you like another drink?"

Mak noticed that Roddy had removed the empty shot glass when she wasn't looking. She was grateful for it. Roy was pointing to her half-finished mineral water.

"Do you want a fresh one?"

She felt the Slippery Nipple starting to take effect. Even with her Amazonian height, drinks tended to take effect quickly. She supposed it was because she only began having the odd drink fairly recently.

"No, I'm fine for now. Thanks anyway."

"Do you mind if I get a beer?"

"No, of course not. Are you kidding?"

He just smiled and called the bartender over. Roddy reacted to his presence with a slight pause. He was used to Makedde being there with her girlfriends. She wondered if Roy picked up on his reaction.

"Hmm, what do you have?" He glanced around the bar. "Could I have a Moosehead, please?"

Mak felt herself relax a little more. *This is just a normal date, Mak. You do remember what a normal date is, don't you?*

Roy turned to Makedde and smiled. "You look fantastic," he said.

Oh, don't blush, Mak. Please don't blush.

Makedde's Dutch complexion had the habit of displaying her emotions a little too clearly. Her cheeks were like red beacons when she felt awkward or embarrassed, and her face was easily robbed of all color when she became tired and stressed.

"Thank you." She desperately wanted to change the subject. "So what's it like working in security? Do your powers differ much from the local police?"

"Oh yeah, you said your father was a detective inspector," he commented.

Sometimes he thinks he still is, she thought to herself and grinned. He still had the respect of the police on both sides of the water, and he certainly still had that unerring desire to know exactly what was going on at all times, particularly in his daughter's life.

"Well, I'm afraid our powers of arrest are pretty much that of every Canadian citizen. We can't arrest someone unless we actually witness them committing an indictable offense. We have a lot less power than the police, who simply need probable cause."

"Right. So if you catch someone breaking a window you can arrest them and hand them over to the police?"

"Exactly. And if I find someone chasing a suspect and saying that they saw such a thing, we could arrest the person and hand them over."

Mak had on occasion heard tales of the frustration of security guards, and now she was starting to understand why.

"Do you have a partner that you always work with?"

"We all pretty much know each other, but we work alone generally, as staffing requirements don't permit doubling up. We have to patrol an area with five hundred and one buildings and over thirty thousand people."

More frustration.

"What happened tonight?" she asked, continuing what was turning out to be an interrogation of sorts. "You said something was sad."

"Oh . . . yeah." Roy paused and a somber, faraway look came over his face. "I, umm, I was called to investigate a bit of a racket at one of the residences at UBC. And when I got there, this woman was banging on the door to one of the apartments, hysterical and crying. She wanted her daughter to open the door for her."

His tone was sincere, and Mak was touched to see this big man talking in such an emotional way.

"What really choked me up though, was that I knew who the woman was," he went on. "I recognized her last name. She has a kind of unusual name, so I remembered it. You see, her daughter was reported missing recently. It was on one of the bulletins."

Makedde's stomach twisted at the thought. "Oh. How terrible," she said.

"I know. I checked afterward to be sure, and it was definitely the missing girl's place. I mean she didn't really have any reason to think her daughter would be in there." He shook his head. "I tried to calm the lady down, but she wasn't thinking clearly. She was obviously suffering from a lot of grief. It's so sad to see stuff like that."

Who is missing? Makedde wanted to ask, but didn't. She could see how much his work affected him, and she thought it was probably a good idea to change the subject.

"Why don't I order a drink, and we'll make a toast to new friends?" she suggested.

Roy broke into a smile and nodded in agreement. "Good idea."

"Roddy, could I have your Martini Special?"

"Coming right up."

"Oh . . . hang on." Mak stopped him by leaning across the bar and reaching out for the back of his shirt. "What *is* the Martini Special?" she asked.

He laughed. "Chocolate."

"Chocolate?"

"Yes, a chocolate martini. You'll like it."

"Okay, Roddy. Whatever you say."

Her drink came in a flash and Roy insisted on paying. After a brief struggle, she agreed to let him. "I'll get the next round," she said.

"Can I have my beer in a glass then?" he asked before

Roddy took off. He turned to Mak. "Just to make it seem a little more fancy," he explained.

Makedde smiled, amused. With his beer in glass and her martini in hand, they raised their glasses for a toast.

Clink.

"To new friends."

Mak nodded. "To new friends."

And to moving on from the past.

CHAPTER 24

Grant frowned when the phone rang. Reluctantly, he extracted himself from Amanda's side and made for the mobile ringing in his coat pocket on the dresser.

Hate that thing.

"Wilson," he answered in a low voice.

"Grant, it's Mike."

He knew it would be.

"What now?" he asked. "Not another one?"

"No, not another one. Worse."

"Worse?" He caught Amanda's attention and held a finger up to suggest that he'd just be a minute. She smiled with her hazel eyes in response. He could see she was tired. "Hang on a sec . . ."

He walked into the hallway and closed the bedroom door behind him. Cherrie was still out with her boyfriend, and the house was quiet and dark.

"Worse? What's worse?"

"Well, not worse exactly . . ." Mike began.

Grant took a deep breath. He was still irritated that Mike had let his brother come along to their last gym session. That was just one more stress that he didn't need. "Mike, stop beating around the bush and just tell me what it is."

"I got a call from my brother . . ."

Speak of the devil.

"He's upset that one of our guys questioned him."

"One of our guys questioned Evan? About what?"

"He was out around the Nahatlatch. Not far from the dump sites."

Grant actually hit his forehead with the palm of his hand. "Idiot. What the hell does he think he's doing?"

"I don't know. Maybe he's just curious."

"Curious?" That man was definitely a loose cannon. Grant found it unsettling that Mike's brother just *happened* to decide to attend a conference on psychopathy and watch the presentation of the Profiler that was helping them on the case. That smelled off to him. Since when did Evan attend conferences on anything? Apparently it was open to the public, though he was sure the organizers must have had psychology students in mind as attendees, rather than bartenders in strip joints. What was his game?

"Curious?" he repeated, incredulous.

"Well, you know Evan," Mike said.

"No, *you* know Evan. I choose to know as little about him as possible." Grant leaned against the wall and ran a hand over his face. He tried to imagine Evan poking around the woods with a flashlight, or something similar. Why? He tried to imagine him getting stopped by the RCMP, asked about his reasons for being there . . .

"He thinks he may be in some sort of trouble," Mike said of his brother.

"What do you mean?"

"Nothing. It's just that he's concerned that they suspect

him now for some reason . . . You know, just 'cause he was out there."

"Well, was he being suspicious? I mean, more suspicious than usual?"

"Now, Grant . . ."

"That was a dumb thing for him to do, Mike, but if he hasn't done anything wrong then tell him he's got nothing to worry about. It's that simple."

"Could you just call that FBI agent up for me, Grant? Just ask him story, you know . . . ask him if my brother's a suspect."

Oh, great. He thought about that. He didn't like the gist of the phone call. What if Evan really was guilty of something? Would Mike be compelled to cover it up? "I'll make the call, but no promises, okay?"

"Fine, Grant, no problem."

I don't like this, he thought. *I don't like this one bit.*

Mike changed the subject. "How's Cherrie?"

"She hasn't come home yet."

"And Amanda . . . ?"

"Same as usual. I'll talk to you later, Mike. I'll make some inquiries."

"Thanks for that, Grant."

He returned to the bedroom and Amanda was there, waiting for him. To him she was the most beautiful woman in the world, even now. Even like this. She had suffered limb paralysis, and it was increasingly difficult for her to speak or swallow. They had to suction the moisture out of the back of her throat so she wouldn't die from inhaling the amount of saliva that healthy people routinely swallow.

Lou Gehrig's Disease was more common in older men, but here she was, not yet fifty, and already the disease was destroying her motor neurons at an alarming pace.

Her muscles were deteriorating rapidly, and through it all that wonderful mind of hers was just as it had always been. She had been diagnosed just over a year earlier, and the doctors said she had a few months left in her at the most.

"Sorry, honey, I just need to make a call, and I'll be back with you in a moment," he told her.

She didn't reply, but he knew she understood.

He grabbed his wallet off the table and walked back into the hallway, carefully closing the bedroom door. He had Dr. Harris's card with the number for his room at the Renaissance Hotel scrawled on the back. Mike had already programmed the number into the mobile phone for him, but he didn't have the slightest idea how to retrieve it.

Dr. Harris picked up almost immediately.

"Bob speaking."

"Dr. Harris, it's Sergeant Wilson."

"Grant. How are you?"

"Fine, Bob. Except . . . Well, to tell you the truth I'm calling because . . . umm. Is Evan Rose on a list of possible suspects in the Nahatlatch Murders Case?"

"Ahhhh . . . He's your colleague's brother, am I right?"

"Yeah, that's right. Look, don't get me wrong, I know he's trouble, but he's not *that* kind of trouble."

"What exactly do you mean?"

Grant did his best to backtrack, realizing what he'd said. "I don't mean anything by that. I just mean that—"

"This is a little awkward," Dr. Harris said. "Perhaps we should get together and talk about this? And I don't think it's a good idea to discuss this with your partner, if you haven't already."

"Why does Evan interest you?" Grant asked.

"He was lurking around the dump sites. He holds a

current hunting license," Bob said. "And he's a UBC dropout."

"I know, but . . . why is that relevant?"

"This is just routine," he assured him. "He was out snooping around the area and we need to eliminate him as a suspect. I'm sure you'll agree. We'll discuss it tomorrow. In the meantime, if you could throw some cold water on the situation with your partner that would be great."

Dr. Harris hung up the phone. "This could get complicated."

Andy shook his head. "You're not going to be very popular with the Mounties."

Bob didn't look too worried. "It isn't a popularity contest. If this guy fits the profile, which he does, then we have to look into it. Thank God he's just family and not actual RCMP. I don't care so much about Corporal Rose, but I want to keep this Wilson onside if I can. He's a good cop. I could use his help."

Andy closed the file he was looking at. The crime scene photos were ugly. They had spent some time roaming around the dump sites and discussing the case with Wilson and Rose, who seemed more relaxed about his presence now. Andy had not worked a lot of serials apart from the Stiletto Killer Case, but his training told him that they were dealing with a very different personality this time around. This guy wasn't messing with the bodies as much. No apparent mutilation. Shooting was much less intimate than what the Stiletto Killer had done.

He and Dr. Harris had decided to work on the case together. It would act as some good apprentice work, and would look great on Andy's CV. But even more than that, he was genuinely interested in assessing the possible danger to Makedde while the killer was loose. He suspected that Bob knew about his ulterior motive, but was playing along anyway.

"What have you got on this guy?" he asked.

"There's no hard evidence of course, but he fits the profile well, and we need to look into it." Bob walked over to the window and crossed his arms. The pose reminded Andy of Detective Inspector Kelley back home—another man he respected a lot.

"Evan Rose, twenty-eight years old, no steady job, lives alone. Known for his antisocial behavior. He's been picked up during bar fights, that sort of thing. Never actually convicted of any assault, though. He's a UBC dropout who may hold a grudge against academics or successful students. The victims were bright and attractive. Maybe his student sweetheart jilted him? Remind me to check into that."

"Doesn't look good, does it?"

The victims were bright and attractive . . .

"It looks good for us if he's the guy. I don't care who his brother is. Evan Rose has just emerged as one of the prime suspects."

CHAPTER 25

Debbie was exhausted. As much as she tried to concentrate on her dilemma and how she could get out of it, she couldn't ignore the hollow ache in her belly. She was starving. She had been restrained in that same spot for almost three days now, and her whole body cried out for release. She needed to move. She needed to rotate her wrists, to walk, to stretch, but she was trapped.

For the moment she let her head hang to one side. She had struggled and screamed and begged and fought, and now she was simply still. She no longer believed she could sway the man who had captured her. She had exhausted all of her strategies, and found a sad, pitiful place within herself that was calm and obedient.

Just do what you want and then let me go.

The man had done many strange and confusing things. Sometimes he seemed to enjoy watching her struggle, but even so, Debbie had heard about the sorts of atrocities that people can commit, and she knew that men in his position could do far worse things. Perhaps he was working his way up to something?

She looked aimlessly around the room, over the wooden floors and into the darkened corners, and saw a pair of strange, lifeless eyes. It was a stuffed rabbit. The small creature stared at her—fearfully, she thought—from its spot on a table to her right.

A great crashing sound ripped into her train of thought, and her captor burst in unexpectedly. She jumped in her chair, sending a rush of pain through her ankles and up her legs. The chair screeched as it hopped back. She screamed and tucked her chin down, locking her eyes tightly shut.

"Stop that!" he yelled. "Stop that!"

I didn't do anything! she wanted to scream, but she was too afraid to speak.

Debbie cringed at his ferocious temper. But he was crying too, actually crying like a child, and through her bleary eyes she saw his fist come toward her, sailing through the air in slow motion, and she tried to duck, but there was nowhere to go.

Her body hit the floor with a thud, the pain in her jaw excruciating. A great black void beckoned her into unconsciousness.

She went willingly.

CHAPTER 26

By the third day of the conference Makedde had a lot of things on her mind, not least of which involved two men and the relentless worsening of her insomnia. She was seriously considering calling Ann.

Things had certainly gone well with Roy Blake the night before, but that hadn't helped her sleep. She stopped drinking after the chocolate martini so there was no hangover to worry about, but she wasn't nearly drunk enough to enjoy an alcohol-aided slumber. She'd had the usual nightmare—her father's uniform, her mother dead.

Roy Blake.

She had half expected an e-mail from him in the morning and she felt a little disappointed when she didn't find one. This feeling vanished though when she almost fell over a large bundle of pristine, cellophane-wrapped, long-stemmed red roses that had been left on the front steps of her flat.

Thanks for the lovely company, the card said—*Roy.*

That felt pretty good—flattering, definitely, and a great distraction from the other male who had recently flown back into her life. She had to do her best not to start thinking about *him* again, just because he was in town. He wasn't there to see her, after all. It was business. And there was no way they could be together.

The schedule on the third day of the psychopathy conference had been interesting, but it wasn't a patch on the presentations given by Dr. Hare or the Profiler, Dr. Harris, on the first two days. Andy wasn't there, or if he was, he was being elusive. Mak tried to convince herself that she was glad of it, but she wasn't. What was he up to in Vancouver? She felt sure he wasn't just sightseeing.

Stop it. Stop thinking about him.

Her answering machine was flashing when she got home, and she hoped it was Roy.

It was.

"Hi, Mak. Thanks for a lovely evening. Perhaps we can do it again sometime? Soon?"

She breathed a sigh of relief. *Yes, that would be nice.* Next message.

"Hi, Mak." It was her father's familiar voice. *"You've had a couple of calls over here . . ."*

That could only mean one thing. The only people that would be calling for her at her father's home on the island were the Tax Department and Andy Flynn. It was not tax time.

". . . from Andy. He called for you twice today. He seems quite eager to get hold of you. He left his number at the Renaissance Hotel in downtown Vancouver . . ."

Oh, bloody hell. Don't give me his number!

Her father carefully said the phone number twice and

finished off by saying, *"If you want my advice, you should probably just call him and get it over with. Otherwise I'll end up becoming your social secretary."*

Cheeky, Dad. Cheeky.

Now her own father was encouraging her to call him. She had a decision to make.

Makedde had to play the message again to get the hotel phone number right. Despite her father's slow and careful recitation, she had tried to block the digits out of her mind the first two times. She jotted the number down on a piece of scrap paper. *Should I?* She dialed.

One ring. "Flynn," was his greeting.

She was caught off guard. Somehow she hadn't expected him to be there. "Ahh, Andy. Hi. It's Makedde."

"Makedde! Hello. Thanks for calling." The tone of his voice seemed so grateful for her call that she found herself feeling guilty for ever having considered doing otherwise.

"How's it going?" Mak asked. She didn't know what else to say.

"Oh, pretty good."

"You weren't at the conference today," she said.

"No." Pause. "Makedde, I'd like the chance to talk with you at some point. As soon as possible, actually."

"Um . . ." *How do I respond to that?* "Sure." It was the polite thing to do, probably also the right thing to do, but Makedde wasn't ready to spend time alone with Andy just yet. "Yeah, that'd be nice," she went on. "It'd be good to catch up."

"Okay. Well . . . what are you doing tonight?"

Tonight!

"Um, I don't think—" she began.

He jumped straight in with an apology. "Sorry. I'm sure you're really busy—"

"That's all right. You don't have to apologize or anything. It's just late notice, that's all."

"Of course it is. It's just that . . ." He paused. "There is something I need to talk with you about . . . in person."

His voice gave her a chill, or maybe it was the words themselves that reminded her of a time when she had begun to suspect him of the most heinous crime. Then suddenly he was at her door, unannounced, pleading to talk with her . . . "There's something I need to talk with you about . . . in person."

"Forgive me," she said. "But that sounds a little cryptic." She let out a short, nervous laugh, and when her laugh was not returned she fell silent.

"I'll tell you all about it when I see you."

That's the way it would have to be. She would have to talk it out with him and deal with it once and for all.

"I'll speak to you soon, then," she said and hung up.

She closed her eyes. Her mind was overwhelmed with a sudden flood of unwanted thoughts—thoughts about Andy, how powerful her attraction to him had been, making love with him in her apartment in Bondi, the candles burning to the floor—and then later, his face peeking through her door from behind the security chain, alcohol on his breath—"Makedde, you have to believe me . . ."—and the way he had looked at her when she was in the hospital, mute and full of stitches, her jaw wired shut.

Makedde decided to try to clear her mind by reading the dictionary. She pulled the great Collins Dictionary out, a full four inches thick and as heavy as a bowling ball. She flipped it open indiscriminately and found herself looking at the M's "mitrailleuse" to "mixed." This was a pastime she periodically enjoyed, but had never tried to explain to anyone else. She loved words and to her the dictionary was rich with expression, but unfortunately it held no interest for her tonight. She put it down and then started re-reading some of the paper, "Juror Sensitivity to Eyewitness Identification Evidence," Cutler, B.L., Penrod, S.D., & Dexter, H.R. (1990). That wasn't any more engrossing. Her thoughts continually wandered back to Andy.

There is something I need to talk with you about . . . in person.

Bloody hell. What does that mean? What does he want from me? Why now?

Makedde walked straight to the bathroom sink, brushed and flossed, and scrubbed her face clean until it was pink and glossy. She was determined to switch her brain off and get some rest. When she slipped into bed it was only nine-thirty.

But she couldn't sleep. Again.

Big surprise, Mak. Big bloody surprise.

It wasn't nightmares that were the problem this time. It was Andy Flynn.

For over an hour she lay in bed staring at the ceiling and willing herself to sleep, but she could not quiet her mind. A loud argument was going on inside her head, heated and drawn out, shouting back and forth between the left and right hemispheres of her brain. Her emotions and her logic carried out a battle while she lay silent under her bed-sheets in the dark.

Damn him, she thought. *Why of all the men in the world do I have to be hung up on this guy? Why? This is so stupid.*

Makedde felt a strong urge to see him, *now*. She wanted to throw some clothes on and march right down to the Renaissance Hotel.

She knew she shouldn't do that.

Makedde had many months ago decided that Andy Flynn was a negative influence in her life. She knew he was bad for her. It wasn't that he was a bad person. He wasn't bad at all. He was a nice enough guy, and that seemed to make her dilemma worse. The problem was that Andy only seemed to appear in times of trouble, and he did not make those times better, he made them worse. Nice guy or not, she knew that. And yet . . .

And yet it was so much easier to dislike him when there were continents between them. Now he was near, impossible to ignore, and she was going to pieces.

My father is right. I have to stay away from him. Those miles of distance were there for a reason.

An hour later Makedde entered the Harborside Renaissance Hotel on West Hastings Street. She had bolted out of bed, thrown on some clothes and a bit of make-up and driven herself over. She feared something like that would happen. She knew her weaknesses too well.

She had rationalized her actions like a student with a Masters in Selfdelusion and had convinced herself that she just wanted to talk to Andy and find out what was going on. He had something important to tell her, and she needed to know what it was. It was that simple. Perhaps she'd find that they would chat for a while and it would demystify everything. Then that would be it. She would know. Finally she would have peace. She would sleep better than she had since his first phone call from Quantico. Hell, she would probably sleep better than she had since they'd met.

Makedde walked up to the reception desk.

"Excuse me. Hello."

The young receptionist looked up. She had a sweet cherub-like face, and Mak couldn't help noticing she was growing out a really bad perm. The young woman's brown hair was shiny and straight until it reached the level of her ears, and then it exploded into fuzzy curls. Mak's eyes were drawn to it in a way that made her wonder if she had been a hair stylist in a past life.

"Good evening. How may I help you?"

"Could you call one of your guests, please? The name is Flynn. Andrew Flynn. Room three-thirty. I also wanted to make sure that he hasn't ordered an early wake-up or something. I don't want to disturb him."

"Certainly, just one moment, please."

Mak looked up at the wall clock behind reception. It was just after eleven. That wasn't too bad. Andy was a bit of a night owl, like she was. If she knew anything about him at all he wouldn't be heading for bed for some time, and nor would he mind her dropping by. And besides, he had said to call him anytime. It was just that she happened to be calling from the hotel lobby. A small issue, really.

"Ahh, Flynn. Yes. If you would like to use the white phone over to my left, you can dial zero three three zero and you will be put directly through to his room. He hasn't put in a wake-up call."

"Thanks for that."

Makedde made her way over to the phone, dialed and heard it ring in Andy's room. She had to admit it was a bit weird. At first she wasn't going to speak to him at all, and now this. She knew that it wouldn't be a stretch to suggest that her insomnia might be affecting her decision-making processes.

No answer.

"If you would like to leave a voice mail message for room three three zero—" the answering service told her.

She hung up. *Damn.*

Makedde walked back to the desk.

"Your friend wasn't answering?" the young lady asked.

My friend.

"No, he wasn't."

"Would you like me to leave a message?"

"No, that's okay. I'll just wait for him for a few minutes perhaps, seeing as I'm already here."

"Please make yourself comfortable," she said and pointed in the direction of the waiting area.

Makedde sat down in an armchair in a far corner of the hotel lobby while she decided what to do next. She was sure she would see him tonight. From her vantage point, she had a good view of the sliding doors that opened onto the street and the elevators that led to hundreds of guestrooms, as well as the hotel's front reception desk. There were some ersatz fern-like plants around the armchair, and when she sat back, they offered a hint of camouflage.

For a moment she felt like a private investigator performing surveillance, a parallel she found amusing. Some part of her relished the thought of surprising him this way, though she wasn't sure why. Perhaps because he had surprised her?

Makedde waited, half-heartedly reading through the *Vancouver Province* for the second time that day, and after only five minutes, a familiar silhouette grabbed her attention. She sat upright. A man had entered the lobby—a tall man in a dark suit, his posture slightly hunched with fatigue. He had short hair, very short at the sides—a cop haircut. She hadn't seen the face, but she was sure it was him.

I knew he wouldn't be far.

A sickly delirium sent a rush of blood to her head. She suddenly felt hot and uncomfortable in her clothes.

Andy.

Her heart pounded.

He walked up to the reception desk, said something to the clerk, and she gave him a room key. Mak noticed there was no nod in her direction from the cherub-faced clerk, but she instinctively stood up and took a step forward.

Then he turned around.

Wrong man.

Mak sank back into her seat behind the plastic fern, but she'd already caught the stranger's eye. He had probably felt her eyes on him before he even turned. The man smiled at her from across the lobby, and Mak responded with a cool nod. She looked down at her newspaper again, heart still rushing, now more with embarrassment than anticipation.

Oh, no.

He was walking toward her.

"Good evening," the man said as he approached. He had a French-Canadian accent. She noted his rough skin, and the smell of cheap cologne. His eyes were friendly as they regarded her, but she returned his salutation with polite reserve. She didn't want to be bothered if she could avoid it.

"Are you waiting for someone?" he asked.

Makedde delivered a smile. "Yes, I am, thank you." She offered a polite and dismissive smile, and pretended to be absorbed in her paper.

She felt his eyes on her for what seemed like far too long, and then he said, "Well, good evening."

"Yup. You too. Bye." She didn't look up for fear that it might encourage him.

When he was a safe distance away, she glanced around the lobby. Still empty. Well, if Andy wasn't answering his phone, where was he? She felt stupid sitting there—really, really stupid. Suddenly she couldn't wait to get out. Makedde stood and crossed the room, and just as she turned to pass the reception desk and make her way out, she spotted a familiar face.

Oh dear.

"Dr. Harris. Hello . . ."

This looks bad.

"Makedde," he said. He seemed suitably surprised to see her in the hotel lobby. "Well. Good evening."

Dr. Harris was smartly dressed in a pressed shirt and slacks. She took in his appearance more thoroughly on this occasion than she had when they first met, distracted as she was by Andy and then Roy. Bob Harris was in his fifties and appeared to take pretty good care of himself, but his face told a thousand tales. He had a mass of crow's-feet, and two deep worry lines between his hazel eyes. His eyelids were hooded and drooped. Makedde thought that he had a kind face, but a weary one.

She smiled at him, hoping she didn't look too red-faced.

"Are you looking for Andy?" Dr. Harris asked her.

"Andy? Yeah. Kind of . . ."

"I just left him at the Sports Bar around the corner." He paused, and seemed to take a quick mental snapshot of her face, her body language, her words. Perhaps the intense scrutiny was only in her imagination. "Is he expecting you?" he asked. "Because I can't imagine him standing you up to hang out at a bar."

"No, no. It was a surprise visit actually. I was just in the area and I thought I'd drop by . . ."

Oh, what an absolutely moronic thing to say, Mak.

But at least she knew where Andy was. He was less than a block away, slugging back beers with his mates. What mates? She wondered who else he might know in Vancouver.

YES! ☐

Sign me up for the Leisure Horror Book Club and send my TWO FREE BOOKS! If I choose to stay in the club, I will pay only $8.50* each month, a savings of $5.48!

YES! ☐

Sign me up for the Leisure Thriller Book Club and send my TWO FREE BOOKS! If I choose to stay in the club, I will pay only $8.50* each month, a savings of $5.48!

NAME: _____

ADDRESS: _____

_____

TELEPHONE: _____

E-MAIL: _____

☐ **I WANT TO PAY BY CREDIT CARD.**

☐ VISA   ☐ MasterCard   ☐ DISCOVER

ACCOUNT #: _____

EXPIRATION DATE: _____

SIGNATURE: _____

Send this card along with $2.00 shipping & handling for each club you wish to join, to:

Horror/Thriller Book Clubs
20 Academy Street
Norwalk, CT 06850-4032

Or fax (must include credit card information!) to: 610.995.9274.
You can also sign up online at www.dorchesterpub.com.

*Plus $2.00 for shipping. Offer open to residents of the U.S. and Canada only. Canadian residents please call 1.800.481.9191 for pricing information.
If under 18, a parent or guardian must sign. Terms, prices and conditions subject to change. Subscription subject to acceptance. Dorchester Publishing reserves the right to reject any order or cancel any subscription.

JOIN NOW!

"Would you like me to go and get him for you?" Dr. Harris offered.

"Oh no. No, that's okay. Thanks anyway. I might swing by, but I really ought to be getting home soon. It's late."

He nodded. He looked like he needed a good night's sleep as much as she did.

"I enjoyed your presentation, by the way. It was fascinating."

"Thank you."

"Have a good evening," she said, finishing with a polite smile. She walked away, leaving the newspaper on a chair as she passed.

Makedde had seen the Sports Bar when she drove past—the neon beer signs and mirrors bearing nostalgic Coca-Cola advertisements through the large panes of glass. It was the kind of distinctly North American establishment where you were asked if you wanted curly fries or coleslaw with your slab of steak. There were several enormous television screens broadcasting a football game, and the place was full of boisterous men, high on sports and alcohol.

She couldn't see Andy, but went inside anyway and took a seat in a quiet corner.

A waitress came over. "What can I getcha?"

"Just mineral water, thanks."

The waitress frowned, then followed it up with an artificial service-smile when she remembered her occupational requirements.

Don't be so uptight, Makedde. You're here to sneak up on an ex-lover, after all . . . "Actually, uh, make it a Slippery Nipple."

The waitress smiled. "Now you're talking."

Okay, the plan: Slug back drink. Feel relaxed. Find Andy. Talk. Go home. Sleep.

Fine.

She tried watching the television, but she still couldn't calm the churning in her guts. She needed that drink.

She tried to put herself in Andy's shoes. He did call her, right? So what was she nervous about? Perhaps her arriving unannounced was a bit strange but that only mattered if she actually decided to make contact. She could still walk away.

By the time she'd finished her second Slippery Nipple, Mak had well and truly graduated from the initial, mellow bliss, and sunk deep into a tipsy melancholy.

Where is he anyway? The men's room?

The waitress drifted past and suggested a Screaming Orgasm.

"Love those," Mak blurted. When she realized her faux pas, she giggled and covered her mouth, then it occurred to her that she might look silly in that position, and she promptly placed her hands in her lap. She nodded and smiled and the waitress disappeared.

Oh, my God, I've lost it.

Mak stared at the TV screen closest to her. Big men in small pants. Everyone grunting and slapping each other's butts. Curious men's business.

The waitress returned and placed two small glasses on the table.

Two?

Mak didn't really know what she was looking at. It must have showed, because the waitress began instructing her on how to drink the cocktail with the wildly pleasurable name. "Take the lime cordial into your mouth but don't swallow it. Pour the Baileys in next. Let it sit in there, then shake your head vigorously from side to side. Then swallow."

She must be having me on.

Mak tried to pay her.

"This one's on the house. Enjoy."

Mak blinked and stared at the little glasses, which responded by swirling around in her vision for a moment. She blinked again and they were still. The waitress was gone. Mak was sure that everyone was watching. Was this an actual drink that people ordered?

Ah, what the hell.

She took the neon-green drink and poured it into her mouth. Straight cordial. Wham. Then the Baileys. She looked up and the waitress nodded at her from across the bar. Oh, yes, mustn't forget to *shake*. She grinned at her with her mouth full and made a show of shaking her head around. She tried desperately not to laugh, but choked on a giggle and dribbled some of it down her chin.

Gulp.

Oh, good God!

Her head did a three-sixty. Every muscle in her body went to putty.

Mak suddenly felt much less self-conscious.

She gave the girl a thumbs up, and then slunk down in her seat.

She must have stared at her lap for a long time, because when she looked up, she found that someone was sitting next to her.

". . . all by yourself," the stranger was saying. He was smiling at her and shifting closer. "Lemme buy you a drink."

Her mouth took forever to respond. Her tongue felt funny. "No, thanks. No more."

He was still speaking. She concentrated on the movements his mouth was making, but still couldn't make out the words. She leaned forward and squinted.

". . . company. Come on, lemme getcha 'nother drink."

Mak recoiled and said, "No. Fuff off."

She blinked slowly, finally comprehending how horrendously drunk she had become, and when she opened her eyes again, he was gone.

She had to get out of there. She wasn't just relaxed—she was off her face, and that was definitely not how she wanted to see Andy Flynn.

Somehow she made it to the exit. The sounds of football and top-forty music faded as she stepped out to the street and raised her hand for a cab. But there were none to be found.

Someone put a hand on her shoulder. She spun around, expecting the stranger with the confusing speech patterns who had approached her inside. Her head spun long after the one hundred and eighty degrees were up, and when her senses finally returned, she found herself nose to nose with Detective Andrew Flynn.

Her jaw fell slack and she stared. Her arm, which had come dangerously close to swatting him when she turned, still dangled high in the air.

No, it can't be Andy. Not now . . .

Her nervous system performed the inebriated version of snap-alert panic and simultaneously displaced the entire repertoire of her motor skills. She was struck speechless and inert.

"Makedde! I thought it was you," declared the man who was either Andy, or the most convincing hallucination she had ever seen.

She stared.

"I thought I saw you in the corner, but I wasn't sure. I thought you didn't drink?" He paused when she didn't respond. She was frozen in embarrassed horror. "What?

Have you joined the SS or something?" He gently brought her arm down to her side. "Hey, are you okay?"

Mortified. Absolutely mortified.

So much for spotting him first. So much for being calm, cool and collected.

He was the same as she remembered, his scent, his presence. The same chiseled jaw and compellingly imperfect nose. The same little scar on his chin, the same dark, short-cropped hair. And his eyes. His gorgeous green eyes. She really wished she was sober.

"I think I need to sit down," she managed to say. She felt ill. Andy stopped asking questions and mercifully led her away from the big glass windows of the Sports Bar.

Hours later, Makedde woke up on stiff hotel sheets. There was stucco on the ceiling above her, and the weak smell of old cigarettes and deodorizer.

She felt absolutely awful. Horrible. Her throat felt sore and her head felt like it was trapped in an airtight bubble. Instinctively, she opened her jaw as wide as she could so her ears would pop. She was depressingly sober, and plagued with a deep, gnawing, unnamed dread. There was something she was unhappy about, but she wasn't awake enough to remember what.

Where am I? What time is it?

An empty glass and the crust off a piece of toast sat on a room service platter on a nearby bench. She'd eaten a bit to make herself feel better after drinking way too much. Someone had suggested it. That someone had been the man she'd come to this hotel to see.

Andy. Oh no . . .

He was sitting on the couch a few feet away. He flashed her a lazy smile when their eyes met. Her first instinct was to look down at herself. She was relieved to find she was still dressed. The feeling of dread decreased a fraction.

"How are you feeling now?" he asked her.

Bloody hell. This wasn't how I planned it.

"Um, how am I feeling? Been better," she admitted, and laughed.

"Would you like some more toast? Some water?"

"No, really, I'm okay."

The hotel room was quiet for a while. She looked around for the digital alarm clock. There was one on the far bedside table, declaring the late hour in neon-red.

Three A.M.

"It's late," he said.

She nodded.

"Definitely late, and a school night."

Was it too late for them? She couldn't decide whether he felt like a stranger, or like a man who had kept her company every night in her dreams for the past year. Dreams and nightmares, of course.

She studied his face in silence.

"May I come over?" he asked, and she responded by nodding.

He stood up from the lounge and walked over to sit on the corner of the bed where she was tucked in, fully dressed in her now wrinkled shirt and pants. She noticed her shoes and socks lying a few feet away. She imagined him pulling them off while she was in God knows what kind of state.

"It's good to see you. I was surprised," Andy said.

"So was I. I was in the area and I thought . . ." She trailed off and then shook her head. "No, that's crap. I wanted to see how you were. You sounded a bit funny on the phone. All that business about needing to talk to me, and then I thought I'd drop in and say hello, you know, nothing major, just say hi and that kinda thing . . ."

"You're even more beautiful than I remember."

Oh no.

"You don't have to say that." *Please don't say that.*

He shifted closer. "I've missed you."

She wanted to kiss him. Damn, she wanted to kiss him. He was close, his lips so close.

"Can I borrow your toothpaste?"

He sat up straight. "Yeah, sure. Whatever you like. Use my toothbrush if you want."

Makedde nodded and struggled out of the bed. She found herself wondering why hotels tuck their sheets in so tightly. She likened it to being shoved into a little envelope that you have to rip open to get out of, and wondered how Andy even managed to get her into the bed like that.

Mak managed to get both feet on the floor and push herself up. She stood, but her brain didn't cooperate. A head-rush caught her and she stayed perfectly still waiting for it to pass. "I'm fine, I'm fine," she mumbled, sensing Andy's attention as she walked over to the bathroom with her shirt somehow tucked up under her bra strap.

The mirror wasn't kind.

Makedde's hair was a mess. Her mascara had held up pretty well, though. A bit smudgy on the lower lids. She brushed her teeth.

Ah, that's better.

She performed what little grooming she could manage, annoyed that she should care what he thought. When she'd checked herself over—no drool, no streaks of make-up—she came out to join Andy on the corner of the bed.

She hadn't been anywhere near a bed with a man in a

year, and the last time it had been with a murderer. The man now sitting beside her had saved her that night. She couldn't stand that thought, it made her feel vulnerable and weak. She felt like she owed him something. She hated that more than anything.

She looked Andy in the eye. "I didn't know if I wanted to see you."

He said nothing, just took the comment.

"It's a bit . . ." She didn't complete her sentence, and he didn't urge her to.

It's a bit what? A bit awkward? A bit spooky? A bit of both?

They sat close to each other, unmoving.

"We'd better get you to sleep," he said, and stood up.

He was avoiding intimacy with her. *A good policy,* she thought.

"I'll take the couch," he went on. "You can borrow one of my T-shirts to sleep in if you'd be more comfortable."

"Oh no. I should probably get back. I can hardly sleep in my own bed, much less here, knowing I'm making you sleep on the couch. No way."

"What do you mean, you can't sleep in your own bed? Is anything wrong? Why aren't you sleeping?"

Mak closed her eyes. He wasn't really supposed to pick up on that. It was just an offhand remark. "I'm fine, honestly."

"Are you going to be okay?" Those green eyes were staring directly into hers now, and the intensity made her uncomfortable.

"Yes, of course. I'm always okay, remember?"

"That's *not* how I remember it."

Fuck you, Andy. That comment stung. She felt like he was holding it over her . . . he had saved her life. Makedde felt a wall go up around her. She crossed her arms. "Okay, so what was it that you wanted to talk to me about?" she asked. "I'm right here, so what is it?"

He smirked and then looked down. When his face was turned away like that she couldn't read his features. What was the smirk about?

When he raised his head again he looked genuinely distressed, and Makedde felt herself panic. *I can't read him right now . . . why can't I read him?* "What on earth is it?"

He swallowed and stood to face her. She watched his Adam's apple move up and down. He didn't look happy. What was it that she was afraid he would say? *I love you? Come back to Australia with me?* What?

"Mak, I don't think this is the right moment to discuss this."

"Why the hell not?"

"Just . . . trust me. Now is not the time."

"You said you wanted to see me and discuss something, and you even suggested we see each other tonight, and now I'm here and—"

"God, I missed your temper." He smiled and moved toward her.

"Oh honestly, that is so condescending, Andy." She stood up, fuming.

Now they were standing side by side, too close, and he was so tall, so beautifully tall beside her. *Damn*. Why did she have to find him so attractive?

"I should be going," she said firmly.

"Your shoes are right there."

"I see them. Thanks for taking care of me."

Again. God I hate that.

"I'm glad you came to see me."

I'm not.

She dusted herself off and headed for the door. "See

ya." She was at the elevators before she realized she'd forgotten her purse. *Damn*. And it was such a good exit, too. She walked back toward his room, her sudden charge of confidence waning a little. He opened the door before she reached it, and passed her the purse.

"Good night."

"Good *morning*. I'll talk to you later."

CHAPTER 27

"Okay, Mak, your turn."

"Gotcha." She readied herself and looked at the man in the puffy suit. "Hiya," she said to him.

She thought she heard him say a muffled, "Hiya" back at her through his mask.

"Mind if I attack you now?" she asked politely.

Was that a growl I just heard?

The man ran at her with his arms outstretched but as soon as he got close enough, she blocked him and forced his arms to one side, striking him in the face with the palm of her hand. The padding of his mask felt soft under her fingers. She followed it up with a knee to the groin for good measure, but before she had got far with that standard maneuver he was turning and grabbing at her throat tight with both hands. "Oh, fuck you then . . ." she said as she tucked her chin down and put her hands together, as if in prayer, and attempted to shove her fingers underneath his . . .

Damn, that's hurting me . . .

"No, Mak," Jaqui Reeves was yelling at her. "Won't

work. Come on . . ." Mak could barely hear for the adrenaline pumping in her head.

I'm rusty . . . Damn, what do I do again?

By now it was really starting to hurt her throat. She considered putting a hand up in defeat, but no.

Makedde screamed, "Noooooooooooo!" as she grabbed the man's wrists and fell backward, pulling him with her. His resistance softened her fall, and the moment her butt hit the mat she raised up her feet and kicked him hard in the face, like a kangaroo does when it rests back on its tail. He went sailing backward and she jumped to her feet, panting.

"Okay, that's it for now," Jaqui said, holding her hands up.

The masked man stopped dead in his tracks and pulled his padded head off. Jason was looking a little sweaty under that thing. He shook his head to orient himself.

"You're a little rusty there, Mak," Jaqui scolded.

"Thanks for pointing that out," Mak replied. "You could have let me keep going, you know. I was just starting to have fun."

One of the girls in the class raised an eyebrow and let out a caustic chuckle at her comment.

Mak turned to her. "I learned this neat trick where you can pull a person's skeleton out through their nose. Wanna see?"

The girl wasn't sure whether to laugh or run. She smiled timidly and scurried away. Jaqui shook her head.

When Mak had showered and changed into her favorite pair of Bettina Liano jeans and a black turtleneck pullover, she waited outside, leaning against the brickwork of the old church building that Jaqui Reeves used for her classes. The space also catered to acting classes, jazz dance and the odd spot of children's ballet.

Makedde had attended the first two lectures at the conference that morning before going to the self-defense class. She was only waiting a few minutes before Jaqui came out to join her. "Caper's?"

"Caper's," Mak agreed.

Caper's Natural Food Market and café was only a few blocks away, and the two women walked there briskly, stomachs growling.

They had first met when Mak attended one of Jaqui's classes as a teenager, and had been friends ever since. Jaqui Reeves was born in Vancouver and she was a true west-coast girl—tall and buff, with platinum-blond hair to her waist. She tended to wear clothes that showed off her impressive, bulging biceps, and in particular, the intricate Celtic dogs tattoo that encircled one of them. She had a few others on her back, and another one on her ankle that meant peace. But she was not trained for a peaceful world. She kept a folding knife in her bra at all times, affectionately called her "Booby Trap," and she was a kick-ass self-defense instructor. Hard-core. Like Mak, Jaqui carried pepper spray wherever she went, and she had a certain double standard when it came to Canada's tight gun laws. She wanted the laws to be tight, she didn't want her country to end up with America's gun problems, but that didn't stop her from owning an illegal weapon or two.

When Makedde had returned from her disastrous "incident" in Sydney, Jaqui got her an illegal Saturday Night Special, and promised her free self-defense classes until the end of time.

"It's good to see you again," Jaqui said.

"You too. Sorry I've been so slack, there's been a lot going on lately."

"I want to—" Jaqui began, but paused as she swerved around an old lady with a walker. They glanced back to make sure the woman was okay. She was. "I want to hear all about it. No editing."

"I never edit with you, Jaqui. That's the beauty of our friendship."

They'd almost reached Caper's. It was a popular hangout, frequented by everyone from university students to hippies, young trendies and seasoned locals. It was fast-service, not fast-food, vegetarian and organic, and always popular in health-conscious Vancouver.

"I don't think Jennifer will be coming back," Jaqui said, speaking of the girl who had chuckled at Makedde.

Mak shrugged. "I didn't mean it like that, honest."

"Yeah, right. How did you like the class?"

They moved up to the glass display of the deli section and simultaneously began to salivate.

"It was great, Jax. You're teaching some new stuff."

"Oh, look at that!" Jaqui pointed at an enormous puffed-up apple pie. It looked like it was a foot high and overflowing off the tin pie sheet. "Save room for dessert. We're going halfers," she said eagerly.

"Next time."

"Don't tell me you're dieting? You're looking a little thin."

"No, no, nothing like that. My appetite just isn't up to snuff."

Jaqui eyed her suspiciously but said nothing.

They slowly moved up the line, and when they reached the counter Mak ordered the vegetarian focaccia with goat's cheese, and Jaqui ordered the spicy stir-fry with Chinese vegetables and cashew nuts. They filled a couple of paper cups with purified water and found seats.

"I love this place. I haven't been here since . . . since we were last here."

"You haven't taken a class for like, five months. I was so offended," Jaqui said, pouting.

"Oh, forgive me. I know I've been all e-mails lately. Bad friend. Sorry."

"You were in fairly decent form today, so I forgive you. Have you been practicing somewhere?"

Makedde laughed. "Oh, no, only on my pillow," she said. "I haven't done a class with anyone else since the time you set me up with Hanna in Australia."

"Aren't you supposed to be practicing other things on your pillow?" she asked, implying the obvious.

Their meals arrived and they both dug in. When she came up for air, Jaqui picked up the conversation right where she had left off.

"So. Come on. I'm waiting. Tell me about this new guy."

Mak gasped. "Oh God, have I mentioned him to you already?"

"Yeeeeeeeeees. He sounds quite gorgeous."

She vaguely remembered the e-mail she had sent the day she accepted Roy's date. *What did I write, exactly?*

"Well, he is that. He's nice, too. Pretty down-to-earth. A security guard. He is very tall—"

"Of course he's tall, you Amazon," Jaqui cut in. "Now tell me he's a total sex god and he sends you to the moon every time."

"Jaqui—"

"Does he give good—"

"Jaqui!" Mak reached over and covered her friend's mouth with her hand. A couple of patrons had looked up. Reluctantly, she took her hand away again and brought her index finger to her lips. "Shhhh," she said. "We've only seen each other once. Well, twice if you include the lunch at the conference. I don't really know that much about him yet."

"So you're not—"

"No. We're not."

"And the detective's back in the picture, eh? Is that what's holding you back?"

"No. I told you I barely know this other guy. I just like him, that's all." She paused and shook her head. "I can't believe that Andy's here." She swallowed hard. "It feels . . . weird. He wants to talk with me about something. I don't know what it's about."

"Oh, I know what it's about," Jaqui said. One-track mind, every time. "Mak, I'm worried about you."

"You're worried about me?"

"Well, for starters I can see you've lost eight, which you didn't need to do. You don't exactly look well-rested either. And by the sounds of it you haven't had sex for like, a year. You're either going to completely forget what it is, or you'll leap on someone and tear them to shreds."

Makedde laughed at the thought. It wasn't an altogether unpleasant idea, with Roy at least.

"I'm just hibernating, that's all. You've never slept with a guy, so what would you know?" she challenged.

"That's because I'm a lesbian, Mak."

"That's beside the point."

"No, it's not. Did you get that thing I sent you?"

"That thing . . . ?" Makedde was momentarily perplexed. "Oh! Oh *that*."

Jaqui lowered her chin and looked at her. She had the Cheshire Cat beat for mischievous looks, hands down.

"You are such a complete hazard, you do know that, don't you?"

Jaqui just grinned. "Have you tried it?"

"You enjoy embarrassing me, don't you?"

"It makes you stronger. Is that why you haven't called me lately? Because I embarrassed you? I bet you didn't even open it. I'm so disappointed . . ."

"Oh, I opened it all right. I get this plain brown parcel from you, and inside I find a little rainbow-colored container with the word 'LifeSaver' written on it, and you bet I opened it."

Jaqui was laughing so hard she knocked her water and it splashed across the table.

"There is something very sick about buying a friend a vibrator, Jaqui."

She was cackling herself and couldn't stop.

"Such a hazard you are . . ."

She stood up and walked to the silverware counter and grabbed a bundle of napkins.

"I'll get it, I'll get it," Jaqui said and started mopping up. When she finished soaking up the liquid she looked directly at Makedde and said, "I just don't want you to forget where your clitoris is."

"Oh piss off, Jaqui. Honestly, could we please stop discussing my clitoris in the middle of Caper's? Would that be possible? Thank you."

One of the waiters walked by and Mak flashed him a tight-lipped smile.

"Enough about me. How's Inelle?"

Jaqui shook her head. "Oh . . . Inelle, Inelle. I think she's seriously going to go back to Sweden."

Mak gritted her teeth. "Bad subject. Sorry. I didn't know."

"How could you have known? Nah, she's such a sweetheart, but ughhhh . . ."

"So you—"

"I kicked her out of the apartment last week."

"No!"

"I had to. She was getting so whiney. It was awful. She wanted to go and I think she just couldn't bring herself to do it."

"Oh, I'm so sorry to hear that."

"Ya know, another heartbreak, eh? Tough as nails," she said, pounding her chest. Despite her humor, Mak detected the emotion in her friend's voice. "I'll be fine. It's for the best." She sighed and shook her head. "Ah . . . women are heartbreakers." She looked at her watch. "Hey, I've gotta go soon."

"Okay. Look, I'm sorry for bringing up Inelle. I hope I didn't upset you."

"Not at all."

But Mak felt that she had. She shook her head and looked out the window, and that's when something caught her eye. "Oh my God . . ."

"What is it?"

"Look across the street. See that guy there?" She pointed.

"The tall one?"

"That's Roy." He was looking in the window of a bookshop across the street. He looked good in Levi's and a black leather jacket. Brando came to mind again.

"Roy? Your Roy? Excellent! Quick, go over and snag him. Mmmm, he looks just your type," Jaqui said, gazing out the window. "I'll quietly disappear and ask you all about it later."

"Oh, don't run away."

"I have to go anyway . . ." and then Jaqui was up and walking away from the table before Mak could protest. "Go get 'im," she said. "I'll call you later."

* * *

"Hi," Makedde said.

Roy spun around and looked at her. "Well, this is a pleasant surprise. Good to see you."

She smiled.

"I called you yesterday . . . you didn't get back to me."

"Yes, I got your message," Mak said. "I was pretty busy." *Making an ass of myself with Andy.* "Sorry about that. It would be nice to go out again."

"Great," he said.

She thought about the roses he had left her.

"Roy, there's something I've been meaning to ask you about. I hate to do this, but you know the roses you sent me? They were a nice surprise, so thank you for that, but how did you know where to send them? I didn't give you my address, and I'm not listed in the phone book." That had been bothering her, even though she knew the answer to the conundrum.

He opened his mouth, then hesitated. He looked caught out.

"You didn't by chance follow me home from the Chilli Bar, did you?" she asked. Mak was sensitive about being followed, especially after finding out that Catherine's killer back in Sydney had stalked her for weeks before abducting her. Mak watched Roy's face to see how he would handle her question.

He let out a long sigh. "I'm sorry. I was worried about you. It was late . . . and I know you said you were fine to walk home alone but I just had to see that you were all right. I didn't mean to frighten you or anything."

Mak shook her head. She supposed it was a thoughtful thing to do, still, she didn't like it. The thought of being followed without her knowledge was alarming, whatever the intention.

"Listen to me now." She caught his eye and held it.

"Please don't ever follow me for any reason. I . . . I have a thing about it. It's just not something I like."

"Sure. I'm sorry. I'm really sorry, Makedde. Like I said, I didn't mean to frighten you or anything, or invade your privacy. I only wanted to make sure you got to your door okay."

Okay.

"Next time just insist on walking me to the door if you're going to do that. Don't follow me."

"But I did insist," he said.

He had a point there.

"I know you did." She looked at her feet. "Anyway, I wanted to talk to you about that."

"It won't happen again. Understood." He saluted her and smiled, and she laughed. He wasn't offended.

"What are you doing tonight?" he asked.

"Studying."

"Oh." He looked disappointed.

She thought of Andy. She had to keep her mind off him. She couldn't push this man away. "But maybe we could catch up when I'm done? Something casual. Why don't I call you?"

"Sounds great." He moved forward and gave her a kiss, his hands brushing her shoulders. "I really enjoyed your company."

CHAPTER 28

Debbie Melmeth woke up and smelled the delectable aromas of venison and garlic roasting in a hot oven somewhere nearby. She sat upright from the snoozing half-slouch permitted by her binds and searched the room with puffy eyes.

The appetizing smells were so potent that she imagined she could actually see the scent itself, like wispy white ghosts creeping under the door and drifting seductively toward her nostrils.

Debbie imagined herself eating—what the food would look like on her fork, what it would taste like on her tongue—what it would feel like in her belly.

Oh, please feed me . . .

The door to her little room opened. She heard footsteps, saw the doorhandle turn, and there he was, standing in the doorway again. But this time Debbie thought he looked different. Perhaps it was because he was dressed differently—in a crisp white shirt and slacks. His hair was combed. Somehow, he looked a little less crazed than she remembered. Actually, at that moment, he looked almost handsome.

To her surprise, he carried a small table through the door. She watched as he walked up to her and set the table down in front of her, then smiled briefly, turned his back and was gone again. Debbie didn't move.

He came back with a tablecloth and some cutlery. She noticed there were two sets. He laid them out neatly on opposite sides of the table and set up a single, long white candle between them. He fished a box of matches out of his pants pocket and struck one. Debbie's eyes followed the flame, and the candle made a tiny crackle as it was lit.

The sight of it was almost . . . almost romantic.

And hypnotic.

Before she knew it he had left the room and returned again with two bottles, one dark and one clear, and as he approached Debbie realized that the dark one was a bottle of red wine. She could see the label—a shiraz. He had glasses as well—two for water and two for wine. He filled her water glass first and placed it in front of her. She was desperate to sip it but her hands were still locked behind her back. She looked to the glass, then up at him. Her stomach let out a long growl.

"Hello, young lady. My name is John," the man said.

He even sounded sane.

"Hello, John," Debbie replied automatically, confused by the sudden turn of events. "I would really like some food and water," she said.

"Oh, I totally understand," said John. "I'll take care of that right away. I am cooking something for us right now. My brother has been very naughty to leave you this way. Has he fed you at all?"

Brother? But he looked exactly like you.

"Well, no. Not really. You, I mean he, he gave me some

potato chips," Debbie corrected herself. "Your brother gave me potato chips, that's all."

Play along. Play along.

"Potato chips!" He looked shocked. "That is it? Nothing else?"

She shook her head. "Nothing else."

"I am so sorry, Miss. That is just awful. What's your name?"

"Debbie. Debbie Melmeth."

"Now, Debbie, I want to help you. I want to try to undo some of the wrongs my bad twin brother has done to you. I would like to take off your handcuffs for a start, but to tell you the truth, I'm afraid that you might hurt me if I do."

"No, no! I won't hurt you. I wouldn't do that," she insisted.

He cocked his head to one side and looked at her. "Oh, I'm not sure." He shook his head. "Perhaps I should feed you by hand until we have talked some, and got to know each other a little more?"

"No! No. I mean, please feed me, please, but I can do it myself. You can free me. I promise I won't do anything."

He cocked his head to the other side, thinking it over.

"I promise! I promise I'll be good."

He nodded. "Okay, Debbie. I will trust you. I am going to uncuff you now, but you have to be nice, okay?"

"Okay."

John walked around behind her and she felt the cuffs come off. Her wrists ached where the cuffs had been, but finally her hands were free. Immediately she reached across and grabbed the water off the table, gulping it down eagerly and not stopping until the glass was empty.

He smiled and refilled it for her. "That's better, hey?" he said and she nodded and grabbed for the glass again.

When Debbie had finished her third glass of water, she crossed her arms in front of her and hugged herself, and she began to cry.

"I am really sorry about all that other stuff with my brother, Debbie. I really am."

She said nothing, just looked at him. He looked sincere, but she didn't know what to think. Where was this man before? Did he really have a twin brother? What if it was the same person? He looked exactly the same. He could have just combed his hair and got changed.

"Hold tight for a moment longer while I get our dinner, okay, Debbie?"

She nodded eagerly. "Thank you so much. Thank you . . ."

Debbie watched him walk away, and feared for a moment that he would not come back. What if this man, her only hope, decided not to help her after all?

But John did come back, just the same, only now he was loaded up with the most beautiful meal that Debbie had ever seen. There were mashed potatoes, venison and roast pumpkin and beans and big cloves of garlic. She couldn't believe her eyes. There were little sourdough dinner rolls and everything.

"Oh my God," she blurted out at the sight of it. "Oh my God, thank you. Thank you so much!"

"I think we'll enjoy this, Debbie," he said and smiled.

She reached out for the food, and tried to grab a piece of meat, but John slapped her hand away angrily.

His smile was gone.

"No, Debbie. No, that's a bad girl." His face changed; his mouth turned down and he furrowed his brow. "You can eat it properly or not at all, do you hear me? Where are your manners?"

"Oh yes, I'm sorry. I'm so sorry," Debbie apologized.

"I'm very disappointed, Debbie," he said, shaking his head.

"Oh no! Don't be disappointed! It will never happen again. I'm so sorry," she said.

"That was very greedy, Debbie. Very discourteous. After I went to all this trouble to present you with a nice meal . . ."

Oh, God, what if he takes it away? What if he takes his food and goes away and leaves me to starve?

"I'm sorry. You're right. I was greedy. I'm sorry." She was dizzy from hunger.

"Okay, Debbie. I'll forgive you, but you have to be a good girl now, okay?"

"Okay," she promised.

He busied himself with aligning everything on the table. It was agonizing waiting while he straightened the napkins and each piece of cutlery. Debbie sat on her hands to prevent herself from reaching for the food again. She kept her eyes down. She could not watch.

"Would you like some wine?" he finally said.

She remembered the drink she had had at the bar and wondered how she couldn't recall anything after that point. How she had ended up in that godforsaken room was a mystery to her.

He must have noticed her hesitation. "It's okay. You have nothing to fear. It's just a shiraz. Do you like shiraz?"

He uncorked the bottle with his wine opener, and the cork slid out with an audible *pop*. With just a touch of the shiraz in his own glass, he sniffed at it, tasted it, and then swilled it around in his mouth. He thought about the taste for a while, as she sat there starving.

"I think you'll like this," he said, and filled her glass halfway, and then his own. "Napkins first."

She raised her hands and forced herself not to look at the plate in front of her. Not yet. It all smelled so incredibly delicious. She fought the urge to grab it greedily. She knew that would anger him, and then she wouldn't stand a chance.

He reached across and placed her napkin in her lap for her, and said, "A toast."

She nodded.

"To us," he said.

To us?

She picked up her glass and clinked it against his.

He took a sip of wine, and she followed suit. She looked to him briefly for approval before launching into her meal. It was okay now, she could eat. It was as though all her senses, all her thoughts had been overtaken by the need to still her hunger.

"Now, just one more thing, Debbie."

"Yes?" she said between mouthfuls.

"I want to ask you something, but you have to be honest with me."

"Yes . . . yes I will be honest with you." She couldn't afford to anger him . . . She knew he could take away the food if she did.

"You have to be honest. You can tell me anything, okay?"

"Okay," she mumbled as she tried not to stuff too much food into her mouth.

"Do you find me attractive?" he asked.

A sick feeling settled on her. Though she continued to eat she started to sense the price she would have to pay.

"You want me, don't you?" John said.

What do I say to that?

"Go on, Debbie. You can tell me. You want me, don't you?"

This could be my chance to escape, she thought. *This man is crazy. If he is the same man who caught me and brought me here and fed me potato chips then he is a complete lunatic and I need to get out of here and this is my only chance . . .*

"Yes," she answered.

"Say it," he said.

Debbie suddenly felt ill. Her stomach had shrunk over the past few days without food. The gnawing feeling had stopped and in its place was a feeling of complete helplessness. She didn't understand why he was asking her such a thing. She was confused. And scared.

"Saaaaaaaaaaay it!" he shouted.

"I want you," she said obediently.

"Say, 'I want you, John.' "

"I want you, John."

He came around the table and pushed her to the ground. At first she lashed out with her arms against the weight of his body, but it didn't take her long to realize this was a fight she wouldn't win.

CHAPTER 29

Makedde came home from the conference worn out. She was greeted by the flashing answering machine. She had promised to meet Roy and it was probably him calling. At the thought of his company, she perked up a little. Should she just invite him over? Talk and watch videos or something? Eat some takeout?

She pressed "play", anticipating his voice, but it wasn't a message from Roy she heard.

"*Hi, Mak.*" It was Andy. "*I missed you at the conference today. Look, I need to speak to you. I don't know what you have planned, but perhaps we could catch up over a bite of dinner tonight? Please give me a call as soon as you can. The number is . . .*"

How did he get my number? Bloody hell.

There was no way she was going to just drop everything for dinner with Andy. No way at all.

No. I want to spend time with Roy, not Andy.

She called Andy back at his hotel and was relieved when the hotel voice mail picked up.

"Andy, it's Mak. I got your message. Sorry, but I'm busy

tonight." It gave some minuscule sense of accomplishment to tell him that. "Perhaps we can meet tomorrow? Take care."

Makedde hung up and frowned.

Part of her really wanted to see him, and she hated that.

Roy Blake came round at eight, right on time.

"Now here's a man after my heart," Makedde remarked with a smile. He stood patiently on her doorstep, waiting to be invited inside, balancing a couple of rented videos, two bags of takeout, a bottle of wine and a bunch of pastel-pink baby roses.

Wow.

"Come on in," she said. "Thanks for this. You really went all out."

He smiled and gave her a kiss as he stepped inside. "My pleasure," he said. "It's great to see you."

He stood beside her and she was struck once again by how exquisitely tall he was. He wore a leather jacket and blue jeans with casual boots. When he took his jacket off she noticed the way it clung to his wide shoulders, a feature she found incredibly attractive in men.

Roy was "just her type" as Jaqui had pointed out. And he had that handsome, boyish face.

Mmm, and he was wearing cologne again.

They settled on the couch and she laid out the takeout with some placemats and plates. He had brought Indian food—butter chicken, lamb korma, some curried vegetables and naan.

"This looks wonderful. Thanks."

"No problem at all. It's kind of you to invite me over," he said.

"So what's in the video cases? What did you pick out?"

He grinned mischievously.

"What . . . ?"

"From Russia with Love and *To Live and Die in L.A."*

She squealed with delight. *"From Russia with Love!"*

"You said you love Bond. And let's face it, Sean Connery is the only Bond, right? I only hope you haven't seen it too many times."

My God, he has been paying attention. Dr. No was still her favorite, but *From Russia with Love* was a close second. Her mood had completely lifted. She was truly impressed. The previews rolled for their video, they clinked glasses and began eating. The meal was delicious and so was the full-bodied red wine he had chosen. What a treat.

They watched as 007 kissed a beautiful bikini-clad woman and whispered sweet nothings in her ear.

"Did you get most of your studying done?" Roy asked.

"Well, not really," she admitted, still watching Sean. She was way behind on her thesis, and this sort of thing wouldn't help.

"Oh! Well, don't let me stop you," he said. "I'll let you work. Or better yet, maybe I could help you?"

She laughed. "It's boring stuff, really."

Too boring, it seemed. Perhaps she should have chosen a thesis topic about psychopaths instead of eyewitness testimony?

"It's psychology, isn't it? That's my pet topic," Roy said.

"It is?" Makedde had seen the movie ten times before, so she didn't mind that Roy wanted to talk. In fact, she soon found that the film made a nice background atmosphere for them.

"Yes," he said. "It was always my favorite subject. I've read a number of the textbooks and I have experience with people who suffer from psychological disorders. No, not any disorders I have." He laughed. "In fact, I wanted to pursue psychology as a profession for a while there, just like you are, but, um," his face dropped a little, "circumstances made it impossible. I had to start work right away to support my family, so the idea of a degree took a back seat."

He has a family!

He must have read her face, because he said, "Oh no, I don't have a wife and kids or anything. No, no. Nothing like that. I've never been married. It's just that my father isn't well and my—"

"Oh," she said. "You had me going there for a moment. Not that there's anything wrong with having kids," she insisted. "But you know . . ."

He leaned over and gave her an affectionate hug. "Don't worry," he whispered. "You aren't about to become a surrogate mom. I'm single and I don't have any kids."

And you're tall and gorgeous and you are not Andy Flynn.

She brought one hand up to his chin and ran her fingertip along the line of his jaw. She could feel the stubble waiting just beneath the surface. He had probably shaved before coming over. She felt the urge to kiss him, and she didn't resist it.

She parted her lips slightly, and they kissed. She liked his taste, she liked the warmth of his mouth and the newness of his touch as his hands moved to caress her shoulders.

Yes. Jaqui was right. I have been waiting too long.

She pushed him down on the couch and kissed him hard.

CHAPTER 30

Sergeant Rothstein of the RCMP Polygraph Division stood in the doorway and quietly eyed Evan Rose up and down. The subject was sitting in the waiting room, flanked by officers, busily filling in the paperwork Rothstein had given him. His lips moved noticeably as he read.

Steroid user? Rothstein wondered, noting his overdeveloped muscles.

Evan wore dirty jeans that strained to fit around his bulging quadriceps. His boots were slightly muddy, his T-shirt rolled up at the sleeves to show off tattooed biceps, and a flannel lumberjack shirt was tied around his waist. *A real bruiser.* He'd been told the guy worked as a bartender at the Blue Fox.

Rothstein had him fill out some standard medical forms to ensure that he was physically capable of being tested and could produce adequate physiological tracings for recording. He certainly looked fit enough, but there was always the concern of drug taking before the test. Hopefully he was clean, otherwise they'd have to postpone.

Having completed the medical forms, Evan signed the consent form for the polygraph, stood up and said, "All right, let's get on with it."

Rothstein smiled. He was eager.

He led him into the office and closed the door behind them, leaving the officers in the waiting room with their arms crossed.

Evan was a big boy. Pretty tall and very beefy. But his cocky attitude seemed to deflate a notch once Rothstein had him alone. He was confronted with a carefully assembled scene—a thick folder marked "Evan Rose," a recent photograph of Susan Walker, and another of Petra Wallace spread out on the desk, and of course the polygraph instrument, with all its wires and tubes.

"Please sit down," Rothstein said, and Rose sat, his eye on the photographs.

Rothstein always made sure he had recent photographs of the victims in cases like these. The killer may not have known the girls' names when he attacked them, so it was conceivable that the name would mean little to him unless he could associate it with a face. This way there could be no mistaking who the girls were.

Rothstein got his attention by leaning forward and slapping his open hand on the desk. "My job here today is to find out whether or not you are the person who did this," he began. "I want you to know that I presume that all examinees who come here for a polygraph examination are innocent and thus truthful regarding the issue for which they are being polygraphed. And I maintain that presumption of your innocence throughout the entire examination until all of the polygraph charts have been collected, analyzed and scored for a determination of truth or deception."

Evan nodded, somewhat nervously. His wide-eyed

gaze rested on the thick folder bearing his name, then shifted to the pneumo tubes. In eleven years as an examiner, Rothstein was well used to this slightly awed response, and the truth was, he was guilty of playing it up a bit from time to time. The subject wouldn't know this, but the folder was topped up with blank sheets. The subject would feel like it wasn't worth trying to lie, because they already had everything on him.

"First off, I will explain in basic terms how a polygraph works, so that you understand fully what we are doing today. A polygraph is simply an instrument that records changes in the physiological activity that is driven by your autonomic nervous system."

Evan seemed dumbstruck.

"Autonomic means automatic or involuntary, so it deals with those aspects of the body that cannot be controlled," Rothstein went on. "There are two branches to your autonomic nervous system. The first one deals with growth and development while the second one is an emergency response system. These two parts operate in opposition to one another, which means that only one system, usually the part that has to do with growth, is in control at any one time."

He watched Evan's expression. He seemed to be following fine.

"The emergency system becomes dominant only when there is some threat to an individual and he or she becomes fearful. For example: if you are walking down the street and someone suddenly approaches you and produces a knife, you will become afraid. That message will go to the brain and the brain in turn will send a message back to the autonomic nervous system to put the emergency system into control. When that happens a series of physiological changes takes place that helps you cope with that situation."

Evan crossed his arms. He was becoming defensive, or perhaps a bit bored of the lecture. Still it was necessary, and Rothstein continued.

"Your heart contracts more quickly which sends more blood throughout your body to provide it with nourishment so it can function more effectively. Your liver secretes sugar giving you more energy and the pupils of your eyes dilate so you can see better. The palms of your hands will also perspire so that you can grasp things more effectively." He raised his palms to make the point. "Just as a baseball player spits on his hands to get a better grip on a baseball bat. These and other changes occur allowing you to run faster, hit harder or lift more so that you can get out of that dangerous situation."

Evan swung his foot up to rest on the opposite knee. He was definitely impatient now. "Are we going to get on with this thing, or do I have to sit through a whole high school class on biology here?"

Rothstein leaned forward. "Listen carefully, Evan. I want you to understand exactly how this works." Evan unfolded his arms, and Sergeant Rothstein went on. "The polygraph test measures a similar response. If you tell the truth you will function at your normal level. If you come to a question to which you are going to lie *you will become afraid of being caught in that lie*." He emphasized that point, looking Evan straight in the eye as he said it. "As soon as you become afraid your body automatically shifts into the emergency system. *There is no way that you can stop it*. All of these changes will take place and I will be able to see them on the polygraph chart."

Evan squinted.

"Any questions?"

"But what if someone is . . . nervous?"

"Don't worry. The state of being nervous as a result of your anxiety about taking this test is constant throughout the test, whether you are very nervous, nervous or just mildly nervous. I expect that all people who undergo a polygraph test will be nervous, but that will not affect the accuracy of the test. Your pulse rate is usually around 70–80 beats per minute depending on your age and state of health but now may be around 90–100. That is the baseline that we will be functioning from. If you're telling the truth you'll stay at that level, but if you lie to a question your pulse will probably jump up to 120. Do you follow?"

Evan grunted affirmative.

"The test that will be used today is called a Zone Comparison Test. Are you ready for me to conduct the test?"

"Yeah, let's get on with it." The bravado was back.

Sergeant Rothstein got up from his seat behind the desk and placed the pneumo tubes around Evan's upper chest and lower diaphragm to measure his breath, explaining their function as he went. "Just breathe normally throughout the test. I will detect if you try to hold your breath, or anything unusual like that. This clamp goes on your fingertip to measure the tiniest changes in your perspiration." Finally he pulled out the arm cuff of the sphygmomanometer aneroid gauge. "This goes around your arm to register any cardiovascular changes."

"It looks like a blood pressure thing," Evan commented.

Rothstein sat back at the desk and looked over the polygraph instrument. "Please sit perfectly still during the test: no finger movements, facial movements, moving your feet. Even if you are nervous, avoid clearing your throat, licking your lips and so on. Each test is only a few minutes long, so just stay still. Simply answer yes or no to each question, not, 'No, I didn't,' or anything like that, and please wait until the entire question has been asked before answering."

Evan swallowed nervously.

"Try not to swallow, please," Rothstein said. "Okay, we will do eight tests today, four with regards to Susan Walker and four with regards to Petra Wallace. We will now begin the first test. Are you ready?"

"Yes."

"Good. Is your first name Evan?"

"Yes."

"Do you live in BC?"

"Yes."

"Regarding any involvement you had with Susan Walker or Petra Wallace, do you intend to answer truthfully to each question about that?"

"Yes, I do."

"Just answer yes or no to each question, okay?"

"Yes."

"Regarding any involvement you had with Susan Walker, *do you intend to answer truthfully to each question about that?*"

"Yes."

"Did you shoot Susan Walker . . . ?"

Andy Flynn waited for Mak in the lobby of the Renaissance Hotel, mulling over Evan Rose's recent departure from the suspect list.

Damn.

Evan had wanted to be polygraph tested—no, he had *insisted* he be polygraphed. And the bastard had passed.

He recalled Rothstein's words, "Look, for all I know this guy could have knocked off twenty banks this month, but in my professional opinion, with regards to Susan Walker and Petra Wallace, he never laid a hand on them. He's not your man."

Evan had passed with flying colors. That meant the killer was still at large, and the case was far from being solved. And the students at UBC—including Makedde— could still be at risk. In spite of his mentor's warnings, Andy felt compelled to say something to her about it. He had to inform her of the danger.

They never really had any hard evidence on Evan Rose, but Bob was right, he had fit the profile and they had to check him out. That he was the brother of an RCMP officer working the murder case only complicated things. It was undoubtedly causing waves within the ranks already, and those who liked the Rose brothers could well become ambivalent toward the outside help that had been brought into their jurisdiction. In any case, Dr. Harris and Andy were supposed to be heading back to Quantico in less than a week. The trouble was, Andy wanted to be sure that the killer was in custody before he left. He wanted to know that he wasn't leaving Mak in any possible danger. At this rate, it seemed unlikely.

Now he was meeting her for dinner and he had to decide how much he should tell her.

True to form, he chose to sit and wait at a spot farthest from the front desk, with his back to the wall and a thin veil of plastic ferns surrounding him. It was a good, protected position which afforded him views of the entire lobby. He remembered Makedde calling this spot in any given room the "Clint Chair"—as in *Dirty Harry*'s Clint Eastwood.

It was shortly after eight when she walked in.

His breath caught in his throat.

Oh, boy.

He couldn't have missed her. She was wearing a figure-hugging black dress and heels. She had a black coat slung over one arm and a small glittery purse in her hand. Understated elegance. With her looks she didn't need to play it up.

Damn she looks good.

Andy found himself looking down at his own clothes to check out what he was wearing. Black dress pants and charcoal-colored dress shirt. No tie. That was still okay. At least he wasn't wearing a T-shirt. He didn't know she would be dressed so . . . well.

"Hi, Andy," she said as she approached. She moved like a seasoned catwalker, but somehow didn't seem conscious of the fact that other people didn't walk that way. Did she have any idea how devastating she looked?

"Good evening," he replied. "You look lovely."

"Thanks," she said, and then all that model composure fell away. She shook her head and put a hand over her face. "That was really embarrassing the other night."

"Forget about it. I could drink you under the table any day," he said.

She offered a laugh that didn't seem all that relaxed. "So, shall we?"

"Where are we going?" he asked. They had agreed on dinner, but she hadn't told him where.

"I'm taking you to Tojo's. It is *the* sushi joint in Vancouver. I was just thinking the other day that it had been way too long since I've been there. You like sushi, don't you?"

Damn. Mak and her adventurous taste in food. Andy's chopstick mastery was not up to scratch, to say the least. He still ordered a knife and fork in his favorite Thai restaurant back home, and he vaguely remembered making an ass of himself in front of Mak while grappling with something called Saang Choi Bao at a restaurant back in Sydney. That was a year ago. His skills had not improved since.

"I haven't had sushi for a while . . ." he said.

"Good. You'll enjoy it then. It's just over on West Broadway. Not too far."

Oh, great.

The restaurant was on the second floor, and they took the stairs. She walked just ahead of him, and Andy did his best not to gawk at the movement of her rounded hips.

When they walked into Tojo's a few heads turned. Mostly to admire Makedde, Andy guessed. Some part of his ego puffed up, until he reminded himself of how "over him" she had seemed just the other day. She was probably only being polite by agreeing to go out with him at all. But then again, she had worn that dress . . .

They passed a busy sushi bar as they were taken to their seats. Japanese men with nimble fingers worked swiftly to create small delicacies with rice and seaweed. He recognized the raw tuna and salmon, but had a little difficulty identifying some items with tentacles and strange skin. The glass case was topped with the biggest wooden sushi boat he had ever seen, and it contained colorful morsels that hardly looked edible. He wondered if he would be able to tackle the dishes they ordered without making a fool of himself.

Right on cue, Mak waved to a mustached man working behind the bar. He had a round, friendly face. "Hey, Tojo," she said, and his face lit up.

He stopped and clasped his hands in front of him. "Good to see you, Mak. It's been a while. Enjoy."

The lighting was low and the restaurant was bustling with customers. Andy imagined it might be difficult to get a booking. He noticed a number of autographed actors' portraits and shots of famous bands framed on the walls in among the more traditional décor.

They were led to a booth in a quiet corner. Lucky for him, it wasn't traditional-style seating, so he could keep his shoes on. He wasn't sure if his socks were ready to impress.

"So, this is Tojo's," she said when they had settled in.

"Nice place."

"Shall we order first, or shall we get straight into it?" she asked.

Get straight into it? He definitely did not want to get straight into a conversation about murder.

"My news can wait," he told her. "Let's just relax for a while."

"I didn't mean to be rude, but you made what you had to say sound so urgent. You've really got me curious."

He could hear the chefs working busily in the kitchen. The aromas enticed him.

"Let's order first," he said, changing the subject. "Actually, why don't you order for both of us? I wouldn't know where to begin . . ."

Mak studied him for a moment. She clearly knew he was avoiding the subject, but she decided to refrain from interrogating him—yet. "Okay. I'll order," she said, opening the menu and looking it over. "Do you like tofu?"

"Not enormously," he said.

"Okay, *Agedashi Tofu* is out. You're a bit of a beef guy, right? How about the *Gyu Sashi?*"

He nodded. *Whatever that is.*

"It's raw."

He tried not to wince.

"Wakame salad . . . *Mori Ten Tempura* . . . that's with prawns and veggies . . . Hey, why don't we try the Pacific Northwest roll? It's fresh crabmeat and avocado topped with scallops and herring roe."

He nodded again. *Isn't that fish eggs?*

"And a good bit of teriyaki salmon for the man with the appetite, hey?"

"That is cooked, I presume."

"Too right."

Phew. At least I know I can eat that one.

The waitress came and took their order. Mak ordered them some sake and Andy refrained from asking for a knife and fork.

A petite woman in traditional Japanese dress offered them a tiny hot towel, saying, "*Oshibori.*" They wiped their hands with it and minutes later, she returned to take the towels away. The sake arrived hot soon after, and Mak poured it into small cups for both of them. Once they were alone, she leaned forward on her elbows and smiled at him. He melted. He used to love that. In fact, he still loved it when she looked at him that way.

"I forget the Japanese saying . . . so cheers," he said, lifting his cup.

"*Kanpai.*"

"Campari," he said in return, and for some reason she laughed. Mmmm, the sake was good. It felt warm in his empty stomach.

Soon their waitress came over with a plate of raw beef with a sauce, and a bowl full of strange little dark sticks . . . seaweed. Weird. Mak motioned for him to try it. He fumbled with his chopsticks a little, but overall he felt that his technique was acceptable. The dish reminded him a bit of *carpaccio,* which wasn't too bad. He avoided the seaweed salad but took to the deep-fried prawns and teriyaki salmon with enthusiasm. He decided that the food was quite edible, after all. But then again, Mak could have converted him to eating cockroaches if she really wanted to.

"I'm sorry if I surprised you at the conference," Andy said.

"Yes, you might have mentioned it on the phone."

"Minor detail," he said.

"Yes . . . minor." She cocked her head to one side and smiled at him. Her deep-blue eyes were just as he'd remembered them. "You look good, Andy. The academy's treating you well?"

"Sometimes. How have you been? Studies going okay?"

"Sometimes," she replied, and took another sip of sake. She smiled and gave him a mischievous look. "When do I get to hear this pressing news?"

Damn. The moment was too perfect. He didn't want to spoil it, and what he had to say would spoil it, there was no doubt about that.

"Mak, what I want to talk about with you is very unpleasant. I'm not sure if—"

"Fine," she cut in. "I can handle unpleasant. What is it? Is it about the trial?" She crossed her arms.

"I wish." He took a deep breath. "Dr. Harris and I are helping the RCMP out on a murder case."

"Mmm. I can see why you didn't deem it suitable dinner conversation. But you know, that never stopped my father." Her father had made assault, fraud and murder into fine conversation at the Vanderwall dinner table.

Andy lowered his voice. "There's a good reason why I want to talk to you about this case. Can I trust you to keep it between the two of us?"

"Of course you can trust me."

"We have three victims so far, all young women found buried near the Nahatlatch River. All apparently shot in the back with a high-powered rifle."

"In the back?" she said.

"In the back."

"Cowardly. That's almost execution-style."

"Almost. One of the RCMP guys mentioned that too, but Dr. Harris says it makes him think of a hunter."

Mak nodded. "You mean, like Robert Hansen?"

"Hansen? Yeah." He hadn't thought of that. "You scare me sometimes, you know that?" She knew far too much about serial killers. Far too much.

She smiled prettily in response.

Robert Hansen was Alaska's most notorious serial killer, a big game hunter who kidnapped, raped and butchered up to thirty women, burying them out in isolated frozen tundra that he accessed with his Super Cub bush plane. The man was a baker by trade, and by all appearances a devoted husband. He continued his depraved secret life for ten years before he was caught.

"Did they come up with anything in ViCLAS?" she asked. The murders had been dutifully recorded on the Canadian ViCLAS, or Violent Crime Linkage Analysis System, with the victimology, offender modus operandi, behavioral and forensic data found at the scene. It had been analyzed ad nauseam by the ViCLAS specialists, but all that work had not led to any strong leads, yet. The victimology however had led to some links with missing persons' cases, which again added fuel to Bob's theory that these were campus murders.

"Nothing too helpful as of yet, but the victimology did lead us to what I am about to tell you."

She leaned forward.

"Two of the 'Nahatlatch women' have been identified as students at UBC. You may have seen the missing persons' posters for Susan Walker and Petra Wallace? The third victim hasn't been identified, so we aren't sure, but we suspect she may also match one of the university's missing person's reports. There have been quite a few reports as of late. Young women, good students, vanishing without a clue. We're really worried that it may not be safe at UBC at the moment."

"God, you and my sister both."

"What?"

"Never mind."

"I'm serious about this, Makedde. There may be a serial killer picking off female students on campus."

She fell quiet.

"What evidence do you have that there is a serial killer here?" she eventually said. "And who is 'we'?"

"Some members of the RCMP originally became concerned, and that's why they asked for Dr. Harris's opinion. And Dr. Harris and I both suspect that the problem may go beyond the three victims who have been found."

"Well, you've got my attention now," she said. "You of all people should know how I'd react, so I hope you're not screwing with me, that's all I can say."

"This isn't exactly something I would kid about, Mak."

"I believe you on that score," she said. "Come on, let's get out of here. I want to hear more, but not here. I don't want to ruin this place for myself."

Several hours and several drinks later, Makedde Vanderwall rose, naked, from the cool linen sheets of a bed on the third floor of the Renaissance Hotel.

She shivered then went out onto the balcony, leaving Andy to his fitful sleep and sticky skin.

Was this what she had come here for? A few too many drinks to drown her sorrows and some late-night encounter with this Australian detective who soon would fly away and be gone? No.

But that's what had happened.

A serial killer. Here. At UBC.

The cold air slapped her skin, and her nipples tensed to sharp points. Mak walked to the railing and looked over the edge. Wet streets spread out below in a fast-moving grid, the traffic flowing past in quick, illuminated blurs of headlights.

A noise.

The sound of feet, and she turned to see Andy shuffling toward her. He was rubbing his eyes, and squinting against the neon city lights.

"Mak?"

"I'm here," she responded. "I'm here."

He stepped outside, and they stood together.

"I love you," he said.

She didn't reply.

CHAPTER 31

Andy woke up alone.

Erotic memories flooded his mind—Makedde seeing him to his hotel door, saying good-bye, and then a kiss, soft at first but growing firm and passionate, her fingertips along the back of his neck, her body pressed up against his. Their mouths melting together, tongues eager, the chemistry still there, undeniable, irresistible. The rest was a blur; naked skin, bodies moving together, pleasure and sweat.

Now she was gone.

Was she okay?

All that was left was an address and a note.

I'd like to see you before you go.
Mak

See you before you go? That bothered him. Did she think he didn't care about her? He'd ask her to come to Australia if he thought there was a chance she would actually say yes.

A newspaper was waiting just outside the door of his room. It looked like it had already been opened. When he read the headline, he knew why.

"NAHATLATCH MURDERS

Female students found dead. UBC panic as RCMP clueless . . ."

Oh damn. It's out.

Makedde would have seen it. At least he no longer had to worry about having told her about the case. Now everyone would know.

He looked at Susan Walker's face staring out from the page. She was a pretty girl. In the photo she was wearing a formal dress, with a gold locket around her neck and a small ring on her finger. She was posing with her fiancé.

Before anything else, Andy decided to go straight to Makedde's house. Even if she wasn't there he thought she might like some flowers for a surprise.

He sat outside her house in his rental car, wondering what to write on the card. What would she be feeling? Would she be happy about last night? Would she be embarrassed?

Then he saw the roses.

What the . . . ?

Andy got out of his car and leaped up the porch steps to Makedde's door. There, on the doorstep, were a dozen long-stemmed red roses wrapped in cellophane.

He bent down and examined them closely, found a small card pinned to the wrap and had to slide the sharp pin out in order to open it.

Mak,
Thinking of you . . .
Roy

He felt a pang of jealousy.

Roy?

Andy got back in his car and drove off. He tossed his flowers in the nearest dumpster.

CHAPTER 32

Makedde emerged from a long shower, still shaken from the night before, and unaware of Andy's early morning visit, or the bunch of long-stemmed roses. She had arrived home at five in the morning and hidden her head under the bedsheets until now.

She checked her watch. It was time. She dialed the number.

"Clinic. How may I help you?" came the voice on the other end.

Mak swallowed nervously. "Hello. Is Dr. Morgan available, please?"

"Who may I ask is calling?"

"Makedde Vanderwall."

"Just a moment, please."

She hoped she had guessed right. Mak had called at nine fifty-five, knowing about the medico's fifty-minute hour, and hoping that Ann was between appointments.

She answered. "Dr. Morgan speaking."

"Ann. Hi. It's Makedde."

"Mak. Hello. Good to hear from you."

"I'm, ummm. My dad gave me your number. I feel a little uncomfortable about this, but, I'm going through
some stuff and I would like to see if maybe you could . . .
Maybe I could make an appointment?"

God this is embarrassing.

"I was hoping you'd call. An appointment would be fine.
I'll fit you in as soon as I can, unless you think you would
be more comfortable if I referred you to someone else?"

No. No strangers.

"No, I don't think I would feel comfortable just talking
to anyone about it. I would rather talk to you. I understand if you are too busy."

"Not at all, Mak. I have to be in the office late this afternoon, so perhaps you could meet me here? I have an
opening from five to six."

Wow, that was faster than she thought.

"I have a photo shoot in town this afternoon, but it's
supposed to finish at five. I could try to bug out early.
Where is your office?"

"Kitsilano, close to you."

Not long before her first "official" meeting with a psychiatrist, Makedde Vanderwall was walking around a Vancouver photo studio sporting a brief, two-piece black athletic
outfit and a pair of warm Aussie Ug boots.

A large, mirrored make-up table sat in one corner of
the studio, illuminated by a row of lights in the style of an
old Hollywood vanity. The studio lights were hot, and she
thought her face might be getting shiny. It was. The make-
up artist was nowhere to be found, so Mak powdered her
skin herself, and used a Q-tip to gently remove some
sleep from one eye. She snuck a look at the wristwatch
she had propped up beside a palette of eye shadows on
the tabletop.

Today Mak was modeling for a local department store. Simple money job—in and out and cash in the bank. It was nearing four-thirty now and she was getting nervous about the time.

She couldn't be late for Dr. Morgan.

Makedde picked up her Starbucks Venti-size latte off the make-up table and shook the container. Half empty. Half full? She brought it to her lips and tilted it back. Cold coffee. Her mouth left a big peachy lipstick stain on the lid.

She thought about Roy. She thought about Andy.

What a complete mess.

The sound of large but graceful feet approaching her pulled her out of her thoughts . . . *Don't think about any of that right now* . . . She spun around to meet the wardrobe stylist, Serge, as he approached with a white Nike sports bra and Lycra pants bearing the "Swoosh." The colorful tags hung cheerily, oblivious to her time constraints, or her man troubles.

"Makedde," Serge said, stopping less than two feet from her and holding out the clothes. "Last outfit, then *fini*." His distinctive accent was French-Canadian peppered with the occasional dash of Japanese. An odd mix. Instead of pronouncing her name "Ma-kay-dee" as it was meant to be, he said it like "Maka-dee" as if she were some kind of sushi.

"The last one?" she asked.

Serge was bald, gay and beautiful, and he'd clothed himself in head-to-toe Versus Versace, or a very good knock-off, she wasn't sure. Simultaneously, they turned their heads to the clothing rack a few feet to their right. She counted six color-coordinated outfits—grey, dark-blue, light-blue, red, red and gray, and finally black and gray. She was still wearing the seventh and the eighth was now in her hand.

"*Oui*. The last one," he confirmed.

His eyelashes were long and dyed jet-black, and she found herself momentarily mesmerized by their movement—like watching black butterflies flutter gracefully.

"Just so you know, I really should leave here in thirty minutes, max. I have an important appointment."

"Audition?"

Mak could only translate his query as far as "Ah, Dijon?" which made little sense in their non-deli environs.

"Pardon?"

"Audition?" This time it was clear.

"Uh . . . yeah," she said vaguely. Something like that.

Serge assumed she was a fledgling actor. People often did. They credited Makedde with movie-star looks and seemed to assume that it somehow came hand in hand with the desire or ability to act. Model-turned-actors were common in Vancouver, or North Hollywood as it was sometimes called. Mak rarely bothered to correct the assumption any more, mostly because it inevitably brought up the topic of her studies. Her present job and her dreams of the future were seemingly incongruous, and she rarely spoke of one in the presence of the other. Like Kipling's *Ballad of East and West*, never the twain shall meet.

Besides, correcting Serge would bring up the question of the true nature of her appointment, and she certainly wasn't about to discuss that.

Just get this shoot over with and get on to making some progress.

Back in model-mode and avoiding conversation, she

turned away from Serge and headed for the flimsy change room. In this case the change area wasn't so much a room, but a small space divided from the rest of the studio by two tall slabs of styrofoam held together with black masking tape. Ah, the glamor. Posing for department store catalogues and changing behind styrofoam wasn't what she'd had in mind when she started modeling at fourteen, but here she was, over a decade later, doing just that.

There was a lone metal chair sitting in the tiny change space, and a wire hanger, bent out of shape, balancing from the seat back. A mangy-looking chartreuse scarf had been folded over, the hanger, and Mak could read the label from where she stood: *100% Polyester. Made in Hong Kong. Fashion TV's* Jeanne Becker once described the color as "fashion designer green." Today it didn't look very fashionable.

She stripped off the black athletic top and shorts she had just modeled, and for a moment stood naked, save for a bland, skin-colored G-string—the uniform model undergarment. She took the change scarf off the hanger and placed it over her head and face, using it to shield the white sports bra from her make-up while she slipped the final outfit over her head.

When she was changed, Mak walked up to the make-up mirror and bent over to move the Lycra into place. She liked the style of the Nike work-out gear, and thanks to her running regime and recent hours spent in the gym, she was looking suitably fit to wear it. Makedde had also slapped on a careful coat of Clarins self-tanner the night before to combat the impending moon tan that marked the approach of every Canadian winter. Now her skin had a subtle golden glow that contrasted well with the stark white top. Hours spent sitting in libraries and at computer terminals could be hazardous to one's modeling career. Preventative measures were necessary.

She pushed a lock of long golden hair behind her ear and looked at herself in the mirror for a moment. She was worried that her lack of sleep and other troubles would get back to her agency, but the only visible clue that Miss Makedde Vanderwall wasn't the picture of health was her slightly bloodshot eyes, which no longer responded well to Visine, and the barely noticeable under-eye circles. Mak was relieved that she didn't look much worse. She had donned a layer of concealer before arriving at the studio, and more again while she was being made up for the shoot. She was exhausted, but she and Elizabeth Arden were conspiring to hide that fact. Starbucks was in on it too. She was up to five Venti lattes on some days; fully five times her normal, pre-insomnia dose.

She doubted that concealer and caffeine would fool someone like Dr. Ann Morgan though.

Therapist. The-rapist.

Damn, Mak. Stop it. Think about clothes. Think about modeling. Or rather . . . stop thinking.

Just when Makedde finally managed to steer her mind back to the job at hand, the door blew open beside her, and a waft of smoke and cold air blasted in. It was Monica, the make-up artist.

"Have a seat and I'll give you a touch-up," she squeaked in her candy-floss voice. She made Melanie Griffith sound butch.

Mak looked at her watch again—four-thirty on the dot. Hopefully there'd be no traffic.

As if in slow motion, Monica popped a wad of Dentine gum in her painted mouth, put one hand on her hip and contemplated her palate. Purple ringlets hung over her eyes, and she flipped her head to one side in an attempt to move them. They promptly flopped back to blur her vision. Eventually she turned her hands to Makedde's face, pointing her fingers outward and running her thumbs along Mak's high cheekbones. After some pointless pawing and fussing about, every movement executed with irritating deliberation, something deep inside Monica evidently concluded that the best course of action was to reach for the powder puff . . . slowly.

All this seemed to confirm Mak's suspicions—Monica was straight out of make-up school. She had disappeared without a trace hours before, and Mak could only hope she would disappear again, very soon.

"I'm in a hurry," Mak said firmly. She could feel a headache coming on.

Monica seemed not to hear. She pummeled Makedde's face with a soft powdery puffball and said, "I think they want hair up for this one."

Oh, good Lord.

Mak tried not to roll her eyes. "I have to leave in—" she looked at her watch again "—twenty-six minutes."

Without warning, her hair was hitched upright into a tight ponytail. Her eyes watered, and the impending headache made a grand arrival.

"God, it's so thick!" Monica exclaimed, pulling and yanking.

Makedde had big hair. It wasn't flat and bone-straight like her sister's. She knew that. She woke up looking like Linda Evans in *Dynasty* every morning. It might have been great if she were born a decade earlier, but she had spent most of her career trying to flatten her blond mane. Now it was the new millenium and she finally had it under control—which of course didn't mean that others did. Especially this girl.

"That's okay, I'll do it."

The make-up artist continued her fruitless pulling and combing.

Deaf as well as inept. *Fabulous.*

"Honestly, I'll do it myself," Mak repeated.

The hands continued to struggle.

That's it!

Mak turned her head sharply, hair follicles just barely holding rank, and gave Monica, a long, hard look. The hands let go. She thought she actually saw a glimpse of fear in her eyes.

I've been doing this for twelve bloody years. I think I can manage a simple ponytail, thank you very much!

In no time at all Mak had brushed her own hair, thrown it into a high ponytail and secured it in place. She took one last look in the mirror, touched up her lips with a fresh coat of gloss and strode off toward the backdrop. Monica was speechless and looked on the verge of tears. Out of the corner of her eye, Mak saw her rush out the door.

CHAPTER 33

Mak stepped out into a rainy street in downtown Vancouver and crossed to her car. She stole a look at her watch—it was almost five. If she hurried, she might still make it.

As much as she was dreading the meeting, she didn't want to be rude, considering Ann was so generously offering her valuable time. She wasn't looking forward to discussing her recent past with anyone, not even a professional, but the time had come. Lack of sleep was affecting things with her friends and family. God, she had even used Roy to try to get over Andy and it hadn't even come close to working!

Damn.

Makedde gave Zhora a pat, unlocked her and jumped in. She threw her model bag onto the cracked, white leather bench seat.

Driving through the city toward the Burrard Bridge, she kept asking herself the same questions. *Am I going crazy? Do I really need a shrink? Why can't I stop these nightmares? Why has Andy come back into my life?*

She made good time across the bridge and down West 4th Street. When she saw the unmistakable giant cutlery at the door of Sophie's Cosmic Café, she slowed down, keeping one eye on the street names and declining numbers. Mak had to circle the side streets several times to find a decent sized parking spot for Zhora. After hoofing it up a small hill to get back on the main street, she steered herself toward the clinic.

DR. A. MORGAN, M.D., FRCPC. Psychiatrist

Psychiatrist. I can't believe I am doing this.

Her name was one of three doctors on the small sign. Mak pushed through the single door to the clinic and glanced at her watch as she walked up to the reception desk. It was one minute to the hour.

The reception area was clean and modern. A curved dividing wall separated the waiting area from the reception desk at hip level. Mak saw a neatly combed black ponytail shifting back and forth beyond the divider, and heard the sound of fingers tapping on a keyboard. When she got close, the receptionist looked up. She was a beautiful woman, mid-thirties, with flawless Japanese features enhanced by glossy lipstick and expertly applied black eyeliner.

"May I help you?"

"I have an appointment with Dr. Morgan."

"Mak-eddie Vanderwall?"

"Ma-kay-dee," Mak corrected her.

"My apologies. Please take a seat, Makedde." She relayed the name perfectly the second time, and went back to her typing.

Mak looked around her. There were two long leather lounges perpendicular to each other in the waiting area. A severely underweight woman sat on the far corner of one next to a potted fern, reading *People* magazine. She wore her hair in a tight bun and was dressed in a neatly pressed beige suit. Her nobby, nyloned knees protruded from beneath her hemline like two chicken drumsticks stripped of the meat. A brown and gold scarf was arranged carefully to mask her thin neck. Mak felt a twinge of sadness for the woman and then chastised herself for her unwelcomed pity. Who was Makedde to say that this woman's visible problems were any worse than her own hidden ones?

A square table between the couches held a stack of earmarked magazines. Mak grabbed a *Time* off the top and chose the opposite corner of the lounge to wait for her appointment. She flipped through the magazine slowly, her eyes barely registering the pages. She was lost in thoughts—the "incident" in Sydney, Andy, Roy, her father and her mother.

She imagined Ann making calculations in her head. Let's see, disastrous affair = ten sessions. Death in the family = twelve sessions. Death of a close friend = twelve sessions. Serial killer = . . . How many sessions is it for a serial killer, again?

The sound of movement coming from the clinic corridor distracted her rambling thoughts. It was Ann, making her way toward the waiting area. She wore a dark, semi-casual pant suit with a cream-colored silk blouse. She looked very smart, and a bit more formal than she had at the dinner table. Mak was nervous, but it was still a relief to see her. She had come to associate Ann with a last chance for sanity.

"Good afternoon, Mak. Nice to see you." She shook her hand. "Would you like to come this way?"

Ann led Mak down a corridor to an office behind the second of four doors.

"It's just through here, Makedde." She held open the door and let Mak walk in first.

The office was simple but elegant. Ann was obviously successful, and had good taste. A modest desk sat in one corner, crowned by a stack of paper in a tray. A small, silver desk clock. A Montblanc pen. A folder was open across the desk, and an unmarked pad of lined paper waited in anticipation of the psychiatrist's notes.

"Please, have a seat."

Ann gestured to a leather easychair near the wall, and took her place at the desk. Her own chair was already swiveled around to face the room, and Mak noticed that Dr. Morgan did not turn her back to her when she sat. There were only a few feet of empty space between doctor and patient, with no desk in the way to create subconscious barriers. Mak was a fan of the set-up, but she wondered about the practicality of barriers when it came time to open her own practice as a forensic psychologist. She might find that she wanted what little barriers she could use, depending on the patient.

Mak settled into the chair. It let air out softly under her weight.

"Are you comfortable?" Ann asked. Her tone was gentle, polite.

Mak took a moment to answer. Physically, yes. Mentally, no. She replied with, "Yes, thank you," regardless.

"Did your shoot go well? I noticed that you weren't late."

Mak thought about how she practically bit the make-up artist's head off.

"Ah, I managed to get away on time."

"So, how can I help you?"

Ann's body language was open and attentive, knees

pointing toward her patient, arms bent in a relaxed position on her thighs. Her large brown eyes were sympathetic but direct. Her gaze didn't waver and Mak was struck by her stillness as she waited for Mak to begin.

"I, um, I've been having trouble sleeping. Insomnia, I guess," she began, "and recurring nightmares. I just can't seem to sleep at night, and when I do it is awful."

God, Makedde, just relax.

"Would you like to tell me something about your sleeping patterns? How much rest are you getting at the moment?" Ann asked.

"Well, actually I've been keeping a diary, so I can tell you precisely." She pulled the little book out of her bag.

Ann looked impressed. "A diary is an excellent idea. I often recommend to my patients that they begin one."

Mak opened her book and read out some of the entries: the nightmares about wearing her father's uniform, the feeling of impotence, the devil-like creature killing her mother, the scalpel . . .

"Very vivid," Ann remarked. "It's wise that you are recording this. So you estimate that you have had on average about three to four hours of sleep per night this week?"

"Yes."

"And always the nightmares?"

"The actual dreams are pretty consistent, and only started this year along with the insomnia, which I've never really had before. But the nightmares have been getting increasingly violent and the insomnia has been worsening." Mak spoke as matter-of-factly as she could.

Now comes the hard part.

Makedde cleared her throat. "You see, there was an incident last year when I was overseas. I think that may have something to do with it." She corrected herself. "I know it does. Actually there has been a lot going on lately. For starters, the past couple of years haven't exactly been great . . ." The words tumbled out and she closed her mouth to stop herself from saying anything more. Her big right toe was beginning to itch again. For months after the microsurgery, she had had no feeling in it at all. Now this itch.

Makedde said, "I'm sure my dad has filled you in," as a way of ending her side of the conversation. There was a definite trace of resentment in her tone when she said it. The psychiatrist could not have missed that.

Dr. Morgan smiled. "Your father told me a couple of very basic details. No specifics. I thought you could tell me at your own pace."

I bet he told you everything.

Mak scanned the room, restless. There were degrees framed and hung on the wall. A tall bookcase held psychology books, some of which Makedde owned—*The Diagnostic and Statistical Manual of Mental Disorders,* fourth edition, *Existential Psychotherapy.* No criminology books, though. No books about serial killers. A box of Kleenex sat on the doctor's desk. A photo of Ann smiling with two teenagers—a boy and a girl. No man in the picture. No Sergeant Morgan.

Will my dad end up in one of those frames?

"That's Connor and Emily," Ann offered when she saw Mak looking at the photo. "Connor lives with his dad at the moment." A flash of sadness passed across her features. "He's a good kid. He could use a little of your ambition though, I think."

Makedde smiled. She still felt agitated and nervous. Her jaw was tight and her toe was really starting to bother her. She felt like taking her shoe off and scratching it to pieces.

The coffee. You need to cut down on the coffee.

Ann was talking quite professionally now. "The way I usually begin with my patients is to ask a series of questions to establish their background and get to know them a little. Perhaps we could begin that way. Then we can explore this problem you're having and hopefully find some sort of solution for you."

"What kind of patients do you work with?"

The doctor's manner changed slightly. She leaned back a touch.

"All kinds. I treat adult patients with schizophrenia, bipolar, dissociative identity disorders, mood disorders. I have worked with a number of patients with sleep disorders. I am confident I can assist you, Makedde, if you will let me. You're a student of psychology yourself. A very good student, your father tells me. I'm sure you understand the benefits of what we can accomplish here, so long as both of us can work together toward the same goal."

Mak looked to her hands again. She made a conscious effort to unfold her arms.

Stop stalling and get this over with.

"I've been struggling a bit lately," she said. "But what really made me finally call you is . . . I did the stupidest thing last night."

Dr. Morgan perked up and leaned forward.

"Remember when you were at the house I got a call from a detective who was involved in the murder case back in Australia? Remember everyone was staring at me on the phone?"

"Yes. I remember."

Mak told her about her background with Andy—the case in Sydney, their brief affair, the way their communication dropped off nearly a year ago.

"Well, he comes to town, totally out of the blue . . . You see, there's a big conference going on at the moment—a conference on psychopathy."

"I've heard about it."

"Andy has been at the FBI Academy doing some training in Profiling, and suddenly now he shows up in Vancouver, attending the conference. He came with an FBI Profiler who was one of the speakers."

Dr. Morgan's eyes narrowed as she contemplated this development.

"You sound like you are not convinced that is the real reason he is in Vancouver."

Makedde thought about what Ann said.

"I don't know. I guess I'm just so shocked. I'm not sure what to think."

The psychiatrist wrote a few notes on a pad of paper, and Makedde remained silent. *What do I think about his showing up?*

"Do you have any interest in rekindling things with this detective?"

"No." The response was quick. Perhaps too quick. "Which doesn't mean I haven't ended up . . ."

Mak grew quiet and crossed her arms again. *Fuck, I slept with him. I can't believe I did that!*

"And how has his presence affected you, Makedde?"

It took Mak a while to answer that one.

He totally screws me up.

"I am totally thrown. It just brings back so many memories." She looked down. "Bad memories." She choked on the last words, and with that, tears welled up in Makedde's eyes. *No dammit, don't cry! Don't!* The tears clung to her lashes and she tilted her head back, willing them to go away. When they finally cascaded down, they stung her cheeks. But she didn't make a sound.

Dr. Morgan held out the box of Kleenex and Mak grabbed a couple. She dabbed her eyes and nose, holding her breath tight, trying to make it stop.

"I'm sorry," she said. She had surprised herself by crying, having thought she had already done her share. She had very little tolerance for her own grief. It was always best to just get on with it.

"You have no idea how devastating it is to accept that . . . that you were . . . helpless," Mak said. "When it really mattered . . . just helpless. And someone had to come along and save you." Mak held her mouth tight and tilted her head back.

"This is a safe place for you to talk about this stuff, Makedde. You need to cry, so cry. There is no need to apologize. You have every right to be upset about your experience."

Dr. Morgan was so calm. She seemed to give off a serene, settling kind of energy that somehow made Mak feel okay about opening up. That was part of her job, of course, and Mak had to admit she was good at it.

It took a while for her to get her composure back.

"Now I can't believe Andy is here. It was so easy to not think of him when he was thousands of miles away, I could leave it all back in Australia. Then he shows up."

"Yes, that'd be hard. Do you feel that it's unfair of him to have come without warning?"

"Yes!" She wiped her nose. "It bloody pisses me off. I mean I know he left messages and I didn't call back, but he could have let me know. He could have let me know what he was calling about."

"Yes. That would have been the right thing for him to do," the doctor said.

"Doesn't he realize what his presence does to me? I mean, he saved my life! He found me naked and bleeding and helpless and he saved me, and I can't forgive myself for that. I had to be saved. If there was any way to relive the past . . . I would do anything to change that. I—"

"Be careful what you wish for," Ann said.

"What?"

"Don't go wishing to relive the trauma you experienced, or you risk attracting violence to yourself. If not in real life, then at least in your dreams. It was bad enough that you had to endure it once, but you have been reliving that trauma in your nightmares, hoping to find a new resolution."

Mak stopped and let that sink in.

My God, she's right.

"I never thought about it that way."

Ann looked directly at her, those intelligent brown eyes holding her thoughts, her secrets. "You were abducted by a terrible person and the police managed to find you before it was too late. The crime was in abducting you, Makedde, not in saving you."

But no one could save my mother. Why should I be saved when no one could save her?

"This detective, Andy Flynn, hasn't done anything wrong, except perhaps being insensitive to your feelings about the situation."

"Oh, he is so bad for me. I can't tell you," Makedde blurted, the tears still running freely down her face. "I don't know what it is about him. I think he's basically a decent man, but something about him just signals trouble. Nothing but trouble." She was on a roll now. "I have actually been dating someone, finally, for the first time since I got back from all that crap in Australia. This guy, Roy Blake, seems really sweet too."

Ann looked up. "Roy Blake?" she asked.

"Yeah. He's tall and good-looking, and he works as a

security guard at the university. I know . . . I know . . . cops, security guards . . . not much difference." Mak took a deep breath. "Nice guy, I think. He looks out for me, he brings me flowers . . ." She was aware that she was rambling. Her thoughts were running off in ten directions at once.

"Makedde, it is a very positive sign that you decided to date someone new. That is exactly what you should be doing. Going out and enjoying the company of some new people. It is a sign that you are moving on—"

"But I haven't finished yet." She opened her mouth to speak, then closed it again. The words were hard. "I ended up in bed with Andy last night. It just happened. I hadn't planned it at all. That is what I meant when I said I had done something stupid. I don't know. I feel like a total . . . slut or something. It's all wrong. I mean with Andy showing up suddenly, and freaking me out with this news about an investigation at the university. The Nahatlatch Murders. And he made it sound like some psycho is actually hunting for victims at UBC. Like he is dragging them out into the wilderness and shooting them like animals . . . and he's hunting for them at my university! And I wasn't doing so hot before that news anyway . . . I feel like everything is out of control here. I'm out of control. I mean; I slept with him . . ."

Calm down, Makedde. You're losing it.

"Did you not want to?" Ann said.

Mak took a deep breath. She thought about that. Yes, she had wanted to. She hadn't planned to, but she had wanted to.

"You are trying to overcome some issues right now. Your insomnia is your body's way of saying, 'Hey, you need to sort this out.' Make sure every step you take is one that will bring you closer to a resolution, Makedde. I think it is wise that you have decided to speak to some-one about this."

No kidding? I can't believe it took me so long.

"I'm not sure what to do now. I've never felt like this." Makedde thought of how she was with Roy, and then Andy the very next night. "I've never acted like this. I am afraid of making more bad decisions."

"Take it easy and look out for number one, okay? And remember that you don't owe these men anything, Makedde. It is okay to ask for space."

But I owe Andy my life.

Makedde didn't say it, but she thought it.

I owe him my damn life.

Dr. Morgan suggested that she see her again in two days, and Mak agreed. She drove home, feeling drained. She lay on her bed for several hours before sleep finally came.

CHAPTER 34

Debbie Melmeth woke to the sound of footsteps. She tried to open her eyes, and was met with a jab of searing-hot pain along the side of her face. Her left eye stubbornly refused to open wider than half an inch in its stiff, swollen state.

She sat perfectly still and squinted in the direction of the sound, the direction of the only entrance to the small room which had held her for days. The footsteps stopped. She watched the doorknob as it turned . . .

No. No, not more!

She had been tricked. *Damn him.* She had given herself to him and it had gotten her nowhere. Now he called her a whore, an animal, and she was confined once more.

Debbie watched as her captor approached, dressed in head-to-toe black, and carrying a hunting rifle.

He placed the gun to her forehead and looked at her without compassion. She did not move a muscle, for fear he would pull the trigger right there and then. The barrel felt cold on her skin.

"Cooperate now, little lady, and you'll be just fine." He

smirked. Then he knelt down and reached for her ankles. She flinched at his touch. She felt the release with a series of metallic clicks.

Should she kick at him? Could she? She imagined the blast of the gun, taking her head clean off, and she resisted the urge. She sat still.

And then he was up again, the cuffs undone, and her arms and legs were finally freed.

My God, I'm free.

She was shoved forward and instinctively hugged herself. Her captor forced her arms behind her again and her wrists were handcuffed together just as tightly as before.

She was ordered to stand.

But she couldn't move. She had neither the will, nor the physical strength. She said nothing, just sat there with her arms behind her back and her raw ankles throbbing in pain. She didn't want to stand. She didn't believe that anything she did would make any difference now. He'd had his way with her and she felt worthless. She didn't believe in anything any more.

"*Up.*" He shoved the gun's cold barrel between her shoulder blades, nudging her forward. "Stand. *Now.*"

Hesitantly, Debbie forced herself to stand. An involuntary cry escaped her throat as she rose and she struggled to remain strong as her knees threatened to buckle. She did not want to fall at his feet. She did not want to lose what tiny shred of dignity she had left.

"Now, walk forward."

The gun barrel jabbed at her, pushing her forward, and then they were moving together in a kind of funeral march, heading toward the door she had stared at for so many hours—for so many days. Then magically, she was through that door, out of that room and walking down a hallway. She'd had visions of making it through that door, but at no time did she imagine it would be like this, with a gun aimed at her back, defeated and used.

"Please—" she began. It was a word she had used many times in the previous days, without success.

Debbie was marched to the front door, floorboards creaking under her feet. The man kicked open a door in front of her and suddenly she saw the dark outdoors. She had started to wonder if she would ever see outside again. It was night and there were no lights anywhere.

The gun stayed pressed to her back as Debbie was pushed through damp grass.

"Walk," came the now familiar voice from behind her, and she did as it said.

Debbie stubbed her toe on something and tripped. She fell forward, felt her balance go, and suddenly hands reached out of the blackness to grab her and hold her upright.

"Careful now . . ." came the voice.

It seemed an odd comment. *Careful or what, I might hurt myself?*

After several meters, the pathway in the grass appeared to end at a wall of trees. Finally, the gun was pulled away and Debbie was in the middle of nowhere, facing the cold, dark forest.

It is time now, she thought. *Time to die.*

She felt a tug at her wrists, heard the click of the handcuffs. They were off. They were finally off, she was free, she was out of that horrible room, out of that cabin but it meant nothing now, and she knew it.

"Run." The voice behind her was emotionless. "*Now.*"

There was no light to guide her way.

None at all.

Her eyes adjusted slowly to the faint moonlight, but even so she could barely see a thing. She did not want to run. She did not want to play this game. If he was letting her go, then he should let her go near a road where she stood a chance of finding help. Not this way. Not in a strange forest, alone.

Instead of running as she had been ordered, Debbie turned toward her captor. Better to face death head-on, rather than get shot in the back, if that's what was intended for her. Slowly she turned toward him, searching for those awful, compassionless eyes that had watched her plead and beg for mercy.

She did not find them. Instead she found great long stalks where his eyes were supposed to be.

Debbie screamed, and started to run.

The Hunter gave her sixty seconds.

Then he adjusted his night-vision goggles, and followed.

CHAPTER 35

It was a beautiful day at UBC—sunny, but with a crisp autumn bite in the air. Mak sat on a bench waiting for Roy, her neck wrapped in a warm scarf against the chill. When she had woken up that morning, she knew what to do. Sleep had helped to clear her mind. She needed time by herself. She needed space.

Mak had called Roy on his mobile and left a message for him to meet her on campus. It was best to just be honest and get it over with. They had barely had a chance to get to know each other, but she had to stop seeing him now. Roy's arrival in her life could have been a further wedge between Mak and her former lover, but instead, she had found herself in Andy's bed as well. She didn't want to be split between two men. It was better to cut it off with both, and be alone until she got her head together.

She spotted Roy approaching along the pathway, right on time. He was dressed in his security guard uniform and carrying a small box wrapped in pretty gold paper.

She knew it would be a gift for her, and that made her want to cringe.

Roy greeted her with a chaste kiss and sat beside her on the bench, smiling boyishly. He had shaved recently and she could smell the Azzaro aftershave. His skin glistened slightly in the sun. His hair was gelled, his uniform neatly pressed. He looked handsome, and she almost didn't want to let him go.

"Hi, Mak." He smiled at her—his face positively lit up. "You look very beautiful today. But then again, you always look beautiful."

Mak gritted her teeth. "Thanks. I, um . . . I actually wanted to talk with you about something, Roy."

He perked up. He shouldn't have perked up.

"Great." He extended his small wrapped parcel. "This is for you."

"Thank you, Roy, but—"

"Would you like to open it now?"

Makedde took a deep breath. "I think we may want to wait on that until I tell you what I need to say. Thanks for the gift, but . . . I just need to talk with you about something first."

He nodded and looked at her with those big brown eyes, his face suddenly serious. "It's not about me following you home that first night again, is it? I'm sorry about that. I was just looking out for you—"

"Roy . . . I don't think we should see each other for a while," she said.

His face dropped.

"There's a lot going on in my life at the moment which I need to sort out, so I shouldn't really be seeing anyone just now. I'm sorry."

He appeared totally confused. "Is it something I did?"

"No, no. You have been lovely. I just would rather be alone."

Roy looked puzzled, and hurt. Yes, he definitely looked hurt.

Am I doing the right thing? Am I ruining a potentially good thing?

"I'm sorry, Roy. It's not your fault. It's mine. I didn't want to just avoid you or anything. I wanted to be upfront about it."

He squinted and pursed his lips. "Is there someone else?" he said suspiciously. She didn't like the look in his eye when he said it. Nor did she appreciate his tone.

"No, not really. It's just me." *Don't bring Andy into this.*

Roy's eyes narrowed. "Not *really?* So there *is* someone else?"

"No," Makedde repeated, more firmly this time. She didn't like this sudden aggression.

"Who is he?" Roy demanded.

She saw a flash of anger, and it made her nervous. She stiffened and sat upright.

"Who is he?" she lashed back. "I just said there is no one else. I don't want to see you, okay? Don't you get that?"

Perhaps that came out a little nastier than necessary.

"No!" he spat. "No, it's not okay. I want a good reason. I want a good reason for why you would lead me on like this. What are you, some kind of tease?"

Makedde's jaw fell open. "Roy!"

He shut up and covered his face with his hands.

"Roy, you are being totally unreasonable," she said.

"I'm sorry. I'm sorry. I shouldn't have said that," he said, shaking his head, berating himself. "I didn't mean to say that. That was wrong. Please forgive me. Won't you give me another chance?"

"I don't think we should see each other any more, Roy," she said firmly.

"But, Makedde, I really care about you." He reached for her hand and she pulled it away. "Will you let me be your friend at least? Please?"

"Just . . . just accept my apologies and go. There's no hard feelings or anything."

"You don't want me?" He sounded like a spoiled child.

"Roy." She was annoyed. He couldn't have missed it. "Don't do that." She gave him a firm and steady "back off" look and felt her body prepare for a possible confrontation. *What if he freaks out and gets violent?*

Roy looked at her for a while and she looked straight back.

"But, Makedde, I can help you. I know what you've been through, and I can help you."

A chill went up her spine.

"Professor Gosper told me all about it. It's terrible what you've been through. I can understand why you're pushing me away, but really, I can help you."

"Professor Gosper told you about *what?*"

"About the man who abducted you in Sydney. The serial killer."

Her blood ran cold.

Her toe began to tingle.

"I'm not going to discuss this with you."

"Don't do this, Makedde. I can help you," he pleaded.

"I don't need your help."

"Don't push me away! I understand you! I can help you!" He opened his mouth again to protest, but stopped, stood up and tossed his gift on the ground so hard that it bounced on the pavement. He stormed off in a huff in the direction he had come.

Makedde sat on the bench and hung her head.

Damn.

That hadn't been as easy as she had hoped.

And he knew all about Sydney!

When Makedde finally left the bench she wasn't sure what to do about the little gold box. If she gave it back it would mean facing him again, and if she left it at his work station or something similar it would be like rubbing salt in his wounds. She wished he had just taken it with him, whatever it was.

I should at least open it, she thought.

Makedde bent over to pick up the little box. It felt light in her grasp, the gold paper smooth under her fingertips. Carefully, she peeled open one end of the neat wrapper and pulled out the box.

Chocolate.

Inside was a large milk-chocolate heart sitting in a bed of crimson gift paper, but his act of throwing it to the ground had caused it to break—right through the center from top to bottom.

The heart was split.

Mak fought a terrible melancholy as she drove home.

In no time at all the weather had turned nasty, just like her day. The clouds had come over as soon as she reached Zhora in the university carpark, and now rain lashed the sides of her car and thunderclouds hung heavy over the city.

You'll see Ann again tomorrow, and then you'll be making progress again. You'll be okay. Don't panic.

But she *was* panicking. Makedde couldn't remember the last time she felt so down.

By noon she had locked herself away in her apartment and had immersed herself in a textbook—*The Diagnostic and Statistical Manual of Mental Disorders.* There was no way she could face the conference, or face anyone at all.

You'll be okay . . . you'll be okay . . .

She flipped the textbook open to page three hundred and twenty, "Major Depressive Episode".

When the phone rang, she didn't move a muscle. Her answering machine picked it up.

"Hi, Mak." It was Jaqui. *"I just got your message. Are you okay? You sounded a little down. I'm worried about you. Call me."*

I'm worried about me, too.

Not long after, the phone rang again, and Mak thought fleetingly of answering it. It'd be Jaqui again.

Her machine got it.

"Makedde, it's Roy. Pick up the phone."

Oh no . . .

"Pick up the phone . . ."

She didn't move.

"Pick up the phone, Mak. Pick up the phone, pick up the phone . . ."

The sound of his voice made her feel cold and she shivered.

Makedde listened to the background noises, the sounds of the wind and the rain. He was clearly calling from outside somewhere. He was calling from his mobile phone, from somewhere rainy and wet, and windy.

Her eyes went to the window, to the trees swaying in the wind.

My God. What if he's outside?

She jumped up and checked that the door was locked, pulled the security chain and went around closing the curtains in every room. With trembling hands she peeked through a crack in the curtain fabric of the main window and scanned the street outside. No sign of him.

I'm going crazy. I can't take this any more.

Breathing hard, she opened the cupboard in the bathroom. Her heart was pounding and so was her head. She pulled out a box of medicines she never used.

There it is.

Makedde popped a small pill out of a foil wrap, and snapped it in half. She slugged it back with a mouthful of tap water. Within ten minutes she felt the drowsiness hit.

It was barely one in the afternoon when Makedde crawled into bed and fell into a deep drug-induced sleep.

CHAPTER 36

Roy drove along the Sea to Sky Highway, frustrated and upset.

She doesn't want to see me any more. Why? Why?

He really cared about Makedde. He wanted to help her. Why couldn't she understand that? He wasn't judging her on her past. He wasn't judging her on what she had been through or what she was going through. He really understood her. He understood her needs.

She was a nice girl, and she had been through so much, but now she was pushing him away.

Why?

He'd stay away for a while and calm down. He would spend the time with his brother and the wilderness, and get his head together, and then he would think of a way to get her back.

Danny would be a good ear to his sorrows. He always was.

Perhaps we'll even go hunting together?

It was Danny's favorite thing. And they hadn't gone together in a while.

CHAPTER 37

"See you next week, Martin."

Dr. Ann Morgan rose from her chair to see Martin Sawyer from her office. He was her last appointment of the day, and it had become a late day, indeed. Another after-hours patient, but Martin had been insistent that he needed to see her right away.

She was pleased to note that the thirty-four-year-old paranoid schizophrenic was responding well to a recent change in his medication. After some time spent using the standard anti-psychotic drug haloperidol with limited success, she had prescribed the olanzapine variety, which was a comparatively new drug. So far it appeared to be working wonders. Martin seemed like a different man from the nervous, angry and confused patient who was first referred to her. He had just been a bit panicked about his prescription being found by his new partner, but she felt she'd eased his mind.

He stopped in the doorway to shake Dr. Morgan's hand vigorously before leaving. "Thank you so much," he said, smiling broadly with crooked teeth.

"There is no need to thank me," she assured him, and meant it.

Although such a positive change was always rewarding to observe, Ann knew that his recovery was far from a mission accomplished. One of the biggest challenges that psychiatrists face is to keep their patients committed to their medication once they feel well again, and Ann dearly hoped that Martin would continue his daily dose when it came time to wean him off their regular appointments. The studies on olanzapine showed a higher level of compliance than with many of the other antipsychotic drugs, and she allowed herself a feeling of cautious optimism about Martin's future as she watched him walk out of the clinic.

With her last patient now gone, her mind focused with neat precision on her next task, and a tiny cloud of apprehension threw a shadow across her heart. Her official day was complete, but there was something else Ann felt she needed to do. She wanted to check a name in the basement files before she left the office, and she suspected that what she would find there would not make her happy.

Ann made her way down the hallway and walked around to the large front desk where the clinic receptionist was busy at the keyboard. "Sai, could you pass me the key for the storage room, please?"

Sai flashed her wise dark eyes in Ann's direction, her neat ponytail snapping to one side like a black whip as she turned her head. Without a word she fished the small key out of the top drawer of her desk and turned her striking, symmetrical face back to Ann.

In Japanese, the name "Sai" refers to intelligence. Ann thought her parents named their girl well. She was by far the best receptionist they had employed at the clinic.

Ann thanked her, and Sai nodded and turned her attention back to her work at the computer terminal.

"Will you be staying on much longer?" Ann asked the top of Sai's head.

Sai turned and looked at her quizzically, broken again from the focus on her work. "I wasn't planning on it. I have a dinner date—"

"That's okay. I'll close up today," Ann said. "I'll be downstairs if you need anything."

Any break from routine in the clinic was unusual, and Ann's comment appeared to give Sai pause.

"Is everything all right?" Sai asked, a worry line flawing her smooth forehead. Such a question was inevitable.

"Yes, everything's fine. I just need to check some old client files and I don't know how long it will take."

Sai nodded.

With the single key warming slowly in her hot palm, Ann made her way toward the rear exit of the building and the staircase that led down to the storage room. The corridor grew cold as she ventured further into the bowels of the building, and she was glad for the warmth of her wool Donna Karan pant suit. She pulled the collar close around her neck.

What if I am right about this?

Ann supposed that she would have to consider her options carefully, but only if her concerns were confirmed. For now she simply had to check.

She made her way to the base of the stairs and was met with the stale smell of neglect as she unlocked the storage room door. Blindly, she flipped the light switch on with one groping hand, reaching around the wall in the dark. The overhead lights came on with a flicker and a dull buzz, the fluorescent tubes illuminating the gray filing cabinets that held every file from the clinic that had been inactive for more than two years. The tops of the cabinets were thick with dust, and Ann was glad she didn't have to come down here too often.

She went for the first cabinet on the left—"A to B"— and pulled a drawer open. Her fingers moved with nimble efficiency to find her target.

BLAKE.

When Makedde Vanderwall had said the name during their appointment, it had rung a bell, but it had taken until today for Ann to place it. As the link surfaced in her mind, Ann found herself wishing she had not heard that man's name coming from the lips of Les Vanderwall's troubled daughter.

Blake . . .

She had to be sure.

CHAPTER 38

Roy Blake's mobile phone rang when he was only twenty minutes from the cabin.

"Blake," he said.

"Hi, Roy, this is Georgina." She was one of the UBC security staff. She usually worked the phones.

"How's it going, Georgie?"

"Good, thanks." The line crackled a bit. He was starting to get out of range. "Sorry to bother you when you're off-duty like this, but someone was calling for you just now. She wanted you to get back to her as soon as possible."

She? "Oh yeah?"

Makedde . . .

"She said her name was Dr. Ann Morgan. She said it was important."

It took him a moment to register the name, and when he did, he felt a wave of panic.

"Sure, Georgie," he managed. "Hang on just a sec while I pull over." There wasn't a lot of traffic around, so he pulled over to the side of the road easily, and grabbed a pen out of the glove box and a piece of wrinkled newspaper off the floor of the cab.

"Okay, what's the number?"

She gave him the digits and he scrawled them on the front of yesterday's newspaper.

"NAHATLATCH MURDERS

"Female students found dead. UBC panic as RCMP clueless . . ."

CHAPTER 39

Now Dr. Ann Morgan had a dilemma.

Roy Blake.

What she knew complicated everything.

When she had seen the newspaper article about the Nahatlatch Murders, it got her thinking. The hunter aspect Makedde had mentioned . . . the Nahatlatch. She knew someone who liked it out there . . . or used to. Someone who had a place not too far away.

The Blake brothers.

Roy and Daniel Blake were an interesting pair. Ann had met them when she hired Daniel to do some basic yard work. He had left one of those photocopied pamphlets at the door. The rates were good, and with Ann's hectic schedule, there was so much that wasn't getting done. But the young man had only worked for her a few times before he showed a great deal of interest in the fact that she was a psychiatrist. He started asking questions about certain conditions . . . things she suspected he was going through. Ann doubted that he had ever talked with anyone about his concerns before. He was confused and he wanted help.

For years Daniel Blake had been told that he had done things he couldn't remember doing. People would say hello to him on the street—people who he couldn't remember meeting. He found things in his room that he thought were not his.

Daniel Blake was a multiple.

Multiple Personality Disorder, Dissociative Identity Disorder—Ann had encountered it before. Like so many psychological disorders, the official name had changed a couple of times in an attempt at a more accurate and less stigmatised term. The essential feature of the disorder involves the presence of several distinct personalities that recurrently take control of the patient's behavior. There is an inability to recall important personal information when the patient is in another one of their personality states, hence Daniel's confusion. The different identities tend to involve complete character transformation, mannerisms and inflection of speech. Even different abilities and languages in some cases.

One of Daniel's personalities was a fanatical hunter.

Ann remembered him clearly. He had not been happy about Daniel being there to see her. At all. He had come out in the third appointment.

Daniel Blake had wanted to be psychologically integrated, but ironically, it wasn't the hunter who got in the way. It was his well-meaning brother, Roy.

The relationship between them was complicated. Their mother had abandoned them and their father at a young age. By the time she met them, their father was senile and in a home—all but absent from their lives as well. Roy had pledged to protect his brother's welfare and the very suggestion that Daniel's condition might require a stay in a hospital had caused Roy to pull his brother out of therapy.

And that was it. After only six sessions, the Blake brothers disappeared from her life.

Until now.

So Mak had met one of them. What could she tell Makedde about the brothers? She could not violate the confidentiality of a patient. What could Mak tell her about them? How much did she know? Did Mak even know that Roy had a brother?

Call it intuition, but those reports about the Nahatlatch Murders were making her think of Daniel . . . or rather his alter ego, the Hunter. Roy had told her straight up that he felt the best thing for his brother was to get out of the city, to stay out there where he could get "his head together". What was he getting up to out there on his own?

If Ann was wrong, if Daniel *was* in an institution by now and she had not been told, if he had left town, even if he was in jail, it would be a great relief.

But what if her concerns proved correct?

CHAPTER 40

After six solid hours of sleep, Makedde Vanderwall woke up drowsy but not distraught. The half dose of sleeping pill had offered her a smooth, dreamless nap. She had bought them for long flights, but had never tried one until now.

Relax. Everything will be fine.

Mak hoped Roy would respect her request for space. Surely he would leave her alone. She just had to stick to her guns, right? And soon Andy would be leaving too. She should just forgive herself for her momentary lapse of reason in the Renaissance Hotel, and get over it. Ann was right, she hadn't done anything wrong. She was human after all and under a lot of stress, and besides, Jaqui would probably be proud of her for giving in to the moment, if she only had the nerve to tell her. Her heart might have fared better without the experience, or any reminders of it, but no matter. That was the final goodbye. Soon Andy would be gone and she would have peace.

And then she could sleep. Without drugs.

And then she could get her thesis done, and she would be fine.

Then the phone rang.

Wearily, Mak made her way to the side table and the buzzing telephone. If it was Roy, she would just tell him off.

She raised the receiver to her ear.

"Hello?"

"Makedde?" An unfamiliar voice.

"Yes."

"Makedde, this is Ann calling."

"Hello. How are you?" she answered, a little surprised by the unscheduled call. "I didn't recognize your voice."

"Did you just get in?" Ann asked.

Automatically, Makedde stole a look at her answering machine in the kitchen. She could see that the message light was flashing.

"I, um . . . actually I was sleeping. You were trying to reach me?"

"Sleeping?" A pause. "Yes, I was trying to reach you earlier."

Makedde had not even heard the phone ring.

"There is something I'd like to ask you about, in person. Would it be possible for you to come over . . . as soon as you can? To my home?"

"Is there something going on?" Mak asked.

"Nothing, going on, per se, but I'd like to talk to you. Don't be alarmed or anything."

"Okay. I'll freshen up and come right over. What's the address?"

She took down the directions. It seemed pretty straightforward, and not too far away.

What was all that? Her head had begun a slow throb. Her instincts told her something was wrong.

* * *

The traffic was light and before long Makedde was approaching Dr. Morgan's house. She checked the address again as she pulled up. The place was quaint, with a border of green shrubs and a set of steps leading up to a welcoming front porch that was lit for visitors. A wreath of dried flowers was on the front door. The house was dark, save for some warm light glowing from within the living room.

Mak parked Zhora easily on the quiet street, pulling into a space right in front of Ann's house, a concept that was quite unlike trying to park near her own place in "cool Kitsilano" as Ann had called it. She cut the engine and sat for a moment in the darkness.

She wants to speak with me about something. That's almost exactly what Andy said.

Mak got out of the car, carrying only her purse, and made her way up to the porch. She rang the doorbell. Within seconds she heard approaching footsteps, and Ann was at the door. She quickly ushered her inside.

"I'm so glad you could come," Ann said. The sight of pinched concern on the doctor's face was unsettling. "Please, make yourself at home."

Ann asked her to sit down then disappeared to the kitchen, presumably to fetch some refreshments. Makedde took a seat on the couch, on the edge nearest to the side table. She noted that Ann was reading *People of Heaven*. Her bookmark—some kind of pressed flower laminated on a piece of pretty mauve paper—was placed right near the back.

"What can I get you to drink? Soda? Wine?" Ann called from the kitchen.

"Just water, thanks," Makedde called back.

Ann walked back into the lounge a couple of minutes later with two tall glasses of mineral water. The glasses were frosty and the ice cubes clinked and fizzled as they moved. She placed Makedde's drink on a coaster on the side table and sat down in the adjacent easychair.

"So, how are you?"

"Fine. Thanks again for agreeing to see me. I think it really helped to get some of that stuff off my chest."

"It's my pleasure, it really is. Thanks for coming over." Her face turned serious. "Makedde, I am aware that this is an unconventional situation, but I wanted to ask you about something, and I felt it couldn't wait."

The unmistakable taste of dread settled on Makedde's tongue. She crossed her arms and felt a lump form in her throat.

"In our last session you mentioned that the man you've been going out with is named Roy Blake," Ann said.

Makedde's stomach tightened. "Yes."

Ann nodded. "Can you describe him for me? Physically?"

Makedde shifted on the couch. She didn't like where this was headed at all.

"Okay. He is, um . . . very tall. Six foot four or something like that." She reminded herself to breathe. For some reason it wasn't coming naturally. "He's a fairly good-looking guy. You know the actor, Vince Vaughn? Sort of like that." She stared off into space as she spoke, picturing him. Reluctantly. "He has slightly curly brown hair and his eyes are brown," Makedde went on. "Clean-shaven. Maybe a few years older than I am—somewhere in his late twenties to early thirties I'd say. He works as a security guard at the university . . ."

Ann nodded to herself again and Makedde stopped her rambling description.

"Yes," Ann said softly, in a tone of both recognition and regret. "The name rang a bell with me when you mentioned him. You see, I worked with a patient by the name of Blake a few years back. I checked my files today to be absolutely sure that I had the name right." She paused. "Has Roy said anything to you about his brother?"

Then the phone rang, breaking the tension of the conversation.

Ann got up immediately.

"Please excuse me. I'm waiting for an important call."

She still looked pretty nervous. Mak found it odd to see her that way.

Ann went to the phone in her bedroom and closed the door behind her. She prayed that it was Roy.

"Hello?" she said.

"Hello, could I speak to Dr. Morgan, please?"

"Speaking."

"This is Roy Blake—"

Thank God.

"Roy. Hello. Thanks for calling me back . . ."

CHAPTER 41

Roy sat in the trophy den, listening to Dr. Morgan on the cabin's old rotary-dial telephone.

"I haven't heard your name for a while. The message said it was urgent."

"Well, I have been going through some old files and checking up on past patients, and I just wanted to know how Daniel is doing."

Roy looked at his watch. Odd that she should make such calls after-hours. "He's fine," Roy said bluntly, a little annoyed to be bothered this way. He'd had a rough day, and this wasn't helping.

"Where is he, exactly?"

Roy frowned. "Well, like I told you when I last saw you, Daniel has been staying out here in Squamish at the cabin. It all worked out even better than I had hoped, really. He's doing very well and he seems to really love it."

Roy looked around him at the animals Daniel had caught and stuffed. He'd become a pretty good hunter, and by far excelled Roy's own abilities now that he had the time to get out regularly.

"He's been very productive. Taken up taxidermy. I'm at the cabin right now, in fact. Daniel loves it here, I assure you. He's in the other room, doing just fine."

"He's not listening in, is he?"

"No."

"Good."

Roy felt increasingly uncomfortable. Just then, he heard a noise and Daniel walked in. He smiled at his brother and sat on the couch across from him.

"So, like I said, we have no need for your help at all. Thanks for calling anyway."

Roy didn't want his brother knowing that he was talking to a shrink about him. That'd only upset him. In fact, any memory of Ann Morgan would upset him. He had wanted to stay in therapy at first, until Roy told him what the doctors had planned for him. Drugs and institutions, Roy was sure. He couldn't let that happen to his own brother.

He had to get her off the phone now.

Roy noticed that Daniel was looking intensely at the newspaper in Roy's hand—the one that had Ann's number scrawled on it.

"I have to go now," Roy said to Ann.

Daniel abruptly got up and walked out of the room. The moment he left, Roy resumed the conversation. "He's fine, honestly. He is very happy. He is very productive out here, and he's not causing anybody any trouble. I said he would be fine, and he is."

"Are you sure?" Ann prodded.

Roy didn't like the tone of her voice.

"Yes, I'm sure." He was starting to lose his patience now.

Daniel came back with a couple of glasses of beer.

"Is there anyone there with him? Does he have any supervision?"

"Well, no. Not really," he said vaguely.

He took the glass of beer from his brother and nodded a thank you to him. They clinked the glasses in the air, and Daniel went back to sit on the couch again. He picked up a magazine and started reading.

"So he is at the cabin without any supervision?"

Roy took a big sip of his beer. "There is no need," he said, purposely vague. "Look, I appreciate your concern, but everything is under control. Thanks for calling."

"Roy—" she began.

"Bye now." He hung up on her and shook his head.

He didn't like her meddling like that. No one had the right to meddle in their lives. She would have put Danny in a mental home if he hadn't put a stop to it. There was no doubt about that. And there was no way he was going to let her back into their lives again, after all this time when everything was just fine.

"Sorry about that, Danny." He took a long swig of his beer.

"That was Dr. Morgan, wasn't it?"

"Excuse me?" Roy said, surprised. He gulped hard to avoid spitting up a mouthful of ale.

"That's who you were talking to, wasn't it?"

"No, just a vacuum-cleaner salesman," he assured him. "They tricked me into calling them back. Made me think it was something important. They can be so pushy, can't they?"

He really didn't want Daniel to know that Ann was snooping around.

Danny seemed to relax and he took another sip of his beer. Roy finished his in long gulps.

When they had downed their drinks, Daniel spoke again. "You're lying to me."

What?

"That was her. I know it was her. Her name is on the paper in your hand."

Damn, he saw it.

Roy was caught. He wasn't sure what to say now. He hadn't wanted to upset his brother. Their mom had always left that to him. He had to protect his brother because he was special. He was different.

"Ann thinks I did it."

"What?"

Daniel pointed to the paper. "And so do you."

The Nahatlatch Murders? Was he referring to the headline?

"Don't worry. I'll take care of it all, Roy. We won't have any trouble."

Roy wanted to ask him what he was talking about, he wanted to know if he was having another one of his episodes, but now words failed him. He didn't feel so well. He felt dizzy . . . sick. The sensation came on sudden and strong.

"Whaaa . . . ?"

The room was spinning, the animals swirling around him, those glass-eyed trophies circling him. He felt incredibly, impossibly drunk.

Within fifteen minutes, Roy Blake was out cold.

CHAPTER 42

"Hi, Andy, it's Bob."

"Hi. How's it going?"

Andy was still dripping from a shower, and he toweled his chest with one hand as he held the receiver.

"We have some progress on the murders," Dr. Harris told him.

"Great."

The Evan Rose lead was at a bit of a standstill since the result of his polygraph, so they'd started on some new leads. The ViCLAS specialist hadn't found any strong links against other reports so they could do little more than hope the offender might do something wrong—reveal himself in some way.

"We ran a rego check on one of the vehicles spotted in the area, and we got a name. It piqued my interest because he works at UBC."

"Really?"

"Security guard."

"Oh, yeah." A percentage of those working in security had in fact been rejected from the police force, and on this basis they tended to treat any suspects with this oc-cupation with special attention. While a bad cop could sometimes slip through the screening process, there were bound to be a lot more cowboys who made it into security—guys who simply wanted a taste of power.

"Bob had him on his attendance list at the psychopathy conference."

"Whoa. Now that is interesting."

"I was wondering if by some chance you'd met him. The name is Blake. Roy Blake. Unfortunately the name doesn't ring a bell with me."

Andy thought about the name. He hadn't met a lot of people at the conference. He had been too focused on Makedde.

"Me either. I met a few professors, that's it."

"Antisocial, were we?"

"Very funny."

"Yeah, I guess you were a little distracted," Bob said.

"Yeah, very funny, ha, ha. Anything else?"

"No. That's it. Just wondering if the name rang a bell."

"No bells, Bob. Sorry."

CHAPTER 43

A black Ford pick-up truck sped along the Sea to Sky Highway, the tires spitting filth onto pavements cleaned by recent rains. The man behind the wheel was hurried but sober, his driving almost reckless, his eyes glued to the road.

The Hunter had borrowed his brother's truck. It was faster than the one Roy always left for him at the cabin.

He had to get into the city fast.

He had a mission.

CHAPTER 44

"I can see how it could be an awkward position," Makedde said sympathetically. She sipped a cup of peppermint tea. "I really appreciate you telling me what you can." She shook her head.

Ann pursed her lips together and clasped her hands. "I'm sorry that I can't be more forthcoming about Daniel's condition. I have to consider the confidentiality of my patients, and if you know nothing about him, then that's that."

"Oh, I wouldn't expect you to compromise yourself professionally," Mak said.

"The brothers are an odd pair, though." Ann said, shaking her head. "They are actually tw—"

Thump.

Makedde and Dr. Morgan looked up in unison, snapped alert by the noise directly behind them.

"Did you hear that?"

Thump-thump.

There it was again.

The sound was coming from outside the door. There

was no mistaking it; someone was moving on the front porch.

The doorbell rang and Ann got to her feet. "Oh," she said with surprise and stood quiet for a moment.

Makedde slowly got up and watched the doctor move toward the front door. It seemed to take forever. It was only Ann answering her own doorbell, but Makedde's stomach twisted into a tight knot at the sight of it.

Something is wrong.

"Are you expecting anyone?" she called out, but Ann was at the door now. Makedde wanted to yell something to her—wanted to tell her to watch out, to get away from the door but Ann was already looking through the peephole, and then she turned, puzzled, "I don't see anyone . . ."

The next sound was the thunderous crash of breaking glass. The racket was not coming from the front door, however—it was coming from behind Makedde. She spun around and faced the kitchen doorway.

Someone was there. They had rung the door and snuck around the back.

Makedde's hands were empty—no protection—no weapon. *Get the gun, she thought. No, it's in the car outside . . . Get the purse . . . Use the pepper spray . . .*

Mak grabbed the small purse off the floor beside the couch and managed to unzip the main pouch with unsteady hands . . . she reached inside . . .

Where is it!?

Within seconds she found the pepper spray and whirled around to face the kitchen again, instinctively unlocking the spray cap as she moved. She extended the pressurized container in front of her with both arms, as if she were aiming the business end of a pistol at the kitchen doorway. She had imagined using the spray many times, particularly in the past year, never quite knowing under what conditions she would need it.

Oh God.

Roy appeared in the doorway.

Roy Blake!

Makedde inhaled sharply. Her heart dropped into the acid of her belly, and her throat seemed to freeze, filling her mouth with a sharp metallic bite.

There was a horrible sense of inevitability in what was happening, and she couldn't place why. It was almost as if she had been expecting this.

Roy was wearing a ski mask, but Makedde was sure it was him. Those large, familiar brown eyes looked straight at her—straight into her. But Roy had no smile for her this time, no chocolates that would split on the ground, no roses, no romantic sentiments. He was not trying to impress her. He was not trying to convince her of anything. He clearly had other ideas.

Roy lunged for her hand as soon as he saw the spray she was holding, but she depressed the button first, releasing a strong pressurized stream of pepper solution directly into his face. She had been told it would accurately shoot up to fifteen feet, and Roy was well within that range. The problem of course, was the ski mask. With his face largely protected, she had to count on Roy inhaling at the right moment, or his eyes being open when the pepper spray hit.

Negative on both counts.

In an instant he was on her, twisting her arm behind her in a classic hold that she had even been taught herself. Despite Makedde's best efforts, the maneuver caused her to drop the spray can in an unavoidable physical reflex. She heard it hit the ground and bounce with a tinny sound, and her heart sank.

Roy was behind her, one of her hands was free, the other pinned painfully between them and no longer holding her self-defense spray. He had locked one arm around her neck, his elbow below her chin. His grip was tight. The air smelled strongly of spray and Makedde's eyes began to water. Her nose would soon start to run as well. She wondered how badly Roy had been hit with it, and if it would affect him at all.

She used her free arm as best she could, attempting to punch out behind her, clawing and scratching at him, but she knew her efforts could not amount to much in that position.

I need the use of my other arm to throw him, she thought. *I need my other arm!*

"Let me go . . ." she growled at him, and then her right shoulder cried out in pain as he yanked it further backward. She screamed more loudly than she needed to, harboring some thin hope of a concerned neighbor calling the police, and an even more remote hope that Roy might actually release his grip a touch if he knew it was causing her a lot of pain.

But he did not ease his hold by even a fraction.

Please don't let him break my collarbone . . . or my rib . . .

It would be easy to snap her bones where they had been broken before. The injuries were little more than a year old. Makedde thought of Ann near the door—everything had all happened so fast, in seconds—and she wondered where the doctor was now.

Roy spun the two of them around to face the front of the room, and Makedde's question was answered. Ann was coming at Roy with a sharp poker from her fireplace. How she had it in her hands so quickly Makedde didn't know, but she was glad to see it. Makedde sensed that Roy was no longer as focused on her. He released his grip ever so slightly, and she stole the opportunity to free her right arm. She pushed her hips forward and squirmed down a bit and his arm tightened around her throat as soon as he realized what she was doing.

Makedde straightened her body and raised both arms back to grab her attacker. One hand firmly grabbed Roy's hair through the knitted mask that covered his head. If her hand slipped and she only had his mask, her grip would be useless. Her opposite hand grabbed his shoulder at the same time, and just as she had practiced so many times, she pulled down and forward in a strong arc with all of her might. With a cry that might almost have been a roar, Mak flipped Roy onto his back, and he fell to the ground by her feet, his considerable weight causing her to fall heavily to one knee.

Makedde had always been told that it was leverage and not size that mattered with that move, but still she was amazed that it could work so effectively on a man of Roy's size.

Not missing a beat, Ann struck down with the poker in a half-moon, the end aimed straight at Roy's face. It was a perfect strike, but he rolled away in time and it only glanced the side of his head. Mak had leaped sideways to avoid being in the way of Ann's blow, and she supported herself against the end of the couch, the side table knocked over, her glass of water broken in wet shards across the wooden floor.

She heard a crashing sound as the poker flew from the doctor's grasp and hit the floor. She turned to see Roy grabbing Ann. And then, horrifyingly, there was a muffled bang—a silencer, and the flash of the muzzle lit up the room.

For a second Makedde thought she had been hit, but

when she saw Ann fall to the floor, she realized what had happened.

"No!" Makedde cried out. "No!"

My God! It's my fault! I rejected him and he couldn't take it! He followed me here and now Ann is dead!

Roy looked up.

Their eyes locked.

You're sick. I never knew you at all . . .

Mak turned and bolted, leaping across the tops of the cushions of the couch, but he was behind her, snatching at her back as she fled. She reached the other side without hindrance, and hit the ground running. The force of her departure caused the couch legs to squeal along the floor.

There was a gun in her glove box. It was her unregistered Saturday Night Special and she knew it was loaded. She needed it—*now*. She needed to get outside and open that passenger door. *Was it locked?* Yes, she had locked it. *Could she smash the windows?*

Roy was shouting, "Where do you think you're going . . ." and Makedde was still running, but now her foot was caught by a hand like a vice around her ankle. She fell to the floor hard, barely lifting her arms in time to catch herself on her elbows.

She screamed for help as loud as she could, and in an instant she was silenced by huge hands around her mouth. He was on her now, gagging her brutishly as he kneeled on her shoulders and upper arms. She tried to kick him in the back with the balls of her feet, but she barely made an impact. She struggled against his weight but it was impossible to win from her position on the floor. He was too big. Once she was gagged, her arms were soon tied behind her back and she was hoisted upright, red-faced and kicking madly.

My God, what will he do to me?

CHAPTER 45

Andy was watching the news in his hotel room when a thought struck him.

UBC . . . the conference . . .

He grabbed for the phone and dialed Bob's room.

"The guest you are trying to reach is not answering their phone. If you would like to leave a message, please do so after the tone . . ."

Beep.

"Bob, it's Andy. A thought just occurred to me. I think Makedde is going out with someone named Roy. I found his name . . ." *On a card attached to some roses for Mak the morning after we made love . . .* "Well, never mind how I found his name, but if he is the guy I think he is, he's a security guard at UBC. Remember her going off with a guy in a uniform that first day at lunch? Coincidence? God, I hope so. Give me a call as soon as you get this . . ."

CHAPTER 46

Makedde Vanderwall was roped to a chair in Ann Morgan's living room, bleeding from a cut above her eyebrow where a nasty bruise was finding its way to the surface. She was gagged with an old rag that smelled faintly of gas and made her want to retch.

Behind her, Ann Morgan was dying—or already dead.

She could feel the doctor's body against her back. If she was still breathing, it was too faint for Makedde to detect. A small pool of blood was spreading around the floor beneath their feet, and that was enough to tell Makedde that she had to fight this battle alone.

The house was in disarray and Roy was busily putting the finishing touches on his efficient job of ransacking and trashing. Every picture had been wrenched from the walls and smashed on the floor. Every drawer had been opened and the contents spilled. He had thrown some expensive-looking items into a couple of large garbage bags. The mirror over the fireplace lay in sharp pieces on the floor where the women had been sitting less than fifteen minutes earlier.

Roy untied Mak and hauled her up, still gagged, her wrists tied behind her back. She fought the grogginess and numb disbelief, and lashed out once—twice—three times, managing only one effective knee strike to the hip flexor of her attacker, missing her real target by a good couple of inches. To her dismay, she found that Roy could control her with ease.

Makedde was hauled out of Ann's house and dragged through the darkness to a black truck, the toes of her boots barely touching the ground. One strong hand remained across her mouth the entire time, working with the foul gag to keep her from screaming. She tried though, but only managed a muffled cry. No one would hear that. No one was on the quiet residential street to see, either.

She tried to think of a way she could get to Zhora. If she could only reach the glove box—the gun. But she needed the keys, and they were in her purse in the house. Could she trick him? Suggest that they take her car instead? No, he would never fall for that. Not Roy. He was many things, that much was clear, but stupid was not one of them. Drawing attention to her car would only force him to move it, removing that telltale sign that Makedde had been at the scene, and had not left of her own accord. Perhaps he was already planning to do just that.

Once I am in his truck and out of this neighborhood, I am dead.

Makedde fought desperately and unsuccessfully to free herself as she was transferred to the truck, aware that he had a gun, but that he would not easily be able to use it while his hands were occupied with her. It all amounted to nothing, however, and soon she was inside, forced to kneel in the passenger side footwell, her face pressed down into the seat like a doomed prisoner about to face the guillotine.

The door slammed.

She wriggled toward the door on her knees, reached for the handle with arms tied behind her back, straining to make contact with her fingertips, but it was too late, the driver was in the other side now, watching her.

Fuck.

"If you try anything, I'll shoot you," he said. He had the gun trained on her.

I am sunk. He could take me anywhere . . . Throw me into a river . . . Shoot me in the forest.

And there won't be any Andy Flynn to save me this time.

CHAPTER 47

"Andy, it's Bob. What were you saying?"

"Are you in your room?" Andy asked.

"Yup."

"I'll be there in a flash."

When Andy arrived, Bob was sitting on the bed with his suitcases open and his belongings laid out around him. He was to fly back to Quantico the following morning.

"Do you remember when you met Makedde at the conference?" Andy asked. "Before we went for lunch? She went off with a guy. He was a tall, young . . ."

"That's right. I remember you coming over all jealous."

"I did not come over all jealous."

Bob gave him an incredulous look.

"I do remember him, actually," he said. "He was a security guard. You say his name is Roy?"

"Well, it could be. Makedde has been dating someone named Roy."

"Last name?"

He thought of the card on the flowers. "No idea."

"Okay, what about the photo on his rego? Some guy?"

"I'll have to check. I didn't immediately recognize him. He still could have been the same guy though. Twenty-nine sound right to you?"

"Unfortunately. And you say your girlfriend's dating him?"

"She's not my girlfriend."

"Evidently not." Bob said, straight-faced. "Well, if this is our guy, she's got one hell of a psycho-beacon going."

"She once called herself a psycho-magnet."

"Well, at least she knows it. Let's give her a ring and see what she can tell us about him," Bob suggested.

But Makedde was not answering her phone.

Andy stood in the hotel hallway, feeling panicked. The phone had rung several times, and the machine kept picking it up. He didn't want to leave a message but he had to contact her—now.

He walked back into the room. "No answer," he told Bob. "I know someone else to call, though."

Andy dialed the number for Makedde's father in Victoria. He felt thankful that he had the number handy . . . until the machine kicked in there as well.

"Damn," he said aloud. "Hello, Mr. Vanderwall, it's Andy Flynn. Please give me a call as soon as possible . . ."

CHAPTER 48

Makedde looked at her captor with hatred and confusion.

Why are you doing this, Roy?

But unbeknownst to Makedde it was Roy's brother Daniel who watched the road intently as he drove them at speed deep into the countryside. When he turned and caught her looking at him, he smiled and let out a humorless chuckle.

And to think I actually liked that smile . . .

Gagged, all she could do was watch out the window, trying to catch a glimpse of something recognizable— the top of a familiar building, a landmark, a highway sign, anything to give her some idea where they were headed.

Nothing. Dark sky and the occasional treetop. Nothing useful at all.

If only she could reach that doorhandle, jump out right now, but they were moving way too fast. Even on the off-chance that she did survive the fall, he would shoot her like a lame horse as she lay wounded on the side of the road. He'd already killed Ann, after all. What if there was another car? A witness? But Makedde thought better of that plan. It was just as likely that he would kill a witness who stopped to help her, wasn't it?

Is he the Nahatlatch Killer? Is he responsible for murdering the UBC students?

It made sense now. Roy was a security guard at UBC . . . he had access to students, he had their trust.

Would he take her all the way out to the Nahatlatch and shoot her there and bury her? Or did he have a new spot now? How much did he know about the investigation?

She thought about the doorhandle again. Could she wrench the door open with her wrists bound? Was it worth a shot? Was it better to die trying, or wait for a better chance?

CHAPTER 49

Dr. Ann Morgan estimated that she was about four feet away from her living room telephone. In reality she had a further seven feet left to crawl. The psychiatrist knew she had lost a lot of blood. It had poured out of the gunshot wound in her stomach and turned her clothes scarlet and her head woozy. Years ago she had saved a stabbing victim on the streets of East Vancouver, stumbling across the scene quite by chance—and it had been bloody. But now for the first time in her life, Dr. Morgan's hands and knees were sticky with blood that was her own.

Ann had already blacked out twice since she was shot, and she feared that she would lose consciousness once more, and never regain it.

911.

911.

911.

All she had to do was to get to that phone and dial.

She had to crawl to the telephone cord and pull the phone off the edge of the table. Simple. It would fall to the floor in front of her and she could pick up the receiver and dial. Three little numbers—*911*—that's all she had to remember and then she stood a chance of living, and she stood a chance of seeing her children again. She could not leave Emily and Connor like this. Not now. They were only teenagers. They needed a mother. Ann Morgan wanted to live to be a good mother, and grandmother. She wanted to live to see them grow into happy, well-adjusted adults, their parents' split a distant memory without lingering consequences. That's what Ann wanted to see.

She thought of Les Vanderwall, and his daughter . . . *Makedde.*

Daniel Blake had taken her. Someone had to be alerted. Someone had to find her before it was too late. *Get to that phone.*

Ann struggled across the hardwood floor of her living room, the hard-backed dining-room chair she had been tied to still weighing her down like a ball and chain. She had bought that chair at an auction with Tony, back when their marriage still seemed salvageable. She had been so happy about the purchase—it was the perfect antique eight-piece dining set she had been looking for. Now she could not free herself from it.

Another six inches along the floor and Ann was making progress . . . she was getting there . . . that phone cord was closer now . . .

CHAPTER 50

Mak was handcuffed to a chair in an isolated cabin outside of Vancouver.

Her captor had discarded the ropes and had cuffed her ankles and wrists. The gag was still in her mouth. She knew that the burglary had been simply staged to account for Ann's death. But why? If he was only after Makedde, why not wait till she left Ann's house and abduct her then?

Or did Roy think that Ann had figured him out?

"Welcome to the Hunter's Lair. This isn't quite how I usually do this, but I'll accommodate you as best I can. This is rather unexpected, after all." He followed up his ridiculous banter by resuming his hollow grin.

Yes, he killed the other girls . . . My God . . . Roy is the Nahatlatch Killer!

She didn't try to talk, or to signal for him to remove the gag. He was playing some kind of game, and she wanted no part of it. He would take the gag off her when it suited him. In the meantime, it was best to observe and to think. She had to keep her head clear. There was so much she didn't know about this man she had dated.

CHAPTER 51

Connor Morgan was hungry. As a growing seventeen year old, he was as bad a cook as his father, but burdened with twice the appetite.

He lived in a messy converted attic above his father's garage. The arrangement worked well because he could live cheaply and his dad let him play the drums as loud as he wanted, anytime he wanted. The noise didn't trouble his father because he was never home. Tony Morgan had been working late hours with the local police for as long as his son could remember.

So the pantry was consistently and depressingly empty. Pizza Hut was quick-dial option number two on the kitchen telephone (his work number being number one) and when Connor wasn't munching on a Pizza Supreme with a stuffed crust and the works, he was picking up takeaway. That's just the way things were. That was the kind of sacrifice he was prepared to make for his drums.

Connor was on his way home after a Dirty Pistol jam session with his pals Jake and Scott when the hunger really hit. He slowed his rusting Toyota Corolla as he neared the Seven Eleven barely ten minutes from Jake's house, and took a quick inventory of the stuff he regularly bought there—a sub with ham and mustard, a Mars bar, a *Penthouse* magazine if Rigby was behind the counter.

For some reason Seven Eleven's finest offerings didn't appeal at that moment. Connor drove right past. He could get by for weeks on end on a solid fare of Tim Hortons, Pizza Hut and the usual Seven Eleven selection, but even he had his limit, and when he reached it there was no getting around it. Sometimes he needed a real meal, and on his budget there was only one place to go for that.

He checked his watch. It was only a little after nine—not too late. Perhaps she had an apple pie going? Some leftover Chicken Kiev or a lasagne? It was worth a try. It was only five minutes further away than his dad's, after all. Perhaps she wouldn't grill him about school or the band.

His mother had got better about that.

CHAPTER 52

The gag was off and Makedde wanted answers.

"So, you brought the others here, too. The 'Hunter's Lair,' as you call it. How? How did you get them to come here?" she asked, as bravely as she could, trying hard not to appear afraid as she sat trapped in the metal chair. The slight, uncontrollable trembling of her lips betrayed her fear.

The tall man before her nodded and folded his arms. "Ah, yes . . . the others. You know about the others. It was the doctor, wasn't it?"

Yes, I was right. The senseless ransacking was all staged and this monster of a human being was cunning enough to change his modus operandi for the task. Even down to the rope he used on her instead of cuffs like these, just in case the forensic pathologists had picked that part up in the autopsies of the Nahatlatch victims. The police might not connect Ann's murder to the other women. There weren't enough links.

She hadn't answered his question, so he went on. "It

was simple, really. A couple of drinks and they come willingly. You women are all the same."

"You mean a couple of Roofies, and they come," she said.

He squinted at her. It was easy to get Rohypnol. She'd seen the reports splashed across the news, linked to assaults on campus where women would wake up in strange locations, unable to recall how they got there. It was too easy—slipped into a drink, Rohypnol is odorless, colorless and tasteless. It could take effect in minutes and often the victim suffered amnesia afterward.

"Rohypnol is not much of a challenge," Makedde spat at him. "It would be a bit like shooting bunnies in a barrel, wouldn't it?"

"You've got a mouth on you, girl."

"I'm sure you're sportsmanlike," *Yeah, like Robert Hansen was sportsmanlike.* "So surely you wouldn't just shoot a drugged-up lady in the back, would you?"

His eyes narrowed. "You're right. That would be most unsportsmanlike. No, I like to even up the game. I like a challenge. I'm fair. You'll see."

What does that mean?

"How many women did you bring here?" she asked.

"Enough to know you're nothing special. Sit tight now," he said with mock politeness. "Don't go anywhere."

CHAPTER 53

Connor Morgan parked in the driveway beside his mother's midnight-blue BMW and slammed the door. Her car was a bit conservative and hardly the latest model, but it beat the hell out of his old junker, that was for sure. His Corolla was loud, ugly and puke-orange— not quite the canary-yellow Alfa Romeo Spider in the poster on the back of his attic door.

Connor was determined to get his beloved Spider once Dirty Pistol went platinum with their first album. His dad had laughed when he told him that. He'd said he could buy him the latest BMW while he was at it. Connor thought he probably wanted that car just to show up Mom.

No sign of any flash new vehicles so far, though. His insurance cost more than his orange Corolla. He felt sure he would tell this story when he was a megastar and people would laugh. Dirty Pistol had the potential to be big. He believed that. He just had to convince Jake to stop writing the lyrics. His best friend was a good singer, but his writing was shit.

Connor hopped up the front steps two by two and opened the door, thinking only of his hunger and that yellow Alfa Romeo Spider. The door was often unlocked, and this time was no exception.

"Mom . . . I'm—" he began as he stepped inside. "Mom? Oh my God, Mom!"

His mother was lying in a viscid mess of blood and shattered glass on the floor in the living room, the telephone receiver in her right hand, the cord wrapped around her forearm. For a moment he thought she had fallen off a chair and hit her head, and a painting had somehow fallen, the glass shattering around her. But that didn't make any sense. Panicked, he looked around the room. The place was completely trashed. He noticed that the chair he thought she may have fallen off was actually tied to her back. What the hell? He saw drag marks along the floor. Someone had come in and ransacked the place! Someone had tied up his mother! Was she dead? Had someone murdered his mom?

"Mom! Oh my God, Mom, are you okay?" he cried. Connor's voice was high-pitched and shaky. He checked for breathing and then wasn't sure if he was detecting any. His hands were trembling too hard to check her pulse properly. He didn't know what he should do. The technique for mouth-to-mouth, the Heimlich maneuver and what to do in case of an earthquake all flashed across his thoughts, all useless. Then he thought of 911. In times like this you were supposed to dial 911.

"Mom," he said again. "Mom, can you hear me? What happened?"

Then he could hear a faint woman's voice. But it was not his mother responding.

The voice was coming from the telephone.

Connor pulled the phone out of his mother's bloody

hand. When he tried to lift it, the cord was caught around her arm and she shifted weakly on the floor.

She is alive . . . Thank God . . .

Connor knew he might start hyperventilating if he wasn't careful. He needed to remain calm. He lay on his side next to his mother on the floor, holding her hand in one of his, the other hand bringing the receiver to his ear. His mother's hand was cool as he held it.

"Hello?" he said into the mouthpiece.

"This is 911 Emergency. Who am I speaking to?"

"Connor Morgan. My name is Connor Morgan and my mother is dying beside me." He didn't know what else to say. He didn't know what else to do, and then it came to him. "My mother is bleeding to death," he said, looking at the blood on his hands. "I think she has been stabbed or shot or something. We need an ambulance right away!" He gave the address to the Emergency operator and she assured him that an ambulance had been dispatched a few minutes earlier, and would already be on its way.

The front door was wide open, and Connor turned to see the Emergency paramedics rush in. He had only ever seen such a thing on television. He sat up with his mouth wide open as they attended to his mother.

"We have a pulse! We have a pulse!" one of them said.

It was the best thing Connor Morgan had ever heard.

CHAPTER 54

Makedde Vanderwall closed her eyes tight and imagined the freedom of running around Elk Lake near her father's home, just as she had done not so many nights previously. She could feel the wind in her hair, see the dark woods and the shimmering reflection of the lake at night, smell the moss and the trees, feel the rush of adrenaline through her body. Freedom.

When she opened her eyes again she was still imprisoned in the trophy room.

He has me trapped like one of these pitiful animals.

She tried to remain calm, tried to convince herself that she would survive. There was a way out. There *had* to be a way out. All she had to do was to figure out how.

He said he was not expecting this . . . he had not been expecting to see her at Ann's house. So perhaps he didn't want to do this to her? Perhaps he was only after Ann? Perhaps she could talk him out of it?

Damn. Why did I have to go out with him? Why did I have to reject him like that, and create this hatred?

It was easier to think rationally when he was not in the

room, but she had to try and remain calm when he returned. She had to. What little control she had at this point was in her own mind and her words, and she had to use those tools if she hoped to escape.

Physically she was doing all right. The cut above her eyebrow had stopped bleeding. The right side of her face was throbbing from being hit during the battle back at Ann's house, but Mak didn't think it was that serious. She could still run, she could still punch, she could still kick. And she planned to.

But even if I can escape this chair, where do I go? How do I protect myself?

She looked around the room for a possible weapon. A pen on the table—useless. There might be knives in the kitchen, if she got that far. But her captor had a gun. She would be no match for him if she simply fought. She would have to get out when he wasn't looking, or she would have to manipulate him into getting her outside, where she could run and hide in the dark.

And then what? Wait to be hunted down in the forest by a psychopath? Wait to freeze to death?

Ann's words came back to her . . . haunting her now in this horrible predicament—

Be careful what you wish for.

CHAPTER 55

Connor held his mother's hand in the ambulance all the way to Vancouver General Hospital. He prayed that she would live, and he made a pact that if she did, he would move back in with her again—even if she wouldn't let him play his drums after nine. He knew she wanted him there, especially since Emily had moved in with her boyfriend, Alex. Yes, if his mother lived he would move back in, and he would protect her, and he would tell her that he loved her and that he had forgiven her for splitting with Dad. And he would mean it.

Connor even promised that he would keep his room clean, and he would do the dishes, just like she always told him to.

And I'll find the assholes who did this and Dad and I will beat them to a pulp . . .

When he arrived at the hospital he quickly found a phone and called his father. But Sergeant Tony Morgan was on duty and Connor could only leave a message on his pager. He left a quick explanation and the number of the hospital. The next person he wanted to call was Jake.

"Hi, it's Con—"

"Do you have any idea how late it is?"

It was Jake's mom.

"Mrs. Webster, I'm really sorry for calling so late, but—"

"Damn right, you're sorry. I didn't ask you to pack it up tonight just so you could wake me up an hour later!"

Jake had mentioned that she was getting a little testy about the noise. They might not be able to jam there any more.

"I'm sorry to get you up, but my mom is in the hospital and I—"

"Ann's in the hospital?" Her voice changed completely. "Oh . . ."

"She was attacked. I found her. It's serious."

When he finally got through to his friend, it took him about ten minutes to convince him that he was serious. By the time Jake figured out that he wasn't just telling a story, he felt really guilty, and so did his mother.

After calling his father and Jake, the next person Connor phoned was Les Vanderwall. He knew his mother would want it that way.

CHAPTER 56

Roy Blake opened his eyes.

He was in a darkened room, the only light coming in under the hall door. He was fully dressed, lying on a bed with a warm blanket thrown over him. He even had his shoes on.

What the . . . ?

He was disoriented, but as his blurry eyes adjusted and his senses returned to him, Roy realized he was in his brother's bedroom. He felt horrible, groggy, it was as if he were experiencing the world's worst hangover.

Roy groaned and struggled to sit up. His head spun, sending a kaleidoscope of colors across his eyes. When the nauseating rush passed, he reached beside him and fumbled around the bedside table to find the switch for the tiny lamp. He recognized Danny's chest of drawers, the heap of dirty clothes in the corner, the movie posters, *Rambo, Predator,* the original *Halloween* and a dog-eared poster of *The Deer Hunter* that Roy himself had given him. His brother's prize caribou rack was mounted on the wall over the bed, straight above his head.

It was well after midnight.

My God! I've been out for hours.

Roy couldn't remember having been that tired. In fact, he couldn't remember lying down at all. Why would he be sleeping, fully dressed, on his brother's bed, instead of on the pull-out hideabed in the den where he always stayed when he visited?

Slowly, he shifted his long legs over the end of the bed and let his shoes touch the floor. He pushed himself forward and attempted to stand, but his efforts were met with an even more formidable head-rush. He fell backward onto the soft bed, and stayed there.

God, I feel so drunk. What have I been into?

Roy decided to lie still on the bed until he felt a little better. He rubbed his scratchy eyes, and when he opened them again, he noticed something dangling above him. There was something hanging from the antlers mounted on the wall. He reached up and touched the dangling gold with his fingertip, and it slipped off and landed beside him on the bed.

Roy stared at it, mouth agape.

A heart-shaped locket.

It was a gold locket, just like the one on the front page of the newspaper hanging around the neck of the murdered girl—the girl who was found at the Nahatlatch by some hunters.

Roy stared at the locket in horror.

"So he is at the cabin without any supervision?" Dr. Morgan had said in that suspicious tone.

My God, what has my brother done?

CHAPTER 57

Gradually, Ann became aware of her surroundings. She did not recognize anyone, or anything, but she realized that there was someone leaning over her with a mint-green smock on. A doctor. He was looking at her intensely. Their eyes met, and he turned away.

A hospital. I am in the hospital.

At first she thought she might have had a car crash. She thought of all the warnings she'd had about not having an airbag in her BMW. Had she crashed her car? No. No. Something else had happened. Something at home.

She felt terrible, and worse than the physical pain she felt was a gnawing dread that she could not place. There was something she desperately needed to recall. Someone was in danger. Who?

"Doctor . . ." she began, but her voice would not cooperate.

He leaned over her again. There were other faces around him now. "Don't try to speak," he said.

A flood of memories rushed into her mind. The filing cabinet. The name "Blake," Makedde . . .

Makedde.

Have they found Makedde?

She remembered the struggle. She remembered the sound of breaking glass, the gun blast, the jolt of pain. The blood.

"Makedde . . ."

"Shhh. Don't speak. Just relax. Relax. You're going to be okay," the doctor said.

"But . . ."

Her body wanted to drift away and she needed to stay with it, to keep alert, to think.

"Just relax."

Somewhere in the background came a voice. "We need to calm her down . . ."

"Makedde was . . ." she tried again, but they weren't listening.

She barely felt the needle go in.

CHAPTER 58

What have you done, my brother? What have you done?

If Danny had got himself into trouble, it was Roy's fault. He should have taken care of his brother like he promised Mom. It was his fault for bringing him out here, and setting him up at the cabin where he thought he wouldn't hurt anyone, where he was away from the prying eyes of specialists and shrinks. Here at the cabin, where he could indulge his love of hunting.

The boys were only seven when their mother packed her suitcases and left them and their father. Their dad was still at work at the time. She had left with a black eye and she had never come back.

"Take care of Danny now, Roy," their mother had said with tears in her eyes. "Protect him. He's the weaker one. He needs you. I'm leaving you in charge, okay? Don't you let him out of your sight. And don't you let your father touch him . . ."

Roy looked back up the wall toward the antlers and the place from where the locket had fallen. As his eyes slowly adjusted, he noticed more things hanging there, jewelry—women's jewelry. There were three gold and silver rings looped over one of the points, and a pendant hanging from another horn.

Roy heard sounds in the cabin—shuffling, movement, a clanging. Someone was awake. It had to be Danny. Perhaps he could explain the jewelry? Perhaps he could explain why Roy had woken up in his bedroom? Perhaps Danny could explain why he felt so horrifically off?

"Danny?" Roy called out, alarmed by the slowness of his mind and body. Then he thought he heard the movements stop. He called out, "Danny?" again, more loudly, and this time his cry was met with the sound of footfalls in the hall.

Soon the door was pushed open and he saw his brother.

"Ah, you're up," he said simply.

"Danny . . . ?"

"Don't worry. I've taken care of everything," he said.

Danny was dressed head-to-toe in black. He wore a zip-up jumpsuit and a vest with various pockets. On his feet were lace-up black army boots. Roy thought he looked like a cat-burglar or some jewel thief from the movies.

The jewelry . . .

"I got rid of her. I got rid of Ann," Danny said.

Roy tried to comprehend what his brother was telling him.

"We won't have any trouble," he went on. "We won't have to run. It's all taken care of."

"What? What are you saying?"

"I got rid of Ann. We won't have any trouble with her."

Roy's head spun once again and he pressed his hand to his forehead. His palm felt cold and clammy against his skin.

"Danny, what did you do? What did you do?" he shouted.

Daniel's eyes went to the locket on the bed, and they lit up.

"I'll show you."

CHAPTER 59

"Do you know where my daughter is?"

Andy blinked and looked at the digital alarm clock in his hotel room. It was twelve twenty-five.

"I said, do you know where my daughter is?"

Andy's voice cracked when he tried to speak. He had been woken out of a dead sleep. "Is this Mr. Vanderwall?"

"Yes. Do you know where Makedde is?"

Andy wanted to ask why he was calling at such an hour, but the question did not seem appropriate. There was alarm in the former detective inspector's voice, and his tone didn't have the air of a social call.

"We tried to contact Makedde earlier tonight, but with no luck," Andy admitted.

He refrained from telling Makedde's father that they had wanted to ask her about a possible murder suspect she may have been dating. They had eventually packed it in for the night, thinking that they would have to wait till morning to ask her what she knew about a man named Roy Blake.

"She's not with you?" Les said in a slightly accusatory tone.

"No. She's not. Is something wrong?"

"My daughter is missing. She's not home. She's not at Ann's house."

"Les, hold on, what are you saying? Who is Ann?"

"Ann Morgan is a lovely dear friend of ours who was attacked tonight. She's in hospital now, drugged to the gills. Makedde's purse was in her living room. Her car is parked outside. She's gone."

Oh Christ, Andy thought.

"I want to know where she is. I'll be touching down at the helipad near the Trade Center in thirty-five minutes and I want you there. It's not far from your hotel. Any cab driver will know it."

"Les, I'll be waiting for you when you arrive," Andy promised, flinging back the sheets even as he set down the phone.

CHAPTER 60

"We have to do this right," Daniel Blake said, eyes ablaze with excitement. "I can't show you unless you do it exactly right."

"Okay," Roy agreed, unsure of what else to say.

Though Daniel was Roy's mirror image, his other half, and the closest person to Roy's heart, there was something foreign about him at that moment. There was something in him that was unsettling, and that Roy had not seen for a long time. It was something he had thought, or hoped, had been banished.

Roy and Daniel knew each other so well. They were twins—split from the same egg, and they were alike in ways that no other person could be. Yes, Roy was the "older" one, born two minutes before Daniel, and he had always taken on the big brother role, but still they were one, they were brothers, they were blood, and they had an unbreakable bond.

Now Roy did not know what to do. This was something else. When Danny was like this, it was as if he was not Roy's brother at all.

"Zip it up," Danny said.

Roy himself was now dressed in identical head-to-toe black hunting gear. He zipped it up as his brother told him.

They had gone out in day gear this way before, but never at night. Roy didn't even know his brother owned such outfits, but he was willing to play along with Danny's wishes so that he could find out exactly what was going on.

"Here," Danny said, passing him a hunting rifle. Roy took it.

"Danny," he finally dared to ask his brother, "how can we go hunting at night? How will we be able to see?"

"It's okay. I've got everything we need. I'll show you. I'll show you how I do it."

Roy considered the consequences of what his brother may have done, the consequences of what he had let his brother do.

Will we have to go south and start again? Or north? We could get jobs in Alaska and no one would ask questions up there. Whatever he's done, we could leave it all behind and start again . . .

The twins walked down the hall, Roy tagging along behind, still in shock, and still suffering some after-effects from the small dose of Rohypnol his brother had given him. Before long Danny brought them to the door of the den.

When the door opened, Roy saw that a woman was handcuffed to a metal chair in the center of the room.

The woman was Makedde Vanderwall.

CHAPTER 61

Mak heard footsteps.

He's back.

But she could have sworn she heard two sets of feet. Her heart rate sped up as she watched the doorknob turn, and when the door finally opened, Makedde couldn't believe her eyes.

Two Roy Blakes.

Two.

Identical.

Both in matching black commando gear. Both armed with rifles.

Holy fuck.

Okay, stay calm. You are looking at twins, Makedde. She fought to keep her breathing even, to slow the panicked racing of her heart. Ann told you Roy has a brother. So, Roy's brother is a twin.

But which one is Roy?

The one she'd fought at Ann's place, the one who had punched her in the eye, the one who had driven her here—had that been Roy?

If she had been dealing with one of them all along, she had to try and keep track of which was which. She had to try to regain his sympathy.

Stay calm. Just try to stay calm.

Gradually, the initial shock passed and she noticed that one of them seemed more animated than the other. Yes, the one on the left was looking at her with absolute bewilderment. Why?

He grabbed the other by the elbow, "Come with me," she heard him say gruffly, and he pulled his twin out of the room.

CHAPTER 62

"What the hell is she doing here!?" Roy exclaimed.

"The girl? She was a witness," Daniel said plainly. "I had to take her, and she's a pretty one, too, isn't she?" He smiled. "It was a perfect stroke of luck. Now, my brother, I get to show you what I do with the girls. It's great fun. You'll see . . ."

Roy felt ill.

"My God, Danny, that's Makedde!"

His brother's expression was blank. The name meant nothing to him, Roy had not told him about Makedde. In fact, Roy had not told him much about any of the girls he had seen over the past few years, for fear that it would make him jealous or cause some discontent. After all, he wanted his brother to be safe and happy up at the cabin, not thinking about what he was missing in the big city, and not feeling as if he were losing his brother to someone else.

"I know her. I know that woman," Roy tried to explain, shaking his head with disbelief. "What have you done? What have you done by bringing her here?"

Makedde had been kidnapped. She had witnessed Daniel do whatever it was he had done to Dr. Morgan. She had seen all of it, and he knew that his brother's plan was to kill her now. And if they didn't kill her, she would have them both in jail for the rest of their lives. He will have ultimately let him and their mother down in the worst possible way.

If they didn't kill Makedde now, they would be locked up forever, and worst of all, they would be separated.

CHAPTER 63

Andy could hear the helicopter. He stood on the bridge that led to the floating helipad, bracing himself against the cold Canadian wind.

Where is she?

He hoped to God that they were all overreacting. He hoped to God that Makedde was okay. Perhaps she was with this man—this Roy Blake—and she was sleeping peacefully, and he was guilty of nothing more than driving around the Nahatlatch and being a security guard at her university. Andy tried to imagine her safe in the man's arms, but his jealousy would not allow it.

The helicopter descended over the water, causing it to ripple into small waves. His hair whipped, with the turbulence and the sound of the blades was deafening. Andy stood with his hands in his pockets, his jaw tensed, wondering how his life had come to this moment; watching a helicopter land in the middle of the night carrying the father of the woman he loved—a woman who did not love him back . . . a woman who might well be in danger yet again.

CHAPTER 64

Makedde sat up when the Blake twins entered.

Here we go . . .

They filed in, one behind the other, and she met their eyes with a steady glare. They stopped less than two feet from her chair, one of them standing slightly behind the other. Her gaze flicked back and forth, trying to find some familiarity, trying to figure out which one of these horrible, identical men was Roy Blake.

Boy I can pick 'em. Or they can pick me.

Can't handle rejection, can you? Makedde thought. *You can't handle anything where you are not in control, you psychopathic bastard.*

She chose the one she thought might be Roy—the less confident one who was standing back a touch, and she shot daggers of hate at him with her eyes. "So you think you could pick a psychopath, then?" he had asked her. Did he know that's what he was? Was that some kind of perverse test?

The two of you combined don't even equal half of a real human being, she wanted to say, but the rifles gave

315

her pause. She would say it before she died, she decided, if that's where this was headed. When the time came, she would say anything she wanted, but she should just observe now. She would watch what they did, she would look for an opening. It wasn't over yet.

The one she guessed was Daniel walked around behind her. She watched the other one again. *What are you two up to? What comes next in this little charade?* The other one appeared to be looking at whatever his brother was doing behind her back.

She heard a door open and close. She wondered where that door could lead. The outdoors? No, there was no draft. A closet space? A bedroom? What was he doing?

Both twins disappeared behind her. She heard something metallic clink, then felt the hard shape of a gun barrel between her shoulderblades. One of the twins bent down in front of her, and she felt the urge to kick him in the face. He reached his hands around her ankles. "You be good now, and we won't have to kill you . . ."

Bullshit.

Her legs were free, but she did not move. She watched them carefully. They would have to undo her arms before they did anything else. The same twin, be it Roy or Daniel, went around to her back, and she felt his hands on her wrists, twisting them, and then the handcuffs came off; a momentary tightening, and then release. Her hands were free.

"Get up."

This is what they did to all of them, she thought with grim surety. *This is when they kill them. This is when they kill me.*

316

"Get up. If you cooperate, you'll have a chance."

They will lead me into the woods and execute me. It's not so messy in the woods. They won't want to kill me in here—not with that shotgun. I would mess up their precious rugs and trophies.

A numbness had taken the place of everything else. She wondered if her nerves had been fried, if she had become incapable of feeling. She decided that this new-found serenity in the face of horror was a proud and beautiful thing that she would hold dear forever, whether it be in this life or the next.

"So what's your game, then? Why the charade? You know me, so talk to me."

One of them went to open his mouth, and the other stopped him. "Cuff her."

He grabbed her wrists and shackled them together again.

Damn.

Fuck you. Fuck you and fuck your brother, and fuck the Stiletto Killer and all the wuss-bags like you who are afraid to act like real human beings.

"Walk."

She hesitated. "You're making a big mistake. You were seen with me." She directed it at both of them. "Talk to me. Tell me why you are doing this. I want to understand."

Don't let them get you outside. They'll shoot you in the back like the others the moment you're away from their precious home. Think of another way. Your legs are free. Run. Run somewhere. She wanted to turn her head to see the door behind her, to see where it led, and as she turned she was bumped hard in the back with the rifle.

"Walk."

If it was a storage room of some kind and they had

more guns in there, they would not be loaded and ready for her to use. The twins would kill her without hesitation if she went for their guns. She mustn't do that—yet. She would have to distract them first.

When they get you outside, they'll shoot you like an animal.

"Move!" She was pushed forward by the gun once more, this time much harder.

She walked. She held her head high and she walked. Roy thought Makedde would make a prime target because of what he had found out about her, was that it? She would be an interesting one to screw with? Well at least he didn't get what he wanted. Not quite. She had her dignity.

The floor moved beneath her feet as she approached the door. She wanted to know which twin was which. She wasn't sure why it meant so much to her, but she supposed it gave her some sense of control to think she knew. Clearly it was part of their game to seem interchangeable, elusive. Why else would they wear those matching suits?

The doorframe moved toward her and then she was through it, out of that terrible room with all the staring animals, all the dumb staring beasts. She was being led down a short hallway—*Don't let them get you outside*—and she considered where she could run to. How much time would she have? None. How much chance had she of outrunning them? None.

Your moment will come, Makedde. Your moment will come.

The front door was approaching now, she was moving toward it, Roy was opening it—that was Roy, wasn't it?—and she could see outside. She could see all that untouched wilderness and she wanted to run through it, run away and be free. She would rather die out there trying. Anything was better than dying by the rules of these twin psychopaths.

A nudge and a shove and she was outside. One step, two. The air was cold. The sky was pitch-dark. Makedde wished for warm clothes, she wished for many things she did not have. She could not see, but now she sensed one of them had more than just a gun with him. He had grabbed something else for them from that room behind her.

Makedde turned her head, dared to turn it and look at what it might be.

She froze.

Oh, no . . .

The man was wearing something on his face. Some contraption with great long crab-eye stalks attached to it. She had seen something like that before. It was an instrument the military sometimes used. What was it?

Night vision.

He had night-vision goggles on.

She was shoved again, and this time she was caught off balance and she fell forward, tried to reach out with her hands but they were trapped behind her by the handcuffs. She stumbled forward and caught her balance just before going down.

She looked again.

The other one was wearing the same horrible goggles now. The eyes were gone, replaced by those stalks.

"Move it," one ordered her.

Shaken, she struggled on. She felt herself start to hyperventilate.

Stay calm, stay calm . . .

She thought of the other dead girls. She thought of what they had been through, what they had endured and how they were left. Had the twins got what they wanted from them? Had they obeyed and been murdered anyway? Of course they had. Had they expected freedom, compassion, mercy?

Shot in the back.

Hunted.

Like animals.

The procession stopped at a spot on the edge of the woods. Makedde felt hands on her, releasing the handcuffs from her wrists. Her arms were free.

"Run," came a voice from behind her. "Now."

They had their night-vision goggles, their guns. Did they honestly think this was a fair game? That she had a sporting chance?

She turned and spoke to their dual shapes in the thick darkness. "You must know that they have an FBI Profiler on this, right? He's one of the best in the world. Sees your type all the time," she spat. "You know what the first thing was that he said? He said you were cowardly. He said, 'Shot in the back with a high-powered rifle . . . a coward.' How does it feel to be a coward, you two?"

Thwack.

One of them struck her on the side of the face with the barrel of the gun. It knocked the words out of her mouth.

"Go. Now."

She turned to them one last time before she obeyed the command, her face stinging from the hit. "How many minutes does a sportsman give his game?" she said defiantly. "How many for the handicap? There's two of you. I have no shoes. None of those . . . goggles."

"You've got sixty seconds. I suggest you get going."

One of the twins fired off a warning shot. It hit the ground somewhere near her feet. A rush of adrenaline filled her body and she set off on a run, as fast as she could.

She ran straight through the trees ahead. She would run seventy-five paces forward, then a sharp left, and another and another. Lead them away from the cabin, and try to circle back. *You can get back to the cabin an find a weapon and hide. But don't get lost . . .*

Go.

Go.

Go!

Her watch glowed faintly in the dark. The second hand seemed to move so fast. She believed what they had said. They would give her sixty seconds. Not a moment less, and not a moment more. They would follow in thirty seconds . . . twenty-nine . . . twenty-eight . . .

Run . . .

Twenty-five paces forward now. Could they still see her through the trees? She had to be out of their sight before she turned off. The woods had to be thick enough to shield her movements. And they would listen for her, too. Forty paces now . . .

It had been forty seconds. She had to run faster, faster . . .

Please don't let me trip.

She ran forward, dodging tree trunks and branches as their great shapes threw themselves up in front of her. Fifty paces, now, and she knew she would not have long before they came after her. Turn soon . . . turn, and run for a few minutes, then another seventy-five paces back toward the road. It had to work.

I can do it. I'm fast enough. I can run in the dark. I can do this.

Sixty paces . . . They would be after her soon. She

looked at her watch—it had almost been a minute—here they come—and then she was falling—*NO!*—tripping over a great slippery patch of moss and gnarled roots. She slid and hit a tree, her already sore wrist scraping painfully against the coarse bark.

No!

They are after you now. Get up! Go!

CHAPTER 65

Roy watched his brother as he raised his wristwatch to his face.

"Okay. Ready?"

Through his green-lensed night-vision goggles, Roy saw the lips move, saw the smile that followed, but somehow it was not his brother.

Roy grabbed him by the arm. "No."

Daniel shook his arm away. "We're in this together now. Trust me, you'll like it."

"You don't understand. You can't do this—"

"Stop wasting time. She's had her sixty seconds. It's time."

Roy held the rifle firmly in one hand, and raised his other, palm up, just as he had done in so many of their confrontations. "You've gone too far, Danny. Let her go," he said softly, trying to placate his brother. "I'll get you some help. It'll be okay."

Chapter 66

Makedde prayed that she had her bearings right, and kept running.

You can do it. Don't give up . . .

Seventy-five paces, now turn. She made a sharp left and tried to run in a straight line again. If she lost her way, if she miscalculated her direction she'd be deep in the woods with no hope of rescue. Even if she hid from them she'd probably die from the elements. Even if she lasted overnight, she would not know her way back.

Then she heard shouting.

BANG!

A gunshot in the distance.

Then another.

They echoed through the darkness, corrupting the stillness. One of them had fired. Had they seen her? They were nowhere near her. Were they? Perhaps it was their way of letting her know that the hunt was on?

Just run . . .

She ran on and on, never slowing, never turning back,

and when the time was right, she turned again and headed back to where she thought the road must be.

And then like a miracle the forest gave way to a clearing, and she could see gravel . . . the gravel road that led to the cabin. Her heart lifted, her breath so hard in her chest, and she was running down the road, which way? There . . . to the right . . . she hadn't quite run far enough.

She could see the cabin.

My God, yes! I can do it . . .

CHAPTER 67

Makedde ran up the cabin steps and inside. When she had been trapped in there, she wouldn't have believed she would have voluntarily returned. But it was the only strategy that might work.

Find any weapon, anything . . . and a phone.

She went to the kitchen first, hoping there'd be a knife. Who knew how long it would take for them to come back? Perhaps they had already seen her turn back this way with their night-vision goggles. She saw unopened cases of beer on the kitchen counter, some leftover bottles, an empty bag of potato chips. She opened the first drawer where she found cutlery, spoons, forks, table knives. Useless.

She looked the other way.

Bingo.

Makedde grabbed a butcher's knife off a magnetic holder on the opposite wall.

Now guns . . . Do they have any more guns and ammunition? Go to the trophy room and find that door . . . Find out what they have in there . . .

Thump.

Movement.

The front door burst open.

She looked frantically around her, knife in her grasp.

Damn! There was nowhere to hide.

There were footsteps approaching, someone was around the corner, coming. It was one of the twins. Only one of them.

When he saw her he stopped in his tracks. "Oh God, Makedde. Are you okay?"

What?

He walked toward the kitchen doorway, one palm up in a gesture of surrender, and the other holding the rifle point down.

He had blood on his hands.

"Stop there," she warned, standing steadily and gripping the knife tight. Her heart was pounding.

"Don't worry. It's me . . . Roy. I was only playing along until I could help you." He shook his head sadly. "Oh, my God . . ." he wailed. "I killed him. I killed my own brother! I had to. I had no choice. He was going to kill you!"

He took another step forward.

"Stop there. Don't come any closer. What happened? Where is your brother?"

"You don't understand. It wasn't me who killed Ann. It wasn't me who brought you here. It was Daniel. He went crazy."

"Roy . . ."

He moved toward her again, the night-vision goggles hanging clumsily around his neck, the rifle still in his hand. "Thank God you're okay," he said.

"Roy, put the gun down," Makedde said.

Roy was coming through the doorway of the kitchen now. "It's okay, Makedde, I won't hurt you."

"Roy, put the gun down, *now*."

Roy looked at her with wide, sympathetic eyes. "Okay . . . Sorry, I'll put it down. I'm so sorry." He bent slowly at the knees, motioning to put the gun down. His eyes never left her, never left the butcher's knife in her hand.

And then she saw it.

The scratch on his right hand.

This is the man who killed Ann, the one I fought with, the one I scratched.

He must have seen her staring, because he looked down at his hand, and realizing the scratch gave him away, brought the gun up . . .

Quick!

Makedde lunged straight at him with all her might, knife extended. She dived across the few feet that had separated them, crashing into him hard. Daniel flew backward from her impact, knocked off balance, and they hit the linoleum floor of the kitchen, Daniel underneath, the rifle knocked from his grasp. Makedde landed right on top of him, her full weight pushing the knife straight down through his black jumpsuit and into his chest. She screamed as she plunged the knife in, and he let out a loud groan, pinned beneath her. His body convulsed as she held the handle of the knife. It was buried in his chest right up to the hilt.

He grabbed her feebly, clawing at her back with hands that were dirty with his own brother's blood, but it was already too late.

She rolled off him and leaped to her feet, shaking uncontrollably.

Ohhhh Jesus . . .

"Fuck!" the man at her feet yelled out with rage, blood spluttering from his mouth.

And then with horror Makedde watched him grab the butt of the knife and start to pull it out with both hands.

Do something!

She saw the rifle.

She went for the gun, and his eyes followed her. "No . . ." he groaned, reaching for it, but he was too slow.

She had it.

Makedde brought the 270 Winchester up to her shoulder. She looked down the sights, aimed it at Daniel's head. She cocked it.

In the small room the blast was deafening.

EPILOGUE

One month later . . .

It was Makedde Vanderwall's favorite day of the year—the day of night, the day when ghouls and witches mixed amicably with mere mortals. On this Halloween night, the sky was illuminated by a bright orange full moon that hung low over Vancouver Island. A full moon on Halloween was a volatile combination. The local cops thought they would be in for a big night, and they were right.

At 7:30 P.M. Makedde woke from the two-hour nap that had been part of her routine on this day every year for as far back as she could recall. She still liked to sleep away the sunset and wake in the dark, just as her mother had her do as a child.

She woke alone in her old bedroom, still in her T-shirt and jeans, and yawned and stretched, arching her back. She looked around the moonlit room, making out the shape of her bookshelf, still stacked with stories her

330

mother had read to her—*Where the Wild Things Are* by Maurice Sendak, *The Gashlycrumb Tinies* by Edward Gorey and the whole gamut of Dr. Seuss, from *Green Eggs and Ham* to *The Cat in the Hat*. Her eyes slowly adjusted and she saw her sweater slung over the chair nearby, and her mother's small diamond stud earrings, which she always wore, on the bedside table.

She felt a stab of loneliness.

I miss you, Mom.

When she was a child Mak was rarely alone, least of all on this day of the year.

She sat up and rubbed her eyes.

Mak was doing her best to find the upside to what had happened in September. She was a survivor, and most importantly, she had ended Daniel Blake's bizarre reign of terror. But she could not forget Daniel's face—the look of homicidal rage and agony as he lay on the floor with the knife protruding from his body, and his final cry as the bullet tore into him, sending him swiftly into death to join his twin—a violent end to a tortured and violent life.

Makedde felt sad for Roy. He had been naïve and made some very poor decisions, but he seemed to have a good heart. In order to protect his brother he had taken him out of the hands of the people who might have helped him. He didn't understand what his brother, in his illness, was capable of. Not even Ann could have guessed, until it was too late.

Ann believed that their father had abused Daniel, mentally and most probably sexually as well. For whatever reason, he decided to pick on the one child. Their mother had found out. That was why she left. No one had been able to track her down since, and probably no one ever would. And their father, the prize hunter, whether he abused them or not, was now a senile old man in an institution.

It seemed unlikely that anyone would ever know the whole truth.

Mak slipped her sweater on and her mother's earrings, and walked in her thick winter socks from the bedroom into the family living room. From the big front window she could see up and down the whole block. The window was adorned with the Halloween decorations her father still pasted there every year; they were at least fifteen years old, depicting a smiling green witch riding her broom across a big orange moon. There would be Santa Claus and his reindeer in that spot at Christmastime and the Easter Bunny in April. Mak smiled at the sight of the old decorations, and wandered over to the side wall to plug in a plastic pumpkin. It glowed brightly as it hung in the window nearest the front entrance, smiling with its single tooth, complementing the Halloween ensemble. Finally she flipped the light switch on for the front porch—a signal that this house had candy to offer the Trick or Treaters.

Happy Halloween.

As she reached the base of the stairs, the phone rang. She turned and leaped up the steps two by two and skidded across the linoleum in the kitchen.

"Hello?"

"Wakey, wakey, rise and shine," came the familiar voice.

"Dad!" Her heart lifted.

"How's my girl?"

"I'm fine, Dad. How are you? How is Ann doing?"

Her father had spent much of the past month with Ann Morgan, who was recovering well. They clearly had something good there, and Mak was pretty comfortable with it. She wanted her father to be happy and she liked Ann a lot, but that didn't stop it from feeling a little weird at times. After all, Ann Morgan was turning out to be her father's first real "girlfriend" since he was widowed. As if that dynamic needed to be more awkward, Ann knew all about Makedde's darkest fears and worst experiences and Mak had witnessed Ann fighting for her life with a fireplace poker. Not exactly a conventional start to their relationship.

"Hang on . . ."

"Hi, Makedde," came a woman's voice. "Happy Halloween." It was Ann.

"Oh," Makedde exclaimed, taken off guard. "Happy Halloween to you, too. How are you?"

"I'm very well. I'm hoping we can catch up again next weekend. I'll be much better company soon, and much more mobile."

"You take it easy, okay? Promise me."

"Deal."

Her father got back on the line. "By the way, the press haven't laid off yet. They don't know where you are, so I'm copping all the flak."

"That's what fathers are for."

"Yup. They're offering five figures just for a photo of you."

"Mmm. My agent would like that," she said. "If they do anything like that behind my back I'll slaughter them."

"And Professor Gosper has been skulking around again. He wants to talk to you."

Makedde let out an irritated sigh. "I know, I know, so he can write my story. How thoughtful of him. Tell him to get stuffed, Dad. If I want my story written, I'll write it myself."

A pause. "Oh dear. I didn't tell him to get *stuffed*."

Oh no. "You didn't? What did you do? You didn't promise I would speak to him, did you?"

How could he do that?

"No. I told him to get *fucked*."

"Dad!" she squealed. "You said that? Such language." She couldn't remember the last time she had heard her father swear.

"You alone?" he asked.

"Presently, yes."

She knew what he meant.

"Call him."

"Yes, Dad, well, have a good night," she blurted, changing the subject.

"You too."

"And thanks for calling," she said. "I love you, Dad."

"I love you too."

Smiling to herself, she settled into the couch behind the witch and her broom. She laid her arms along the back of the seat and rested her chin, looking out the window at the children dressed up in their costumes and wandering around under the streetlights. There was an alien here, a Dracula there, one of them was a fairy, a Frankenstein, a Dalmatian.

I will give him a call, she thought.

Andy had come across from Vancouver to visit her now that Dr. Harris was back at Quantico. They both agreed that it was a little too intimate to have him staying in the Vanderwall guestroom, so Andy had splurged on a nearby B&B—the cheapest accommodation possible. For the past two days he had been renting an undersized bed in the maid suite in the house of a rather frightening old woman with some strange opinions and too many cats.

He planned to leave for Australia in about a week, but she figured he wouldn't last another day in that place. She'd have to save him. If he was good, that is.

He had dropped a few not-so-subtle hints about getting back together, but she wasn't so sure. *You are not over the shock yet,* she told herself. *Don't go running into his arms hoping he'll save you from the memories of what has happened here.* But she did want to see him, and she didn't want to be alone on her favorite night of the year.

Perhaps she could make him wear face paint and answer the door in a big cape or something? That'd be amusing.

The number of his B&B was tacked to the bulletin board next to the phone. She dialed.

"Hello?" An older lady's voice.

"Hi, I'm calling for your guest, Andy Flynn."

"Oh, hang on. He's just here watching TV," she said.

Mak chuckled to herself.

"Hello?"

"Hi, Andy. It's Mak."

"Oh, I'd know that voice anywhere," he said. And she certainly knew his.

"Would you like to come over?" she asked, feeling a bit like a naughty teenager with the parents away. "We could order in and watch all the vampire and werewolf movies on TV. Whaddya say?"

"You want to drag me away from the Charlie Brown Halloween special with the haunted pumpkin in the pumpkin patch and all that? I'm enjoying it, you know."

Mak couldn't restrain a giggle.

"Get me outta here," she heard him say in a low voice. "I was hoping you'd call."

"I did recommend the Honored Guest, didn't I? But nooooo . . ." She laughed. "Well, I wouldn't want to drag you away from Charlie Brown at grandma's house. But the *Legend of Sleepy Hollow* is on next, so if you need someone to cling to when you get scared—"

"I'll be right over."

Grinning from ear to ear, she made her way back to the window.

Rain had begun to fall outside. She saw some children being ushered under shelter by their parents. Some had opened umbrellas and were rushing home, and others shivered and waited for it to pass. Hopefully it would clear up. It was never as much fun traipsing around in the wet. It was hell on those Dracula capes, not to mention the pasty ghoul make-up.

The rain depressed her, and she thought again about what Ann had said.

Be careful what you wish for.

In the end Makedde supposed she got what she wished for—another chance to prove herself, to save her own life. In some ways, she felt whole again.

"You came to save me," she'd told Andy, "but I didn't need saving this time . . ."

Andy and her father were rummaging through her apartment for clues when news came that she had called 911 from a cabin deep in the woods of Squamish. She hadn't needed anyone to save her this time, though she suspected that she might not have made it back to the cabin safely if the brothers had not fought. Their quarrel had given her time that the other victims were not afforded.

Debbie Melmeth's and Susan Walker's families had both contacted her. They found some solace in knowing that their daughters' killer was dead, but nothing would bring their children back. Nothing anyone did could change that fact.

Whatever great being or force shaped Makedde's life, it had an infinitely bigger picture in mind than she did. Now, more than ever, she was convinced of that. Whatever her fears were, they would come true. But what she was only just realizing was that rather than being a curse, adversity was in fact a great gift. For once your greatest fears come true, you are no longer burdened by them. You have survived, you are stronger, and you are free.

The doorbell rang.

Makedde peered cautiously through the peephole and saw Andy's familiar face.

"Aren't you going to say trick or treat?" she asked, opening the door.

"What?"

"Never mind. Come on in."

Andy was wet from the rain, dressed in jeans and a leather jacket, and carrying a bottle of wine.

They sat up that night and watched the Halloween specials on TV, periodically answering the door for adventurous Trick-or-Treaters who still rang the bell despite the weather. In time, the visitors dropped off, and they hugged close to each other in silence on the couch. There was no need to talk.

Makedde gave in to her sleepiness around one. She kissed Andy goodnight and saw him to the family guestroom, not wanting to send him back to that awful B&B. But nightmares came to her quickly. She was running, and there were monsters, horrible monsters chasing her—twin vampires and zombies. She heard their footsteps behind her as they followed, fast—too fast even for her athletic strides. She was breathless, panting and running, and then somehow all was quiet. She had reached an oasis in the dark, a temporary haven behind a great gnarled tree like the ones in the forest when the twins had hunted her down. And then a noise . . . a crack of twigs . . . no, a scraping, somewhere . . . the sound was real, and she opened her eyes with a start.

NO!

There was a sound.

A real sound.

In real life.

She leaped out of bed. There it was again. It was coming from down the hall.

Daniel . . . with Roy's blood on his hands . . .

But he's dead . . . I killed him . . .

Andy was already in the hall, standing in his boxer shorts, his eyes wide. He had heard it too.

"What is it?" she whispered, coming up beside him, heart pounding and trying not to tremble. He gave a cursory glance at her dressed in underpants and a T-shirt, but said nothing. He was half-naked too, so what could he say?

"It's coming from the sliding doors at the back," he said quietly. "I think someone is trying to break in. I'll go check it out."

Makedde followed, and when he looked back at her and held up his hand as if to say, "Stay here." He saw from the look on her face that she wasn't staying anywhere.

They crept down the hall together.

At the end of the hall, they turned to look into the kitchen. Through the opening on the other side, they could see the sliding glass doors of the balcony, and blackness beyond.

Silence.

They moved closer.

They were a mere five feet from the glass doors when a sudden "Boo!" pierced the silence, and a gruesome green face emerged from the dark to blow a big raspberry against the glass. Huge white lips squished up against the glass pane, the pink tongue writhing. Ghoul make-up. It smeared against the glass in a pasty mess, and in seconds the teenager ran away to the laughter of his hiding cohorts.

"Oh, bloody hell!" Andy exclaimed. "Kids!"

They collapsed together in a relieved and shaken heap on the kitchen floor, holding one another in their underwear, laughing.

"You were more scared than I was!" Makedde cried, barely able to form words through her laughter.

They held each other when they drifted into sleep. That night Makedde slept soundly.

She didn't dream.

TARA MOSS

FETISH

Mak is young, beautiful—and in grave danger. An international fashion model, she arrived in Australia on assignment, only to find her best friend brutally murdered, the latest victim of a serial killer with a very deadly fetish. Before she knows it, Mak herself is caught up in the hunt for the killer...and trapped in a twisted game of cat-and-mouse. Who can you trust and where can you turn when you are the dark obsession of a sadistic psychopath?

JEFF BUICK

AFRICAN ICE

A diamond formation worth untold millions, hidden deep in the jungles of Africa. Many have tried—and failed—to find it. Can Samantha Carlson do the impossible? The president of Gem-Star thinks so when he hires the geologist to lead a team into the Democratic Republic of Congo and return with the diamonds' location.

Samantha is aware the odds are against her from the beginning, but she knows what she's doing. Plus, Gem-Star has provided an escort team to protect her. But Samantha's expedition is about to turn into an all-out battle for survival. There's another team on a mission in the jungle. Their goal: kill Samantha.

R. BARRI FLOWERS

STATE'S EVIDENCE

Assistant District Attorney Beverly Mendoza has been selected to prosecute a disturbing case: the murder of a judge and the rape of his wife. The defendant, Rafael Santiago, once vowed to get revenge against the judge and his wife. It seems like an open-and-shut case. But appearances can be very deceiving.

At the same time, detective Stone Palmer is investigating the rape and strangling of a young woman. Career criminal Manuel Gonzalez is in custody, but he pulls the rug out from everyone when he claims he's the one who murdered the judge. Could it be a case of mistaken identity? Or two desperate, violent men out to manipulate and beat the system?

SMILING WOLF

PHILIP CARLO

Anne Fitzgerald is young, beautiful and intelligent—but she may also be dead. She disappeared after interviewing a mysterious man named Santos Dracol, and it's up to detective Frank De Nardo to find her. But the more De Nardo investigates, the deeper he descends into a shocking world of dark clubs and darker perversions, hidden in the shadowy underbelly of New York City. It's a world of power, sex…and blood. It's certainly bizarre, and De Nardo is convinced it's deadly. But will he be able to prove it? Will he be able to stop Dracol and his followers before another body is found?

A HARD TICKET HOME

DAVID HOUSEWRIGHT

McKenzie is an ex-St. Paul cop with time on his hands. That's why he's doing a favor for an old friend with a sick daughter: Nine-year-old Stacy has been diagnosed with leukemia, and the only one with the matching bone marrow that could save her life is her big sister, Jamie. But Jamie ran away from home years ago—and disappeared.

McKenzie starts with Jamie's seedy last known associates. But the trail doesn't lead where Mac expects. It takes him to some very respected businessmen. And every time he starts asking questions, people start dying…in very unpleasant ways.
